AF405580

THE DREAMING MOON

DAVID E RAGLAND

Copyright 2022 by David E Ragland

All characters and events are fictitious. Any resemblance to any person, or persons, alive or dead is purely coincidental and unintentional. Some locations exist and some are fictitious. None of the events in this book occurred at any of the actual locations.

IF YOU ARE A VETERAN AND NEED HELP VISIT WWW.VA.GOV IF YOU NEED IMMEDIATE HELPTHE VETERANS' CRISIS LINE CONNECTS VETERANS IN CRISIS AND THEIR FAMILIES AND FRIENDS WITH QUALIFIED, CARING DEPARTMENT OF VETERANS AFFAIRS RESPONDERS THROUGH A CONFIDENTIAL TOLL-FREE HOTLINE, ONLINE CHAT, OR TEXT. VETERANS AND THEIR LOVED ONES CAN CALL 1-800-273-8255 (PRESS 1), CHAT ONLINE AT VETERANSCRISISLINE.NET, OR SEND A TEXT MESSAGE TO 838255 TO RECEIVE CONFIDENTIAL SUPPORT 24 HOURS A DAY, 7 DAYS A WEEK, 365 DAYS A YEAR.

YOU ARE NOT ALONE.

Table of Contents

MISSION MIAMI BEACH

They couldn't see anyone on the beach as far as the clandestine pair could see. The full moon left a shimmering silvery aura and the ocean lapped at it like a hungry cat. The moon's reflection crossed the water and lit the beach with just enough light to make a flashlight unnecessary. Iridescent organisms twinkled in the churning surf. It was perigean spring tide, so the waves were sometimes up to three feet which is high for Miami Beach. Each wave crash created an incredible display of natural fireworks as the iridescent organisms were thrown into the seaweed riding in the surf. It was eerily quiet as two shadows waded out waist deep into the salty swells then returned to shore just a few minutes later. With their business finished, they headed for the Fourteenth-Place dune crossover. A quick stop at the shower rinsed the sand and salt from their legs and feet. Then it was onward to Ocean Avenue and into the crowd of the rich and those going broke to live like the rich. It was Easter weekend and the weather had been especially cooperative for the spring breakers that were arriving in droves. To the late-teen and early twenty-somethings, it was a week for fun in the sun and all-night clubbing with the plastic people. Some of whom were so pale from living at night that they could've been the basis of a modern-day Stoker novel.

Ten minutes of walking later, the shadows that had waded into the surf, Matt, and Misha, were back in their rapidly failing car heading south toward home. They hated driving up to Miami Beach and had only done so tonight because of something that had to be done. Fulfilling a promise to a friend.

They lived in Marathon and hated the drive up, especially the part on US 1 from the new bridge over Jewfish Creek. It was especially unnerving because the tourist crowd was always hurrying south toward Key West leaving a trail of death and destruction in their wake, and to top it off it was Spring

Break. The road was often closed due to accidents and more often just too many cars, so many Keys' residents tried to avoid this stretch of road or tried to make the drive at a less busy time.

Living on a tight budget in the Keys means you can't afford to waste a trip north, so on the way home they stopped at the supercenter for supplies and a few niceties. After suffering the late evening big box store crowd of shopping zombies and freaks, they headed for the Card Sound Bridge. Most tourists headed directly south on US 1, so Card Sound is the preferred route for many of the Upper Keys dwellers. It also meant a stop at a famous waterfront bar for a beer or two just before crossing the bridge and returning to life.

The restaurant claimed the best conch fritters in the Keys, but Matt and Misha knew better. The fritters that were self-described as the best were the same deep-fried balls of dough and minced conch served by at least fifty other establishments from here to Key West. Neither Misha nor Matt would eat them and stuck to the beer. The main reason for the stop, at least for them, was the beer and bathrooms. It was a long dry trip down to Marathon from here, especially at this time of night. That is if you wanted to avoid cops and the tourist traps, which they did. With two beers each down, it was time to head across the bridge and south. Matt drove. He always drove because Misha was happier drinking a beer and looking for interesting things on the side of the road, plus her shoulder injury still caused trouble with shifting the gears. She also liked to roll and smoke joints and driving interfered with this activity. Matt was not a big dope smoker these days he but did take an occasional toke, just to remain social. He did drive with a beer between his legs though and drank it when he felt no cops were within sight.

The nineteen eighty-eight Alfa Romeo Spider convertible Matt and Misha owned had seen so many better days. The body was in decent shape, but the leather seats and interior had suffered from exposure to the weather. The top had become useless long ago and that, in turn, rapidly sped up the interior's deterioration. Heavy rains also periodically wreaked havoc on the electrical system requiring Matt to trace and repair wires and circuitry. Then there was the endless search for online parts stores with replacement components that they could actually afford. It was getting near impossible to keep the car running and both he and Misha wished they could just sell it and go carless. The problem with being carless in the Keys is that you were subject to bus evacuation in case of a hurricane threat, and nobody wanted that. A second six-pack was needed by the time they got to Islamorada and now it was back to the cheapest stuff available from the gas station. Sometimes, Misha wanted to say, "To hell with this life" and head north to New York or west to Los Angeles, find a decent job and be normal. Even so, she had known for years that big city life was not in her stars and made the best of even the less than desirable parts of her life in the Keys. Matt was oblivious to the hard parts of their life; he could only see the good things about life because of the way he made his living in the area.

ESCAPE FROM THE MOUNTAINS

Matt Luna didn't begin his adventures in life in Marathon, it took many years for him to arrive in the Keys. He has been born poor in a small West Virginia town. During his youth, he was only able to experience the beach in North Carolina and New Jersey while visiting family/ That's how he fell in love with the ocean. He did reasonably well in school but since he had no special status, no college recruiter sought him out. That meant he had to find his own way out of the hills or be a coal miner like most of his non-college bound classmates. He weighed options and chose to join the Navy since that came with both career training and travel on ships. The recruiter said he would be able to stay out on the water as much as he wanted and maybe more. His visions of the high seas were the kind that only a mountain boy could have, forged by movies, short vacations by the seaside and occasional deep-sea fishing trips.

After basic training, he was assigned as a machinist's mate, which was fine with him because it meant lots of shipboard time. He spent as much time as possible at sea, volunteering for any mission that kept him on sea duty. This wasn't hard because of the never-ending wars in the Middle East meant ships were always on patrol in the area. Most sailors wanted off the ships as fast as possible, and that helped Matt easily stay at sea. He loved his shipboard life, including the storms. The only issue was essentially living without regular female companionship. He had been on sea duty for two years before the accident that ended his career.

It was a relatively calm day. They were in the middle of an underway ship-to-ship resupply was when a rogue wave caused the ships to list away from each other. Matt was on deck and had turned to secure a pallet when one of the metal cables between the ships snapped. The loose end hit him in the back just below the last rib and broke his spine. He instantly went unconscious, crumpling to the deck. His shipmates good training helped prevent further injury as they reacted to prevent further damage from unsecure lines and supplies. After being immobilized on a stretcher, he was moved to sickbay and stayed there until the ship was near enough to a land base for a helicopter transfer. The ship's surgeon successfully stabilized the fracture but was unable to perform the surgery to install the metal rods necessary to hold Matt's spine in place and allow proper healing. So, three agonizing air transfers later, surgery was performed at Bethesda Naval Hospital. It was a miracle that he was not paralyzed from the waist down.

DETERMINATION

At Bethesda, surgeons implanted two stainless rods into Matt's back, one along either side of the spine. Neural exams had already shown that there was going to be some nerve damage and that meant possible issues with walking. It was three weeks before the full extent of any damage could be assessed though because not all the x-rays and scans in the world could predict what actual weight bearing would reveal in a matter of seconds.

When Matt was helped out of bed for the initial try at weight bearing, he was unable to control his left leg well enough to stand on his own. For now, at least, unassisted walking was out of the question. The neurologist, orthopedic surgeon, and physical therapist all agreed that intense physical therapy and nerve stimulation might help. But the real key would be Matt's determination and willingness to put maximum effort into the plan.

Matt resolved that he would walk again, without someone's help or a walker, and he worked to make that happen every moment that he was awake. When he wasn't in physical therapy, he was sneaking off the side of his bed and doing squats. Initially, he would have to hold the bed rail for support, but after three weeks he could do twenty squats without holding the rail. When in bed, he did isometric exercises, trying to isolate muscles according to a chart he had requested from the physical therapist. After eight weeks, he was walking fifty feet between parallel bars and every day it became easier to walk on his own.

The work was not easy for Matt because he was in constant pain. At first, he tried taking the pills the doctor's prescribed, but after a few weeks, he felt the addiction coming on. This is where he could have given up and just let the drugs take over his life. That wasn't Matt though. He decided he would have to deal with the crushing bolts of pain from his spine and legs differently. After managing to get a laptop and Internet access he found instructional basic yoga videos to follow. He struggled for weeks to get his body to cooperate with some basic stretches and poses. His primary care doctor noted Matt's determination and granted free access to the physical therapy area, as long as a staff member was present. Matt also studied papers from the medical and non-medical community on self-hypnosis and using your mind to help heal your body. It all began to work and after a few months passed, he asked to be discharged from the hospital into an inter-service transition unit, a wounded warrior detachment, where he could have some independence, but also would have support when needed. After a thorough assessment, Matt was transferred to a transition unit where he fast became friends with Misha. She was recovering from injuries sustained in a mortar attack on her Army unit. Her injuries included a shattered right shoulder, traumatic brain injury and some shrapnel damage to her face. They were not physically attracted to each other, at least no at first.

MUSICAL ESCAPE

Both Matt and Misha had the common dream of getting out of the transition unit and back to normal duty, or at least back to normal life. The goal of the transition unit was to help decide whether someone was better fit for return to military duty in some capacity, medical discharge, or some other type of separation from the military. Sometimes it took several months to make the determination. During that time, there were classes on finances, benefits, medical issues, job training, resume building, and a myriad of other topics. Matt and Misha were in these classes together but seldom said more than a quick hello to each other. They were rapidly becoming loners. This was actually Matt's normal behavior, but Misha was used to being doted over and was having a little difficulty adjusting to the loneliness. It was unusual for either of them to speak a word to anyone, other than instructors and counselors. The change in attraction came on a warm, sunny Saturday afternoon. Matt had wandered into the recreation room. He was alone because it was the weekend and almost every other person in the unit had family to go home to, or was off with visiting family members in DC, or something. Some were well enough to pursue leisure activities and liked to stay at hotels on the weekends. Matt often came to the rec room to read and sometimes listened to the old CDs that had been donated to the unit on an ancient boom box with headphones. Today, he was listening to a CD of a late 1960s group called The Doors. His parents had been fans and the group's music was always on in the house, or in the car, while he was growing up. The familiarity of the songs brought back happy memories of childhood.

MICHELLE

Michelle Pomeroy was from Ann Arbor, Michigan. She had joined the Army, just as her mother and grandmother did, to see the world. Her mother was one of the first women to make the rank of Command Sergeant Major and her grandmother had been one of the first women to make Colonel. Michelle had no aspirations of such high ranks and enlisted as a medical specialist, mostly because she had volunteered at a local hospital as a candy striper and then worked there briefly as a nursing assistant. She thought that the experience would be the ultimate test of the medical profession for her and that would decide if she would try to go on to be a doctor. Her grandmother had been a nurse in the early Vietnam war era and had always said that being an Army nurse was the most rewarding thing she had ever done in her life. Her mother had been a personnel specialist and, other than for the travel and benefits, was not overly enamored by military service.

In basic training Michelle's name was quickly shortened to Misha and the moniker stuck. She soon started introducing herself as Misha and most of the people she served with had no idea that was not her real name. Men came and went from her life without knowing her full name or anything about her family. None of them ever seemed interested in anything more than her body and, after a few sexual encounters, moved on, or were emphatically told to get lost. Misha had been both blessed and cursed with her looks. She had straight, strawberry-blonde hair that normally hung to the middle of her back, long slender legs, and large breasts. She found out, by the time she was fourteen, that almost all males liked large breasts, and she felt like was hit on by every passing man. By the time she was sixteen, she had become jaded and began seeking out troubled relationships for the extra attention. That's when, at her grandmother's strong urging, she decided to start volunteering at the hospital. She liked the work. So, at the first opportunity took a medical assistant class then was hired full-time in that role.
Misha's enjoyment of the work, along with some urging from her mother and grandmother, eventually led her to the Army recruiter's office and her enlistment. That was five years and one re-enlistment ago, now. In that time, she had made sergeant, her grandmother died, and her mother began having debilitating bouts of alcohol and post traumatic disorder related depression. Her father couldn't handle her mother's mental health problems and wandered off, never to be heard from again.

LIGHT MY FIRE

Matt was sitting in a lounge chair, in the recreation room, headphones on, listening to a CD in the recreation room when Misha came in and finalized her decision to approach him. Matt had his eyes closed and was unaware of her presence, just a few feet away. He started singing along with the music, "You know that it would be untrue, you know that I would be a liar, If I said to you, Girl we couldn't get much higher…C'mon baby, Light my fire…" Misha knew this song too, and began thinking about good times at home with her mother as she sat down across from Matt. He suddenly felt a presence and opened his eyes. Her eyes lit up as she smiled. He smiled back.Taking off the headphones, he asked, "Was I disturbing you?" She looked at him and, in an unsteady voice, said, "No, I was actually thinking about joining in!" They continued to look at each other until she asked, "How long has it been for you?" Matt had no idea what she was talking about, and his facial expression showed it. She clarified further, "Since a girl lit your fire." Matt turned redder than Misha did, and seeing the possibilities, quietly said, "I can't remember and seriously don't even know if everything still works." Misha said coyly, "I don't remember when either, but I am pretty sure that everything on me still works. Maybe we could go somewhere and see about you?" Matt felt some nerves activate that had been dormant since the injury. He sat up, to get closer to her, and said confidently, "I think that is the best offer I have ever had! Hell, let's just go all out and get a hotel room. If I am going to fail, it might as well be spectacularly!" She laughed and signed on to the recreation room computer to look for a hotel. Half an hour later, they were in a cab headed for a Days Inn near the base. It was the only place that they could find within ten miles that had an available room.

The cab ride was quiet. Both of them silently worried about the possibilities of the upcoming encounter, and whether it was going to work out like each was thinking. They were also a little antsy because the desire for sex was rapidly building inside each of them. Matt had leg braces on, and Misha had a metal contraption that held her arm rigidly out about eight inches in front of her chest. The padding and position hid the true size of her breasts and that may have been why she was not being actively pursued by men in the unit. The check in at the hotel was easy, Matt paid. Then it took fifteen minutes to get to the room because of medical limitations. Once inside the room, there was sudden awkwardness until Matt broke the ice by saying, "Over a year." Misha immediately said "Longer for me." That was the needed transition and they managed to begin kissing. That heated their desires hot enough to get them naked and, on the king, sized bed. Matt's body cooperated without hesitation, and everything seemed to have resumed normal functioning. Misha's arm brace dictated that she had to be on top and the whole first episode lasted less than two minutes. Matt felt embarrassed but Misha said, "Now that we know everything works, we can relax and do it as often as possible until Monday morning." Matt kissed her left breast since it was the closest thing to his mouth.

Misha rolled onto her back without any intention of covering herself and Matt rolled over to look at her and said, "I can't believe that I missed how beautiful you are." She said, "It was probably due to the mechanical devices and this scar on my face." A piece of shrapnel had split her cheek in a way that was going to need extensive plastic surgery to remedy. Matt said, "We're all scarred, don't let it get you." They lay naked and talked about nothing until nature said more sex was possible. This cycle happily repeated until it was time to leave for the unit on Monday morning with only a break for a pizza delivery and exhaustion.

They arrived back at the transition unit in a cab together. The sergeant in charge saw them get out of the cab. He intuitively knew what was going on and made a very loud announcement to the people in the common area, "Nothing! And folks I mean nothing is to be said about Matt and Misha arriving back here together after being gone all weekend. People, you *will* let them have some happiness! God knows there ain't enough of it around here." Everyone instantly knew that violation of this suggestion would put them on a permanent shit list and decided not to mention it. Matt opened the door to the common area for Misha and they looked up at the several people already there who were also looking to see who just arrived. The smiles on the new lover's faces said volumes and everyone uttered a nonchalant "Hi,", almost in unison, and then went back to their conversations, as if nothing unusual had happened, while secretly thinking how good it was that this happened. Since people came and went constantly from the unit, no single event was of any focus for more than a few minutes and life quickly resumed its normal lassitude.

At the first opportunity, Matt made arrangements for him and Misha to stay at the Navy Lodge, on Virginia Beach, the following weekend. When he told the sergeant about his and Misha's planned absence from the area over the following weekend, the sergeant said, "I will authorize a three day pass for both of you if you want to stay through Monday." Matt said, "I would like that. I will see if the room is available for another night and if Misha is agreeable." The lodge could not get them the extra day, so Matt quickly arranged for a hotel. Later, when Matt told Misha about his plan, she said he was being awfully presumptuous and that she would have to think about it. His face changed suddenly to the saddest thing that she had ever seen, so she quickly let the pressure off with, "If we weren't on duty, I would kiss you. Of course, I want to go and would stay a week if we could." Matt sighed relief and, with newfound humbleness, said, "Lesson learned. From now on, I will always check with you before making plans that involve you." She smiled and said, "I think we will be making a lot of plans that involve both of us and we can just discuss them together as we make them." They were now getting dangerously close to being late for the first class of the day and hurried to the upstairs classroom.

BEACH BABY

It was a long week in the barracks and since fraternization was strictly forbidden and stringently enforced, both Matt and Misha were more than ready to go on Friday afternoon. They took a taxi to a rental car place and then drove to Virginia Beach. Traffic was terrible and it took five hours to get to the hotel. Matt's legs and Misha's arm issues made it take an extra thirty minutes to get into the room. Sex happened before the bags were unpacked. Showers were taken and then they took a slow stroll down the boardwalk to dinner.

Over dinner, Matt opened up a little and said, "Since you offered to light my fire, I have been happier than any other time in my life. I know this is only our second weekend, but I feel something is happening." Misha looked him straight in the eye and said, "I know something is happening, so don't turn into an asshole. Please." He answered, "If I head in that direction, please hit me upside the head. I promise to do my best to never be an asshole to you." She said, "I will do just that, and we'll see where this leads. Meantime we have a beach, time off, and a place to screw. Let's have some fun." After dinner, they walked a little on the beach and found a spot to sit. Matt said, "I like this," and snuggled up to Misha. She snuggled back and smiled as they stared at the moon rising out over the water. There was no talk for the next five minutes, just two lovers enjoying each other's warmth and touch. It was Misha who finally broke the silence and said, "If you buy me a drink, I'll take you upstairs and give you something special." Matt said, "You've got yourself a deal!" The next morning, Misha woke up to find Matt looking at her and asked, "How long have you been doing that?" Matt said, "Not long enough, you seem to get more beautiful by the second." She said, "Hold that thought while I go to the bathroom."

A few minutes later, she opened the door and asked Matt to please come to the bathroom. He did and she said, "If I run a bath will you wash me? This arm is a problem, you know." He said, "Absolutely!" She ran the water, and he carefully washed every inch of her body. By the time he finished with her hair, she thought that only a man capable of great love could be so gentle and attentive. She smiled and spoke. "You should rinse off then join me back in bed." He insisted using the handheld showerhead to rinse her off then dried her with one of the large towels. He thought about how he had hesitated to book a handicap accessible room, at first, but was now incredibly happy that he had because of the bathroom's size. He touched her with the towel like he was shining a fine porcelain doll. She left the bathroom walking on air. Matt quickly showered and rejoined her in bed. She pulled him close with her good arm and said, "Let's make love and then go to the beach again for a while." He agreed by rolling on top of her and sliding his head down her torso, lightly kissing her skin as he did. He noticed the Goosebumps of her approval and made certain that she was happy before kissing his way back up her belly.

He helped her put on a bikini then pulled board shorts on over his leg braces. He rubbed her down with sunscreen and applied some to his legs, face, and arms. She used her good hand to rub lotion on his back. Out on the beach they basked in the morning sun, and by eleven o'clock, they were both done with the beach, for a while. They suggested food at the same time and smiled at each other. He put on a shirt and helped her with a sundress, leaving the strap off her bad shoulder. There was a restaurant nearby serving a brunch style meal, complete with mimosas. Afterward they helped each other back to the room. Once inside, they helped each other strip and rinsed off before taking a nap. There was afternoon sex, the beach and then dinner and drinking at a nearby bar until after midnight. Back in the room, drunken sex kind of happened and they woke up to bright morning light, from a poorly closed curtain. They laid in bed a few minutes just staring at each other until it got uncomfortable. Without consideration of morning breath or anything else, they began passionately kissing and holding each other as close as possible. They both had to urinate but that was secondary to the moment. A full five minutes of embrace still left them wanting more but needing to answer nature's call took precedence. Something had happened, in the moment before the kiss, and they both had felt it. The three-day pass seemed to be a lifetime of happiness but was over way too soon.

THE NATURE OF HEALING

Misha was scheduled to have surgery for more structural repair to her shoulder and potentially remove the arm brace on the Wednesday after the Virginia Beach trip. This was a topic of discussion during the trip and they both knew that Matt was only going to get authorization to visit her in the evenings. It was also unlikely that he could be there for emotional support before the surgery.

It was fortunate that First Sergeant Bixby was on duty Wednesday morning and when he saw Matt and Misha saying goodbye, he intervened. He came over to the couple and said, "Petty Officer Luna, you will accompany Sgt. Pomeroy to the hospital and supply moral support until she is discharged You will have no duties here until that time. Is that clear?" Matt and Misha looked at First Sargent Bixby and he was smiling. He quietly said, "You kids seem happy, keep it that way. I'll take care of everything here," then he walked away.

At the hospital, Matt convinced the medical specialist assigned to prepare Misha for the surgery to allow him to help. The medical specialist was unsure, so Misha begged her to let Matt stay and convinced her it was okay. Matt mostly held Misha's hand, and soon he was walking beside the gurney on the way to the operating room. At the operating room doors where he had to break away, he kissed her hand and said, "I will be beside your bed when you wake up." His eyes showed all the concern of a man in love. Misha saw the look, smiled, opened her mouth to say something but at the same moment the pre-surgery medications kicked in, and she faded out.

In the waiting area, Matt paced the floor, did some web surfing, watched television, and chit chatted with other people also waiting for four long hours. In the operating room, surgeons removed metal pieces from Misha's shoulder blade, detached the rod inserted into her arm where the brace was attached and added bone dust to help the remaining fractures heal. Most of the extensive bone damage had healed beautifully, but there was some noted muscle atrophy that might create a temporary issue. After all Misha's internal sutures were put back where they belonged, sixteen staples closed the surgical wound. After discharge, she would have to be in a special frame to hold everything in place for at least ten days to minimize the chance of motion causing accidental damage.

Misha arrived in the recovery area unconscious and securely strapped to a special rotating bed that held her completely immobilized. This was so she could not damage the surgeons' handiwork while everything began healing. After about an hour Matt was finally allowed into the recovery area to see her. By this time, she had almost regained consciousness, but was now under the influence of painkillers and in a foggy state. She recognized Matt and mumbled a, "Hello". He said, "How are you doing, beautiful?" then kissed her forehead, which was almost the only available spot not covered in dressings, covers, and her new metal brace. The bed she was strapped to was designed to keep her immobile but also allow her body to be flipped, turned, and tilted, without physically moving her body. Matt examined the mechanics of the bed and asked, "Can I get you anything?" Misha managed to form a response, "No, just please stay with me." He came back with, "I'll be here until somebody makes me leave."

A few hours later, Misha was moved to the orthopedic ward and given a private room because it was the only room available. Matt stayed close by. When he had to leave the room for a procedure, he always returned immediately. Eventually though, he had to eat and take care of his own needs. To help her not feel alone, he waited until a few minutes after she was given pain medicine, that's when she would generally sleep for a few uninterrupted hours. The first time he had to return to the barracks and get some clean clothes, First Sergeant Bixby caught him asked about Misha's condition.

After Matt gave his report, First Sergeant Bixby informed Matt that he was authorized to stay with Misha until she was discharged and able to return to the barracks. That is, if that was what he wanted. Matt wanted to do this, and after a few minutes of small talk headed for the shower.

Misha was in agonizing pain and asked for pain medication more often than she was allowed to have it. She essentially slept, or more accurately was unconscious, for three days. Matt held her hand tight during the worst of the pain between injections for pain, telling her how nice it was to be able to spend time with her and reassuring her it was going to better very soon. On the fourth day, she was unhooked from the monitors leaving only a catheter that had to be monitored by the nursing staff. The staff visits became less frequent. Matt learned how to reposition the bed and a nurse taught him how to massage Misha's legs and arms to help her peripheral circulation. He did the massages almost every hour because he could see that they made Misha feel better. On day six of Misha's confinement to the special bed, she developed a fever. Matt noticed she felt very warm while massaging her. He had added a head massage to his massage routine and saved it for last. When he felt her sweaty head and wet hair, he alerted the nurse on duty. The nurse came, checked Misha over and took her temperature. It was 103. The doctor was notified and soon a laboratory technician came for blood and urine specimens. Two hours passed and it was determined Misha had a urinary tract infection. The nurse came in and told Matt he would have to step out while she removed the catheter.

Later, when Matt was allowed back in the room, Misha told him that she had a problem. The nurse arrived and Misha stopped talking. The nurse placed an IV in Misha's arm for administration of antibiotics. Knowing that Matt was always there, the nurse showed him how it worked and asked to call her if he noticed any of several things happening. With that, the nurse left. Matt asked, "What kind of problem are you having?" Misha said, "I know we haven't known each other for very long but I need a very personal favor." He said, "I think by now you should know that I will do anything that I can for you." She said, "Good, because this is embarrassing to me, and I hope it doesn't cause you a problem." He said, "What, already?" She said, "Can you go somewhere and find some of those wipes for people with hemorrhoids?" He looked at her and said, "I've seen that area and I didn't see any problems." She smiled and said, "Please just go get some wipes." He realized this was not a negotiation, said, "Okay," and prepared to go.

Upon Matt's return, he said, "Got the pads, now what?" She answered, "Could you please clean me?" He asked, "Where?" She said, "You know." He said, "Okay." He gingerly wiped her bottom with one of the pads, threw it away and washed his hands. She said, "Is it possible that you could open my legs a little and do that again?" He smiled and said, "Okay, tell me if I get too personal." He opened her legs by adjusting the bed and she said, "My ass itches like you would not believe, please help me?" He carefully and very lightly wiped her again and she said, "You can be a little firmer." He cleaned her for the third time as she instructed him. With that done, she asked, "After you wash your hands, could you do the front?" He said, "No problem." He washed his hands and carefully cleaned her as she again instructed him. He finished and went to wash his hands again. She saw that his effort had an effect on him as he walked past her head. He gently closed her legs and placed the cover back over her. She asked, "Matt, why do you treat me so good?"

Matt looked at Misha, puzzled, and asked, "How else would I treat you?" She said, "You really don't know me that well and yet you are willing to take direction and wipe my ass without question?" He said, "What else would I do for the woman I am in love with?" She smiled and said, "I love you. I've known it since we met but didn't want to scare you away by telling you too soon." He said, "How could you know that when you met me?" She replied, "Sometimes, you just know." He smiled back at her, and said, "Then I think I we have been on the same wavelength since minute one." She cringed and added an urgency to her voice, "I need some pain medicine, please see if I can get some." He found a nurse and fortunately, it was time for Misha's next dose of pain medications. Soon, the nurse came into the room and announced that there was a new procedure for pain medicine. It had to be directly injected and not given through the IV. She asked Matt to step out and gave Misha the injection in her hip.

When Matt came back into the room, Misha was crying. She said that the nurse just told her that her pain medication was not only now only by injection but only every twelve hours. He asked her, "What's wrong with that?" She was choked-up and said, "I don't think it's going to be enough. And, on top of that now my ass hurts from the needle." Matt leaned over and kissed her. She whimpered, "Thank you." He smiled even bigger at her and asked, "What can I do for you, baby?" She said, "Please, always call me your baby." He said, "No problem, *baby*." She smiled and slipped into unconsciousness.

Having a urinary tract infection and no catheter in, meant Misha had to urinate often. The nurses and medical assistants sometimes were busy, meaning it took more than a few minutes for help to arrive. By the second day, Misha was asking Matt to help her, which he did without issue. By the third day he was helping with all her bodily functions, she was embarrassed but had only two choices, letting him help or trying to hold and wait for someone from the nursing staff. Matt continually assured her that he had no problem helping her with anything that had to be done. She was continually embarrassed. But, since he was always willing and never had anything negative to say, or even gave her a strange look, she suffered the indignity of the situation. On the tenth day x-rays showed that healing was right on track, and Misha was unshackled from the tortuous bed. Her arm was now immobilized under her breasts using the new brace.

Even though Misha was no longer strapped to a bed, the days of immobility meant that she had trouble walking. Matt massaged her legs and supported her while she got her land legs back. He also insisted on taking her by wheelchair to the sunroom for some changes in her environment. She was resistant, at first, but soon liked the feeling of the sun on her newly repaired, but still very painful body. During the past week, Matt had been reading a book, which had been left in the waiting room, aloud. It was *Triggerfish Twist* by Tim Dorsey. When Matt finished the book, he went to the nearest bookstore and got another Dorsey novel, *Torpedo Juice*. Misha began reading Triggerfish Twist and halfway through the book, she started talking about moving to Florida. Matt quickly agreed that Florida was the place for them.

A few days later, Misha was discharged from the hospital. Matt helped her to get resettled in her barracks room, back at the transition unit. Now she only had pain pills and Matt was unable to stay with her in her room. He came by and helped her get to the recreation room during his lunch breaks, and in the evenings. Three days later, it was Friday, and Misha decided this arrangement was beyond unacceptable.

When Matt came to get her that evening she said, "Let's get out of here." Matt said, "I don't know if your arm can take it." She said, "Don't worry about that, I need to get out of here." Matt called a taxi, and they went to the same Days Inn where they had first escaped the transition unit. They even got the same room. Once they were inside the room, Misha said, "Help me get undressed, I seriously need some of your special attention." He was still unsure, but she was not and began trying to pull her dress off with her good arm. Matt joined in to help and then was very careful to be very gentle during the sex that she wanted so badly. Afterward, Misha said, "Can we get a place together? I really want, no need, you beside me every night."

Matt didn't hesitate in saying, "I think we can do that." They spent three hours online looking for a place to rent and quickly found out it was going to be financially draining. Further searches found that there was an extremely limited supply of affordable places nearby. This was the direct result of consolidation of many separate military medical, and ancillary service units, in the area. This was also why Matt, who was Navy, Misha, who was Army, and First Sergeant Bixby, who was a Marine were all in the same unit. Everyone who had been displaced or reassigned by the consolidations had snatched anything affordable up, months ago. The only time and reason anything affordable ever came available was the turnover of personnel. The next day, Saturday, they toured a few of the available offerings and found out it was going to be tougher to get out of the barracks than they thought.

Matt realized that he had a lot more patience these days and thought about what had changed in his life. Then he realized that it was Misha and caring for her. She saw him deep in thought and said, "What 'cha thinkin' bout?" His reply came slowly, "Taking the best possible care of you." She smiled and hugged him. He said, "Maybe we should think about getting a car and then a place to live." She smiled and said, "I haven't been able to spend any money for months and have some saved." "I bet you do too, except you have been paying for a lot of things we do. Let's do both, pretty please." He said, "Okay baby, let's do it." They submitted an application to rent the fourth place that they looked at then took a taxi back to the hotel.

In the evening, they searched online for a car. After some tender love making, Misha slipped into the bathroom and took two pain pills to cover the painful aftereffects. When she returned to bed, he asked her if she was okay, she lied and said, "Yes." He had doubts but let them go as she made it obvious, she was not done with sex for the day. She let her pain out in the sounds produced during the encounter and tried not to reach climax since she was sure that the accompanying muscle spasms would cause severe pain. Fortunately, the double dose of painkillers dulled her senses, and her shoulder also survived another encounter, mostly undamaged.

Sunday morning came with a gale force thunderstorm with blowing sheets of rain moving sideways. This put a severe damper on car shopping. They hung out in bed and by afternoon the storm had subsided. They got out of bed to go look at some cars. With limited transportation options, they simply went to the nearest dealership and Matt financed a used Toyota Camry that they both agreed was the best available option.

The week of waiting for the apartment began to drag as soon as the sun came up on Monday morning. At least they had the car, and they began to escape out into the surrounding areas in the evenings. Approval for the rental came on Thursday and they drove over to decide which, of the two open units, in the building, was right for them. It was a quick decision, Misha made it based on the proximity of the door to

the parking lot. She was actually thinking of Matt's inability
to walk over a hundred feet without difficulty, which had
become secondary to her issues.

THERAPY

I took two trips to move everything to the new apartment
from the barracks that Friday evening. It might have only
been one, but the Matt and Misha's physical limitations
meant only so much labor could be done at one time. The
weekend was low key, and they managed to get thing
relatively where they belonged. On Monday, Misha went to
the doctor. He looked at her records, did a short examination
then told her she had to start physical therapy immediately.
Then on Tuesday, Matt went to see his doctor, who told him
that he needed additional physical therapy to stop some poor
muscle alignment.

When they reported to the hospital together, they were
assigned to different therapists, but the same daily time slot
after they explained that they had limited transportation and
how much easier it would be to have appointments at the
same time. Not only did this allow them to travel together, it
helped with accountability. Matt could see Misha during her
physical therapy and noticed she was cringing and seemed to
be in pain.

That evening, he mentioned that he saw her struggling
during physical therapy. She exploded, "What do you know
about my pain? I am doing the best I can and it's not up to
you to judge me and how I'm doing!" Matt retracted, not
knowing what just happened. After a few tense moments, he
said, "I'm sorry." She ran into the bathroom slamming the
door behind her. Alone, and in control of her environment,
now she began wondering what had just happened and
broke into tears.

Ten minutes passed before Matt knocked lightly on the
bathroom door while cautiously asking, "Are you okay in

there?" He could hear the weeping in her voice as she answered, "I'm okay, be out in a minute." He went back to the futon that served as both their couch and bed. A few minutes passed before a bleary-eyed Misha popped a pain pill and exited the bathroom. She headed directly for Matt, standing in front of him and in a voice that was failing said, "I'm sorry, I didn't mean what I said." She dropped to her knees in front of him and choked out, "It hurts so bad, I don't know if I can do this." He touched her shoulder and said, "I know about pain, you know that about me. I just don't know what happened to my beautiful and loving girlfriend." Misha put her head on his knee and said, "I love you, please don't leave me." He said, "Why would I leave you baby, I love you. We just can't be having these episodes, it's too scary." She said, "It's the pain and the stress, not you. Please hold me." He did and soon she was asleep. He folded down the futon and very carefully got her stretched out and covered up. Wanting to let her get settled, he stood at the kitchen entranceway eating potato chips and watched at her as she slept. Unseen forces caused her face to contort and cringe. He thought about the pain and nightmares that stalked him and wondered if it worked the same for her. Eventually, he lay beside her and after a few hours, she nudged him.

He awoke expecting something horrible and instead heard, "Matt, I love you" He rolled over, and they looked into each other's eyes for a few seconds. He finally said, "I love you too Misha, please don't attack me like that again. I was scared you were going to leave me." Her immediate reply was an assuring, "You are my Prince Charming, how, or why, would I ever leave you." His brain was stumbling in the *how* part of what she said, and he managed to get out only, "Okay." She moved to kiss him, but a shooting pain scrunched her face up and he reached out for her. The moment broke into a hundred pieces, and she asked, "Would you get me my pain pills from the bathroom?" He did and when he picked up the bottle noticed it had about ten left in it, the fill date was three days ago, the dosage was one every twelve hours and there were originally thirty in the bottle. He noted the name of the pills and left the bathroom with the calculations repeating in his mind.

Returning to the living/bedroom, he handed her the pills and said, "I'll get you some water." She said, "A cold beer would be better!" So, he got both of them a beer. When he saw her take two of the pills, he pretended he didn't notice. He thought that maybe she really was in that much pain. Sunday turned into a blur of beer and pizza delivery since they had almost no food in the house, nor any pots and pans to cook in, anyway. Monday morning arrived with the pizza box, still containing three slices sitting on the counter. Matt carried it out to the dumpster as they left the apartment. He remembered putting the box in the refrigerator, which meant Misha must have been up during the night. He drove them to the unit, where they reported in then immediately went to the hospital for physical therapy. Matt isolated Misha's therapist while Misha was in the bathroom and asked him about her pain medication. The therapist seemed to understand that Misha was taking too many of the pills, but apparently failed grasp Matt's concerns.

That evening, Misha had another meltdown. Afterward, when she was calm again Matt said, "Baby, I don't think you realize it, but … Those pain pills are making you a little crazy. I think we should talk to your doctor about it." Her face went hard, and she firmly said, "I'll deal with it, so please drop it now." She stopped the conversation by suddenly changing her demeanor and giving him a come-hither look, accentuated by pulling up her dress to reveal only bare skin. He fell for her diversion and after he fell asleep, she took a pain pill along with two shots of the vodka that they had picked up on their way home from the hospital, at her insistence. It seemed to provide immediate relief, so she crawled back in bed beside Matt and fell into a dark, restless sleep. The next day she did go to see her doctor and he gave her a prescription for muscle relaxers to help the pain pills work better and hopefully cut down on the number of narcotics needed.

That evening, she took a muscle relaxer and a pain pill along with two double shots of vodka. She felt relief and there were no explosions or issues that evening. She used this good feeling to seduce him into multiple sexual encounters to deflect talking about pills, alcohol, and pain. He was happy that she had gone to her doctor and thought all this positivity was a result of that visit going very well. It wasn't, and when she got him to sleep, she quietly partook in another round of pills and vodka. The week passed with dinners of Chinese take-out and pizzas. On Saturday they went to the Post Exchange to purchase some basic housewares and then over to the Commissary for groceries. The last stop was at the liquor store where she grabbed two one and a half liter bottles of vodka. The day was already half over when they got home to set up housekeeping. She cooked some broiled salmon and steamed vegetables for dinner. Everything seemed to be fine, and the weekend passed without outburst or meltdowns. A state of bliss had seemingly settled over their abode.

They both worked hard at physical therapy, and everything went very well all week. The next weekend passed without incident and Matt thought everything was back to normal. This bliss continued for six more weeks. One evening moving to Florida came up again and they decided that they had to go for it. As they were probably beyond returning to full military duty, they both decided to request medical discharges as soon as possible.

FALLING DOWN

It was mid-fall and a morning rainstorm had soaked everything. Unusually large raindrops had knocked down many leaves prematurely leaving a green coating on the roadways and sidewalks. Matt was walking toward the transition unit with a song in his head when he hit a slick spot in the fallen leaves. He woke up three hours later in the hospital wondering what happened. Once he was awake, there was a CAT scan then soon after, orthopedic technicians applied a traction device to help hold his spine in place and relieve some of the pressure. Misha arrived an hour later. She had been at her own doctor's appointment and had made it all the way back to the unit before finding out what had happened. She spent all day with him but by evening felt a need to go home where she could take care of her own pain privately.

Around five, Matt said that she should just try to get some rest at home and not worry about him because he was going to be okay and had the nursing staff to look after him. She agreed and went home. Six shots of vodka, a muscle relaxer, and a pain pill later, she was in bed trying to sleep. After an hour and two more shots, she finally passed out. Soon, dreams came floating into her head and not good ones. Images of the attack that resulted in her original injury raced through her mind, but somehow the timing was all out of sync. This version had the wrong people in it! People that she knew to be alive were being killed. Finally, the dream climaxed and woke her up, fully drenched in sweat. It was close to five in the morning and even though she had slept, she felt exhausted. But, since it was almost time for the alarm, she got up and took a shower. The hot water helped her relax a little and she only needed a single pain pill to make it to the transition unit and report in. First Sergeant Bixby soon sent her to the hospital to be with Matt, much like he did with Matt when she had surgery. He did have some unspoken concerns though. His seventeen years of dealing with hard driving troops, and his own past, allowed him to spot a sergeant with a problem pretty quickly. He thought about what to do with Misha off and on all day while processing five discharges and one set of orders that allowed an eager young troop to return to his unit.

At the hospital, Misha had trouble sitting still and she couldn't focus on reading to Matt. By noon, she was so bored and cranky that Matt told her to go back to the unit and return sometime in the evening. She left but went home instead of going back to work and had a liquid lunch. After a short nap, she got up and headed back to the hospital. Three blocks from the hospital gate, she ran a red light and narrowly missed being run over by a cement truck. The blaring sound of the truck's horn quickly blasted her back into a sense of reality. She pulled over. After regaining a little composure, she continued on to the hospital. Before getting out of the car, she took another pain pill and had a shot of the vodka that she had brought, just in case of emergency.

When she got to Matt's room, she told him of the near accident, and he smelled the vodka. He asked her, "Baby, are you drinking and driving?" She said, "Yes, I just can't help it. My shoulder hurts so badly that I can't function. And now, dreams of the attack are haunting me, but they're all jumbled up." She began crying and he tried to comfort her, but the medical devices trapped him in the bed.

He had talked to a drug and alcohol counselor earlier in the day as part of the hospital protocol and he very cautiously asked Misha, "Baby, will you talk to the addiction counselor, please. I am worried about you." She looked at him and a little rage appeared in her voice as she replied, "See this arm, it's been strapped to my chest for so long that I don't even know if it will ever work right again. My shoulder was blasted into pieces, and it hurts. It hurts so fucking bad that I can't take it any longer." Matt reached for her hand, and she pulled it away and screamed, "Who the fuck are you to tell me what to do and when to do it, you don't know about my pain!" With that, she stormed out of the room.

A nurse that happened to be passing by the room stopped when an all too familiar conversation floated out the door.

She followed Misha to the door and asked her one question, "Do you love that man?" Misha's tear-streaked face added emphasis as produced the words, "He's everything to me and yes I do love him very much. He's just being an asshole right now." The vodka cloud hit the nurse's nose and she firmly asked Misha, "Are you on active duty?" Misha said, "Yes ma'am, realizing the nurse was wearing a gold oak leaf on her lapel." The nurse, Major Burke, said, "Come with me soldier." Misha followed.

At the substance abuse counselor's office door, Major Burke told Sergeant Pomeroy, "You now have two choices and there is only one right one. You will either go inside this office and be put into rehab, or I will have a chat with your commanding officer." Misha countered, "I only had a drink to calm me down, Matt is lying in bed and may never walk again." Major Burke countered, "Young lady, I have been around a lot longer than you. I can see by your sunken eyes and skin tone that you have had a problem for a while. If it's a medical issue, let's get down to the emergency room, if it's not…" She pointed at the abuse counselor's door. Misha's swirling mind still had enough military discipline for the words to come out of her mouth through the alcohol fog, "I'm going to go in and ask to be put into rehab." Major Burke smiled at Misha and said, "Please do your best, I am betting that Matt doesn't want to lose you. I will let him know what happened and where you are."

Misha knocked on the door and entered when given permission. The counselor asked questions and Misha provided the expected answers. Two hours later, Misha was in a locked rehab unit with a twenty-eight-day sentence. Major Burke stopped by and told Matt what had happened, and he thanked her for helping. She smiled and said, "Now, since you will have to help her keep herself in order, you will have to keep yourself in order." He knew exactly what she meant and thanked her again.

Matt slept better than he had in weeks, knowing Misha was safe, at least for now. Misha was angry and cursing everyone and everything that crossed her path. She was in a co-ed unit with twelve other persons in various stages of recovery and had only a sweat suit to wear. Her pain pills were now on a strict schedule, and she begged for them constantly until she would finally pass out. Nightmares came, they all involved Matt dying and her waking up in a cold sweat. The shower did not help so much this time and she went into a depression that left her just sitting on her bed. Fortunately, the staff had a lot of experience in this exact situation. They got her into a group session with people who had suffered similar situations. Her rehab days passed. and since Matt was unable to get out of his bed to visit, she went through all the stages of withdraw and denial alone. This was mostly because her support group only met for two hours each day leaving her mostly to her own devices. The group discussions about similar experiences and problems did help though and began to the alleviate the nightmares. However, a potentially bigger problem might be developing. The group, and the facility population in general, consisted of mostly men. And some of them were starting to show some interest. It was certainly a great temptation to commiserate, but she resisted. She even tried to project that she was not looking for companionship. Fortunately, at the next meeting the group leader announced again that there was a zero-tolerance policy against fraternization within the group and the rehab facility in general. The penalty was expulsion from rehab and disciplinary action under the Uniform Code of Military Conduct. Failure to successfully complete the program would, and there was great emphasis on the *world*, include the loss of pay, rank, or both. Twenty-three days passed before Matt was able to get a wheelchair to visit Misha. They talked through a plexiglass barrier for the maximum allowable time of ten minutes.

Misha didn't like seeing Matt in a wheelchair, and it scared
her to think that he may be confined to it forever. She had no
idea how to manage it, and cautiously asked him, "Are you
doing okay? How are your back and legs doing?"
Intertwined with, "I miss you so much, baby." Matt replied,
"It's only five more days; I am doing okay and can walk short
distances again. Everything on me is working, as far as I
know, and I can't wait to get out of this place and be together
with you." She asked, "When are you getting out?" He said,
"The day after you. The doctors won't discharge me without
someone to help me at home." She said, "What if I'm not
able? I still have pain and my next surgery is only a month
away." He said, "We can deal with this bump, if *you* still
want to, that is." She said, "Of course I still want to. Why
would you ever think otherwise?" He said, "Because you
seemed to be putting pills and booze ahead of me and it's
kind of hard to deal with that kind of rejection."
She said, "I have learned a lot here and think that type of
behavior has passed. You have to be supportive and tell me if
I start slipping, though. The whole thing just snuck up on me
and took over." He said, "I will be so happy to get back
home with you." After a deep kiss visiting time was over.
Misha said, "My wardens are telling me it's time to go, so see
you later." He said, "Only a few more days, baby." She was
escorted back into the locked ward, and he slowly made his
way back to his room.

HOME AGAIN

Misha was first to get out of the hospital. When she got
home, she dumped out all the liquor in the house then went
out and got some basic groceries. She had a frozen pizza for
dinner that evening. She planned on cooking steak and baked
potatoes for Matt's homecoming the following day.
She reported into the transition unit the next morning and
suffered a tongue-lashing from First Sergeant Bixby. She

broke down and he ignored her tears, which had no effect on him. When he finished, he asked her what she had to say for herself. She struggled for words as she said, "I didn't mean to become addicted; I thought my pain was unmanageable and just fell into the trap of self-medication." He asked, "Have you completely fucked up your relationship yet?" She said, "Matt still says he loves me, and I love him. So, I don't think so." He said, "You're lucky! And, by the way, I have gone out of my way to let you two have some happiness, so don't make me look like a fool! Got it?" She said, "Yes First Sergeant, I have it together now." He said, "Life's hard enough, don't make it harder. Now go get your man from the hospital and take tomorrow off. Remember, I'm giving you this time off in the hopes you are not planning to fuck things up." She said, "Thank you, First Sergeant Bixby." He waved her out of his office.

It seemed to take forever to get Matt out of the hospital. He could only walk about a hundred yards before needing rest and it was at least three hundred to the car. Misha offered to get the car and pick him up, but he said he had to walk at every opportunity, or he may have permanent wheels. She helped him walk to the car. Once they got to the apartment, Misha said, "Can we have sex without it hurting you?" He said, "God, I hope so. But you may have to perform some acrobatics." She said, "We had to do physical training in the rehab unit, so I can do about anything that doesn't require my right arm." They quickly figured out that she had to be on top and keep all her weight off him. They managed to get through it and started figuring out how to make it easier, for the next session, while she cooked dinner.

Dinner turned out excellent and afterward they cuddled and watched a movie on a laptop since they had Internet but no television. After a few hours, they went to bed on the futon. In the morning, Matt was very sore, and it took several minutes and a hot shower before he was able to walk with any normality. Misha was terribly upset and thought about vodka for a few seconds before shaking it off. After the shower, Matt said he was cooking breakfast and began peeling potatoes. She went into the kitchen area and offered to help. It was a good morning to be together.

After breakfast, they began looking for job prospects in Florida. The biggest obstacle was that neither of them had any professional training other than her being a nursing assistant and him being qualified to be a deckhand who was physically unable to perform the duties of that particular job. There would certainly be some disability assistance but that would never allow them to buy a Florida house. Matt said, "I liked taking care of you, maybe I can get some training and work in the medical field and we both can get a job at the same hospital." She said, "You could do that easily. They told us that the VA might help with training." He said, "I'll get to checking on that first thing tomorrow." She added, "I think I want to at least get up to LPN level." He asked, "What's that?" She laughed and said, "Licensed Practical Nurse, I just need to check Florida's requirements."

Misha discovered that since she had completed the Army's second level Medical Specialist training program, with the clinicals, that she would be allowed to take a test for Florida licensure after completing some required courses. Matt would have to complete an entire program, from scratch, to get any kind of license and still might only provide a chance of being hired by any hospital. Neither of them was destined to make any significant money.

The next morning, they reported in to First Sergeant Bixby and asked to be processed for medical discharges. He told them that it was going to take some time because of the backlog in scheduling the counseling sessions required. He asked them to describe their plans. Matt said, "I am going to get into nursing school and Misha is going to get her Florida nursing license, we have already been looking for a place to relocate." First Sergeant Bixby thought for a second and asked, "Why Florida?" Misha said, "The weather is always warm, which will be good for Matt's back and the population is older and requires more medical attention, which should keep us both employed." First Sergeant Bixby said, "Sounds good. But, have you considered pay versus cost of living?" Matt spoke up, "It will probably always be tight, but we think the tradeoffs are worth it." First Sergeant Bixby said, "I'll get you two on the schedules, when does your lease end?" Matt told him the date and since it was less than four months away it was not going to be an issue.

The next week, they finished the personal finance classes, started the benefits awareness training, and began the applications. Educational benefits were the next class. Both Matt and Misha decided to use the money they had managed to save through the military educational program to go to school in Orlando and applications went out.

Christmas came and they used the holiday to drive to Orlando for a week to check things out in person. They had both been accepted into training programs and wanted to drive by the school and check out rental places. They had just over a month before they were scheduled for discharge and needed to start getting it together. The put in two applications for rental apartments near the school and then they drove to Cocoa Beach to add some enjoyment out of the trip.

They were surprised at the coolness of the water and since they were not going to be swimming a whole lot, stayed on the beach and explored the area in the evenings. They found Canaveral Groves Hospital and decided it was the place where they wanted to work. The week off passed quickly and they begrudgingly drove back to Virginia. The nine hundred miles on I-95 ticked away, slower than anything they had ever experienced. There was much joking talk about turning around and living on the beach, as bums.

The sun seemed to be shining on Matt and Misha. Their training applications were accepted, apartment buildings approved them, their discharge processing was moving along without incident, and they were in love. Misha was first to receive her discharge and was rated at fifty percent disability by the military and still had no idea about the VA. Matt received news that something had happened to some of his paperwork and there would be a delay processing his discharge. This was the first hiccup, school was scheduled to start in a week and it was now estimated that he would not be discharged for at least a month.

They decided it was better for her to go ahead and move to Florida, start her classes and he would follow as soon as possible. First Sergeant Bixby did everything he could to speed up Matt's paperwork, but he was just a cog in the wheel and had extraordinarily little power to change the timeframe. Matt would have to move into the barracks for the time he had to remain behind. He was able to take a few days off to help with the drive down and get her settled into the new apartment. He would then have to fly back to DC, take public transportation and then a cab to get back to the transition unit but decided it was worth the hassle to get Misha set up.

IN THE SUNSHINE STATE

On the trip back up, Matt knew it was going to be a long month. He changed his application for training to the next class, which started in three months and was turned down because the class, and the next one after that, was already full of a special offering made to local high schools. After much agony and discussion with Misha and First Sergeant Bixby, Matt decided his only choice was to take the medical assistant class and at least start getting experience until a slot in a nursing program was available.

The separation and changes were hard on Misha, and she bought a bottle of vodka. The next day, a classmate looked at her and said, "Are you feeling, okay? You look terrible today." Misha said, "Rough night, I'll be okay soon." There was a slight slur in Misha's voice and her classmate, Debbie, said, "You need a different source of stress relief, let's have some dinner tonight and I'll hook you up." Misha agreed and a time and place was set.

The day droned on, and Misha was in the bathroom throwing up several times. By evening, she was starting to get re-hydrated and felling somewhat better. She made the meeting with Debbie, who immediately said they should go for a ride before eating. They did and Debbie drove them, in her pickup truck. She drove to a park and after selecting a secluded parking spot, lit a joint and passed it to Misha. Misha was hesitant but followed Debbie's lead and soon the second joint was gone. Misha decided this worked better than her muscle relaxer pain pill combo and after adding two beers felt great.

Misha began buying her own dope and smoking it daily. She didn't seem to have any pain, but all her grades dropped at least one full point. Matt had no idea what was happening, he was having his own issues and had just found out that the rating board was recommending seventy percent permanent disability retirement for him. The process slowed after the decision, for some unknown reason, and his discharge date was moved out a few more weeks. He missed Misha more each day. She seemed to be having the same problem and rationalized that it was the cause of her studying problems and subsequent drop in grades.

When Matt's discharge finally happened, he thanked First Sergeant Bixby for everything and got a final lecture about not fucking up his life by letting Misha get re-addicted to pills and booze. Matt thanked the good sergeant again and headed for the airport with everything he had in a large rolling suitcase that was difficult for him to maneuver with limited leg and back function. He made it through the public transportation system and after three hours arrived at the airport only to face a two-hour delay. Misha was getting ready for Matt's arrival by smoking extra dope and not drinking beer so he wouldn't smell it on her breath. She was watching the flight status on the Internet and when the two-hour delay was announced decided to take a nap for an hour. Misha woke up half an hour after Matt was due at the airport and panicked. She drove to the airport, as quickly as she could and as she was crossing State Route 528, her cell rang. It was Matt telling her the plane had just got to the gate and he would call her again as soon as he got his bag. She drove to the cell phone waiting lot and tried to find a place where she could light up without detection. It was simply too busy, and the anxiety of the late call was working on her nerves. A lot of cars left all at once and she quickly smoked half a joint before Matt called. She put out the spliff and stashed it in the ashtray before heading over to the passenger pickup at area A.

She got out of the car as Matt approached. She hugged him, kissed him, and then said she would put his bag in the trunk if he would drive. He accepted her offer and soon they were in the car. She reached over to kiss him again and he said, "Have you been smoking?" She coyly replied, "Yes, I got a joint from a classmate and it really helps the pain." Matt's stomach dropped. She saw his facial expression and said, "It's not that bad, I'm not abusing anything. I just found that if I smoke a joint and have a few beers, I don't have to take pain pills but twice a day instead of four times, and I actually feel better. I was hoping you would be alright with it." He said, "If it truly keeps you off the pain pills and heavy drinking, I'm okay with it. I want you to feel good and be happy." She said, "Thanks for not being mad." He was mad but decided it was not worth the drama of mentioning it. They arrived at the apartment, and it was immediately obvious to Matt that Misha was not the ideal housekeeper. It wasn't horrible, just very untidy and unlike a disciplined soldier. She got his bag inside and announced her desire to immediately get to the bedroom. Matt went along and twenty minutes later, they were lying naked in bed looking at each other. Matt asked her, "Are you sure you aren't heading back into addiction?" She said, "Marijuana isn't considered an addictive substance and I never drink more than three beers. In fact, usually I just have one beer and a joint at bedtime to help dull the pain and let me sleep. I'm telling you, I am feeling so much better these days." Matt was secretly relieved because this meant he didn't have to be a total non-drinker anymore.

Things were perfect between Matt and Misha and after a week, he started his nursing assistant training. They checked on VA benefits but were unable to navigate the rules, so they gave up. Since Misha had a head start, they both finished their program within a week of each other. She took and passed the nursing test and got her license and he got his certification as a nursing assistant, commonly called a CNA.

CAPE CANAVERAL

Matt and Misha wanted to get jobs that allowed them to work together, or at least work the same shift. Cape Canaveral Hospital was the first to offer this and soon they were both ready to start the night shift. Since working the overnight was not the most popular thing, it was relatively easy for them to get the same floor, but different duties kept them apart for most of their shift.

Matt was doing all right with walking these days and could operate the mechanical lifts and devices used to assist patients effectively, so that was initially what he was assigned to do. Misha was not considered a real nurse by some of the staff and got assigned to the hardest and the messiest jobs available. This was also a rite of passage since she was the new kid.

Soon there they established a pattern and after finding an apartment in Cape Canaveral, Matt and Misha began going to the beach in the mornings after work to smoke dope and relax as the day was just beginning for most people. At work,

Matt was not doing as well as Misha. He had a tough time with the acutely sick people and their demands. He soon found that it was the dying people that he could relate to far better. He began seeking more assignments to care for terminal patients. A nurse noticed this and asked him, "Matt, you ever thought about working private duty?" He replied, "What's that?" The nurse said, "There are a lot of people who can't be with a family member who is terminal, in a coma, or in some other severe state and they hire nursing personnel, who are off duty, to sit with them. There can be some good extra money in it if you can handle it." Matt said, "How is that different than what I do now?" The nurse said, "On private duty your job is to be there for one patient and only help the nursing staff if needed." Matt said, "I can manage that, but need to talk to Misha before I start. Can you tell me how to start?" He was introduced to an older woman who had spent the last week with her terminal husband and looked like she may collapse at any moment. The nurse introduced Matt to her and said, "Matt here is considering starting to do private duty, are you interested?" The woman, Martha, said in a soft grandmotherly voice, "I have to do something, staying here around the clock is starting to kill me." The nurse said, "The going rate is seventy-five dollars a shift and sometimes insurance will pay it. Normally, however the family pays the sitter cash and then seeks insurance reimbursement, if it is available." Martha looked at Matt and asked, "When can you sit for a shift?" Matt was off the next night and without thought said, "Tomorrow night." He had meant to discuss this with Misha first but the urge to do it was just too compelling.

When Misha and Matt were sitting on the beach watching the early morning surfers, Matt told her about the upcoming private duty. She said, "I wish you would have told me about it before taking it. I need you at home." He said, "We have each other all day and it's just a test. I'm not sure how often the work is available or if I can even handle it." She said, I'll go with you tonight and help you. I know you are having a hard time with a lot of things they make you do, even if I don't mention it. I see you struggling to walk after moving a patient and how hard it is for you to get back up, after cleaning something off the floor. Maybe this is actually a good thing." He kissed her and they went home to make love and get some sleep.

That night, Matt and Misha arrived to relieve Martha, who was surprised by two people showing up. She said, "Why are there two of you, I can only pay for one." Matt said, "This is Misha, she is a nurse here at the hospital and she is going to sit with me. It doesn't change our deal. This is my first time doing this and since she loves me, she offered to provide support." Martha smiled and said, "No hanky-panky, Max may be dying but he still has a moment or two every now and then." Matt said, "There will be no hanky-panky, you should go get some rest and let us take care of Max." She said, "If he gets restless, I read Moby Dick to him, he loves that book for some reason, and it seems to calm him down. The place where I stopped is marked. Do you mind?" Matt said, "No problem, that's what I'm here for." She said, "I hold his hand sometimes because I want him to know someone is here with him." Matt said, "I will take good care of him, and you should not worry while you're gone, I'm sure that he wouldn't want you getting sick over this." Martha thanked Matt and then said goodbye to him and Misha.

Misha waited until Martha was gone to say, "You managed that very well, honey." Matt thanked her and said, "Let's see what I've gotten us into." They entered the room proper and found Max in an agitated state. Matt walked to the bed, checked all the wires and tubes, and said, "Max, I'm Matt and this is Misha, we are going to be here for a while so Martha can go home to get some rest." Max seemed to calm down a little, Matt and Misha sat down. It was boring and soon Matt picked up the well-worn copy of Moby Dick and checked to see where the bookmark was. He found it was on page one and asked Misha if she minded him reading it aloud. She said, fine with me, so he began. *Call me Ishmael…*

The reading seemed to have an effect on Max and the heart monitor showed a marked decrease in rate, missed beats, his breathing evened out a little and his blood pressure dropped on the next reading. Matt read most of the book over the night and at one point when he touched Max's hand, he had a vision. He thought it was just a combination of the book and him being tired, but it wasn't. Misha noticed something too but was in a big chair half-asleep and didn't fully wake up to mention it.

Matt pulled his had away and a few seconds later touched Max's forearm again. The same sensation and vision returned, and Matt decided to see where it went. A few seconds passed and Matt was on a sailboat without any land in sight. He could smell the salt and feel the wind on his face. Max stirred, broke the contact and Matt returned to reality. This was startling to Matt, and he stepped away from the bed. Max became restless and Matt returned to reading.

Morning came and a freshly showered and happier Martha arrived. She handed Matt a wad of cash and said, "When can you do this again?" Matt said, I am off again in five days, so I can do it then. Misha smiled and they left for the beach.

At the beach, Misha commented about this new opportunity by saying that if he thought that it was going to be better for him than actually working for the hospital, he should pursue it. He said, "I think that I will have to try it a few more times before making any decisions. The week passed and Matt was now spending the night alone with Max. After reading for a while, he touched Max's forearm and was again on the ocean aboard a sailboat. The stars seemed so real and so close that Matt felt like he could reach out and touch them.

When Martha arrived in the morning, Matt asked her, "Did you guys ever own a sailboat?" She said, "How did you know?" Matt said, "I didn't, it was just a guess based on

Max's love of Moby Dick." She said, "We had a sixty-footer, right after Max retired from the Navy and sailed around the world one year. It was the best time I think we ever had. Thank you for reminding me about that time of our life." Matt said, "You're welcome and I can sit more often, if you like." She said, "Every other night would be nice, but you know Max is not long for this world, the cancer has almost finished with him." Matt said, "I'll take the work as long as it's available." He then went to hospital personnel and asked to be placed on part-time nights and since there always seemed to be a shortage of male nursing personnel, he was allowed to work two nights on Misha's schedule. He went straight home anticipating getting in bed with Misha.

That night, Matt and Misha worked together and talked about the recent changes during slack periods. Misha was still a little uncertain of Matt's decision. He had absolutely no uncertainty and, over the night, convinced her that it was a good plan. She hoped so and knew that the seventy-five dollars in cash, per shift, was a little bit more than he made working directly for the hospital. Health insurance was not an issue since they both received care from the Air Force base not very far to the south or could go to the VA clinic on the mainland.

Max died on the next shift while Matt was there. Matt knew instantly what had happened and thought it was a strange coincidence that a thunderstorm rumbled in at that precise moment and a long rolling thunderclap seemed to shake the room. When the thunder passed, Matt sensed that the room seemed emptier and sure enough, the ECG machine was flat lining and Max was gone. Matt touched his forearm, and the sailing sensation did not come. He called the nurse on duty and then helped clean and prepare Max for the trip to the morgue. It was not distressing for some reason because he somehow knew Max was happy where he was now.

Matt had never been very religious and didn't quite know if he believed in a heaven or hell. He just thought that Max simply no longer inhabited his physical body, and thus it was no longer necessary. He couldn't even think it through enough to explain it to Misha, so he decided not to bring it up. Martha arrived in tears, but still managed to thank Matt and shove a wad of cash in his hand. She hugged him, thanked him again for being so kind to a dying man and then left. Matt put the money in his pocket and began to leave, wondering where he would pick up more work. He made it about fifteen feet before an older woman approached him and said, "Martha said you sit with people who are dying. Can you sit with my husband?" Matt said, "I have to work a regular shift tonight, but I can tomorrow night." She responded, "That would be perfect, I understand it is seventy-five dollars a night." Matt said, "That is correct." She said, "I will see you tomorrow evening at seven then. My name is Bella, and my husband is Hank. He's in room 251." Matt said, "I'll see you then." He continued on his way out and, while waiting for the elevator, was approached by a man. The man said that he had a dying son and asked to be next in line and even offered one hundred dollars a shift.

HANK AND BELLA

Matt arrived at Hank Parsons' room a few minutes early and Bella was starting to gather things to go home for a few hours. She asked Matt if he would please take good care of Hank. Before leaving, she called Matt into the hallway, "I don't think he will make it through the night, he's not breathing very well and was awake today for the first time in a week. I told him you were coming, and he said that I had to go home. This happened to my mother when my father was dying. He sent her to the store for some Ginger Ale and died a few minutes after she left. I guess he just wanted to spare her from seeing it." Matt said, "I will take good care of Hank and hopefully he will still be here in the morning." With that, she returned to the room, kissed Hank, told him that she loved him and began crying as she left the room.

Alone with Hank, Matt could hear the labored breathing and the sound of building congestion. Matt carefully repositioned his charge and the gurgling temporarily abated. Looking around the room, he discovered a copy of the bible and picked it up. It was a well-worn, leather-bound copy of the New Testament and the dedication page said it had been presented to Hank at his and Bella's first wedding anniversary in appreciation of his service in Korea. Matt flipped through the pages and found passages marked in highlighter.

When Hank became restless, his breathing hard and raspy, Matt began reading the marked passages. Matt did not grow up in a religious home and had little exposure to the Bible, so it was a few minutes before he got used to the rhythm and language of the passages. He read at least seventy-five passages and Hank seemed to calm down and breathe more easily. It was four o'clock in the morning when Misha showed up and asked how things were going. She said there wasn't anything going on in her area, so the head nurse let her take a pager and come to visit. A hug and kiss seemed to cause the pager to activate, and she left to return to her ward. Matt returned to Hank's side and touched his arm. There was an immediate feeling of calmness that came over him. Hank's body seemed to jerk a little and then Matt felt the energy in the room change. He checked for a pulse and breathing and found none. He knew from reading Hank's chart that there was to be no resuscitative effort and pressed the nurse call button. The nurse on duty was Tony who came along after around five minutes. Tony stuck his head into the room and asked, "Can I help you?" Matt said, "Mr. Parsons has passed away." Tony said, "I see, I'll call for a doctor to pronounce it." Ten minutes later, all the lights were on in the room and the on-call doctor signed the paperwork making Hank Parsons officially dead.

Matt cleaned up Hank's silent body and prepared him for the ride to the morgue. A technician with the special morgue gurney arrived and the body was transferred from the bed. This gurney was special in that the stainless-steel tray that served as the bed slid off the frame and into the morgue's refrigerated compartments. Bella arrived as the technician was about to leave the room. She asked the two men, "Can I have a final moment or two." Both said, "Yes," almost in unison, Bella handed Matt money, and he and the technician went into the hallway, closing the door behind them. Matt put the money in his pocket without any thought.

After five minutes, Matt and the technician began to worry and knocked on the door. There was no answer. Matt knocked again and asked the technician to please find Tony. The technician walked to the Nurse's Station and soon returned with Tony. Tony knocked and again there was no answer, so he cautiously opened the door and saw Bella on the floor beside the gurney clutching the sheet she had pulled off Hank as she fell. Tony rushed to her and snapped, "Call a *code blue!*" Matt pulled the cord on the wall and an alarm went off at the Nurse's Station and in the Emergency Room." Tony began CPR and Matt joined in. The room became a flurry of activity and the morgue technician quietly wheeled Hank away thinking that he might be coming back for Bella in a few minutes.

Matt took over chest compressions and on the second one, felt one of Bella's ribs snap from her sternum. This was not something that he had been warned of in training and it took him by surprise. Tony saw Matt's reaction and said, "Happens all the time, just keep trying." Matt could feel that Bella was no longer in her body but went through the motions, like a professional must do. The doctor arrived and after a quick exam, pronounced her dead. Further exam found the reason, her left pupil was twice the size of her right, and the doctor said the cause of death was almost certainly a massive stroke. Matt assisted with the cleanup and then helped the morgue technician load the next body onto the sheet covering the cold, shiny tray.

Matt reflected on how someone was usually called by their name while alive but as soon as they were dead, healthcare personnel tended to refer to them as *the body*. He realized that he did it also and realized that it was common. He thought it might be an unconscious mechanism to help the worker's cope with the sudden transition between life and death. His thoughts were interrupted by Misha arriving and asking if he was ready to go.

At the beach, Misha noticed Matt's mood and asked, "What happened?" Matt said, "Mr. Parson's died, and his wife arrived as we were getting the body out of the room and asked for a few minutes. She had a stroke and died while we were in the hall waiting." Misha said, "Her heart must have been broken beyond repair and sent a rush of blood up to allow her to join him." Matt looked at the horizon and thought about this while they smoked a joint.

CHANGES OF FORTUNE

Arriving at work, Misha was told to report for a mandatory drug test and her stomach dropped. She did as instructed though and tried not to think about what was going to happen. She found Matt and told him what happened, and he pulled her into a supply room and said, "They will make you either take rehab or dismissal and once they know you're positive I'll probably be selected for a test." She asked, "What do you want to do?" He said, "I have private duty gigs lined up. So, I will resign in the morning and work the private duty so we will have income beyond our retirements, and you should do the rehab so you can keep your license." She said, "Shit, I don't know if I can actually do another round of rehab." He said, "We have to do something, baby. And fast" She looked lost in thought for a second and then responded, "Okay, I'll do the rehab and you can do the private duty thing. Then I want to move further south so we can try to start over at another hospital. I'll probably always be on the testing list here." Matt agreed and they returned to work.

In the morning, they waited until the personnel office opened and then she asked for employee assistance drug and alcohol rehab, and he turned in his resignation. They then went to the beach for a short visit and home to sleep because Matt had work in the evening.

After Matt left, Misha watched a movie on the laptop while drinking a beer. Afterward she decided that since she was going to be in rehab and couldn't drink or smoke for a month, she might as well go for it. After finishing all the beer in the house and smoking a couple of joints, she decided to walk over to the convenience store and get more beer and some munchies. On the way home, a man approached her and tried to pick her up. She said no thank you I already have a boyfriend and sped up. The man was persistent, and she finally was scared enough to break into a trot. The man seemed to be considering running after her and she sped up. She arrived at the apartment, ran inside, and locked the door. Her buzz was gone, and it pissed her off. She found another movie to watch and began drinking and smoking again. The excitement of running from the man wore off and her shoulder began hurting. She took two pain pills and went back to drinking.

Matt arrived home in the morning to find Misha passed out on the couch with a beer can in her hand and the laptop on the floor. He rushed to her and tried to wake her, she was unresponsive, so he checked for a pulse. Finding that she had a pulse, he settled down a little and began looking around. He found ten empty beer cans and evidence of at least seven joints consumed. Lastly, he noticed that her pain pills were on the counter. He checked the bottle, and it had plenty in it, so he decided she hadn't overdosed.

Matt carried Misha into the bedroom, stripped her and put her in bed. She had gotten mad at him the last time for leaving her clothes on and complained about how the clothes restricted her and made her sore for two days afterward. He decided to do some laundry because he needed some clean clothes for the shift he had arranged for that night. He began checking pants pockets and discovered that he had forgotten to remove the cash that Martha had given him. He counted two hundred fifty dollars and wondered why she had overpaid him so much. A few minutes later, he found the cash from Bella, and she had given him five hundred dollars. He put the money in a jar and hid it in the pantry. Then, he started the washer and decided to crawl in bed with Misha.

SURVIVING REHAB – ROUND TWO

Misha got a call about two in the afternoon with the expected news. Her drug test was positive for cannabis, and she was relieved of duty and told to report at eight the next morning at the selected rehab facility. It was an inpatient program for the first two weeks and then ten hours a day for two more weeks. Misha approached the whole thing with trepidation and Matt worried it was going to be a long-term issue that would split them up in the long term.

Matt continued to work at night, relieving families of their deathwatch duties and got leads on people needing services in nursing homes and hospice facilities. It was strange because, he thought that the hospices had a high level of personal care for their patients and that would negate any need for his services but there was demand. Misha attended drug rehab classes and suffered being constantly hit on by the males in the class. She was bored and lonely by the fourth day and hated being there. Matt was not allowed to visit during the first two weeks. Supposedly, this helped the rehab patients break bad relationships and start fresh. It didn't, it mostly caused the patients to develop relationships with each other and arrive back to reality as a pair of addicts that mostly helped each other back into rehab, jail or worse. She tried to hide in her room, but group meetings prevented her from total seclusion.

The rehab program had a remission rate of around sixty percent but managed to retain their contracts with several large businesses in the area because the re-admissions were spread out among all of the businesses and therefore had little effect on one business at any given time. Then there was the tendency to simply blame the patient and not the program. This was, after all, a money-making venture with owners and investors that expected profits. Misha was caught up in the whole business aspect of the operation and was being shuffled through the system robotically. Since she had to either complete the program successfully, or potentially lose her job and nursing license, she had much motivation toward success. The men were becoming obnoxiously blatant in their attempts to get her alone for a while by the end of the two weeks and she almost fell for one of them. He was a charmer and their similar circumstance made him even more attractive. She fought the urge to surrender and made the two-week mark without demerit to her morals.

Matt had worked every night since dropping Misha off and picked her up after an especially hard night with a young man dying of melanoma. He had to present himself to the staff before she was allowed to leave with him, and they only saw a man who looked strung out. He explained to them that he had just worked fourteen straight twelve-hour overnights and then explained to them what he did. They all knew that was enough to string anybody out and allowed Misha to leave with him after he promised to take a few days off and help her. It was Friday morning, and the sun was having a tough time poking through a layer of nimbostratus cloud cover.

PARADISE FOUND

Misha held onto Matt like she was going to be torn away by hungry lions as they walked to the car. She was so happy to be out of the facility that she wanted to run to the car and speed off before they decided to make her come back inside for another round. No one chased them down and they made it to the car unscathed by rampant felines. Matt opened her door, and she noticed two backpacks sitting on the back seat. Matt got into the driver's seat and said, "We have until Monday, so we are going to the Keys for the weekend. She said, "I need some attention, it's been a long two weeks." Matt came back with, "We are going to be in a hotel in Marathon in a few hours and you will be getting so much attention that you might have trouble walking for rest of the weekend." She smiled and giggled a little while saying, "I guess that'll work, let's go!" Matt headed over to I-95 and then southbound.

Misha was wearing a dress and as they headed toward Miami at eighty-five miles per hour, she asked Matt what he packed for her to wear. He said, "Bikinis and dresses, you always look so good in those sun dresses." She said, "What about underwear, bras, and things like that?" He smiled and said, "None, you shouldn't need them where we're going." She said, fine, "I don't need them now then." With a sly grin, she slipped off her panties and threw them in his lap. He said, "You shouldn't do things like that to a man driving you down the road at ninety miles an hour." She said, "What fun would it be any other time?" He smiled and the miles ticked away.

Misha reclined her seat and napped as they entered the Florida Turnpike at Fort Pierce. He woke her up as they crossed Jewfish Creek, on the new bridge with, "We're about to enter the Keys." She sat up, looked at Lake Surprise and said, "Not quite what I expected." He said, "Me either, but we'll see what happens in the next fifty miles." After getting through the stoplights and traffic of Key Largo, it seemed that the Keys in the postcard began to appear sporadically. By Marathon, they felt like there had been a transformation. They checked into the hotel and were in the bed seconds after entering the room. After a short nap, it was time to go exploring. They drove past a hospital and instantly looked at each other with the same thought in mind. Just then, the trip became a mission to find a place to live and a job. Neither of which was going to be easy because they were definitely not the first couple to have this idea. They had blackened fish sandwiches at Keys Fisheries sitting at a picnic table overlooking the water. It was far more romantic than either imagined and the headed back to the hotel for more together time.

On Saturday morning, the sun rose with a splash of color behind a few tall cumulous clouds that looked like mountains in the distance. It was a lovely day and they drove side streets and US 1 seeking for rent signs, read every paper that they could find and searched the Internet. The hospital did have openings, so Misha filled out an online application but not Matt. When she said it was his turn, he said, "I think that I just want to continue the private duty work. I'm sure there will be opportunities down here." She said, "That's fine with me. Now, let's go get a tropical drink to celebrate." He said, "Really? Won't that blow your rehab?" She said, "No, they only test for drugs unless you were there due to alcohol." He was unsure but said, "Promise to not let it get out of hand?" Her look told him to shut up, and he did.

It was not a drunk-fest night, but several drinks were consumed. The hotel room rocked until early in the morning and then went quiet. They barely made checkout time and then he drove them back to Cape Canaveral. They were not in a hurry, so they made a stop in Miami Beach. It was not what they expected even if there were a lot of people who seemed to be enjoying it. They got off the Interstate in Fort Pierce and took A1A the rest of the way up, stopping just north of Sebastian Inlet for something to eat. It was nine thirty, at night, when they arrived back at their apartment, and they immediately went to bed. Misha had to report to rehab at seven in the morning.

ESCAPE

The next week did not allow a lot of interaction between Matt and Misha because he was working at night, and she was going to rehab during the day. They managed to meet a few times and have sex but mostly it was just passing each other coming and going.

Misha finished her required rehab. She was allowed to return to her nursing duties after a warning that only one chance was granted, and she could be fired for another incident. She knew this was complete bullshit since two of the floor nurses had both had been to rehab twice and she knew for a fact that both were still smoking pot regularly. The shortage of personnel to fill certain time slots and to do certain duties guaranteed almost constant employment, as long as you're not purposely killing patients. Two weeks passed and she and Matt got back on the same schedule. Some days later, she got a call from the hospital in Marathon. The interview was by phone. Since she was okay in the State license database, her supervisor had given her a good reference and she was a disabled veteran, it was a successful interview. A start date was negotiated that allowed only two weeks for her to get down to Marathon and find a place to live. She and Matt both knew that it was not going to be easy but were determined to make it work.

Matt said that he could stop sitting in a week and they could go then. Misha gave a one-week notice and Matt told the people he was currently working for that he would be gone in a week. Unfortunately, Matt was done in four days because a patient died. He spent two days at the apartment packing while Misha finished her time. They had accumulated quite a few more things and now needed a U-Haul to move. Misha didn't want to drive the car by herself, claiming it caused her shoulder to hurt, so they rented a truck and a car-hauling trailer.

A mutual decision not to smoke dope until after Misha's initial drug test was made early in the trip, somewhere around a stop for fuel just before getting on the Turnpike. She figured the test would happen on day one of the job and stuck to the beer she bought while Matt fueled the truck. She drank the better part of a twelve-pack while Matt drove. The trip down to Marathon took ten hours due to her need for pit stops, the general slowness of the truck pulling the car on the trailer and traffic. Matt started suffering from back pain, from loading and driving the truck, but tried to keep it to himself so Misha wouldn't worry and have an excuse to drink more. They had found a transient motel while driving around during the last visit and decided that it was going to be there home until they could find an apartment. Matt had called and arranged for a long-term room a few days earlier while packing. When they got there, it was dark and Matt asked Misha, "Do you mind if we wait 'till morning to unload and just get a pizza for dinner?" She slurred, "No problem, I'm too tired to do anything anyway." Matt ignored her drunkenness and apparent uncaring attitude, attributing it to the big changes happening in their life.

They slept on the motel bed and after Matt decided that it was suspect, covered it with one of their blankets and then a sheet. As they lay there Misha said, "I will help you unload in the morning, as best as I can but right now, I want to break in our new place." He agreed by rolling closer to her and starting to kiss her. Not long after that, they were both sound asleep. The next morning was off and on rainy, so it took a long time to get their belongings into the oversized hotel room. It was a surprisingly tight fit and they both said that a storage unit was probably in their future. Matt quickly suggested, "We should really try to deal with it and not spend any extra money until we're both working again." The first thing they decided to do was to find a non-tourist place to hang out at, since the motel room was very restrictive. This search took two days before they stumbled into a small bar where the tourists failed to go. It was not on the water, near a resort or on a main road and it was obvious that the crowd was all locals. At the bar, Matt ordered a beer and Misha got hit on. She looked at the offeror and said, "Let's get something straight here. I am with Matt, here, and I will be working at the hospital starting next week, he deals with dying people. This looks like a place we might hang out, so don't push my buttons already." The man shrank into his barstool and Misha ordered herself a beer. The bar resumed its buzz and soon there were introductions and discussions about living places and arrangements. Once it was known that Misha and Matt were not just slumming, the attitude toward them changed and by the end of the night, they were well on their way to being considered locals. The bar had a small TV and room for a band, but it looked like no one had played there in years. It also regularly served a few food items that required minimal preparation or attention.

The real reason the bar had a kitchen was they cooked fish that the patrons brought from tourist charters. The tourists would go out on the boat, fish, keep everything that was legal and then, at the end of the day decide they couldn't deal with the catch at the hotel. Most didn't want to pay to have it frozen and shipped home. So, the crews ate a lot of fish. There was a fish fry every Friday and Saturday night and anything left was cooked on Sunday afternoon. Misha and Matt discovered on Friday night that the term *fish fry* was a bit of a misnomer. The fish was cooked in many ways and the regulars all brought something to share like Coleslaw or potato salad. The bar survived by charging a dollar for each plate and the increased alcohol sales. A lot more people showed up on Friday and Saturday, so the beer and wine sales shot way up. It also helped that most of the patrons walked or rode bicycles, which greatly reduced the fear of a DUI, which led to greater consumption.

NEW JOBS

The move to Marathon went smoothly. They were both excited about this new life journey, so the confinement of the hotel room never became an issue. On Sunday afternoon, while at the favorite local hangout, someone finally asked Matt what exactly it was that he did. When he explained it, the inquirer was at first taken aback and then just stared at him. Soon, everyone there knew Matt's occupation was sitting with people who were dying. He had three job leads within minutes and his first gig lined up by the time the bar closed at five in the afternoon.

Monday came and Misha went to the hospital and Matt went to a nursing home. The Key's rate appeared to be a hundred dollars a night and after all was arranged, Matt went to have lunch with Misha at the hospital. She was happy that he was already working and then told her news, "I 'm finished with personnel, had my drug test, and start working tomorrow night. Can I come with you tonight to help get back into the night rhythm?" He said, "I don't see why not. What time do you think you'll get out of here?" She said, "No later than two, so we can nap before going. Can we eat there?" He said, "I guess that they have food there and a nap sounds like a good idea."

This was the first nursing home job for Matt and soon after arriving, he knew this particular assignment was not going to be a long-term. Jim Young was at least ninety years old and his wife, Mae was almost as old. Mae had been sitting with Jim around the clock for two weeks because she was sure he was going to die at any moment. Matt decided that, based on the odor, Jim's care had been neglected for at least a week. Once he got Mae to promise to go home, clean up and get

some rest, he and Misha began cleaning up Jim and his bed.
They found that there were two bedsores on his right butt
cheek and the bed seriously needed changing.

After getting Jim, and his bed cleaned up, Misha went
looking for something to eat. The staff was sparse after
visiting hours and she discovered that the only food available
was by delivery. She went back to Jim's room and after some
discussion with Matt, went out to pick up some Chinese
food.

Morning came and Mae returned looking exactly like she did
when she left the previous evening. Matt was concerned
about her, but she seemed to be cheerful and handed Matt a
crisp hundred-dollar bill as she went to the bed to check on
Jim. She saw Jim was in a clean bed, turned and seemed
comfortable so she turned and said, "Can you come again
tonight?" Matt said, "Sure, see you at seven."

Matt and Misha went to Coco Plum Beach for sunrise. They
found that a yoga group met there at that time and quickly
decided they needed to find another place to get back into the
smoking at sunrise habit. The days were hot, the motel room
was kept dark, and the large window air conditioner made
enough noise to block out the nearby construction and road
noise. It was still too short a time between getting home,
getting up, eating, and going back out to work. They both
were working from seven in the evening until seven in the
morning and that seemed to be the best pattern for their life.
The only rule was that they had to have either Friday or
Saturday night off for the fish fry and Sunday afternoon
gathering at the local hangout.

Thursday night rolled around, and it was stormy. Matt was
still taking care of Jim and Jim was especially restless. Since
Mae had not given any information about what Jim liked
when he was younger, Matt went by the library and checked
out a Tim Dorsey novel called *Hurricane Punch*. He was
reading to Jim and at around two in the morning he noticed
Jim was especially still. He touched Jim's left forearm and got

a feeling of being on a boat on a moonless night with stars everywhere. Matt was thinking about the brightness and number of the stars and after a few minutes, Jim was no longer there. Mae arrived at about the same time, for some reason, and thanked Matt for his time. She handed him a hundred and said she would have to sell the boat now. Matt was surprised how well she was handling Jim's death and wondered how she knew when to arrive. She solved the mystery, in a way, by saying, "Today is our seventieth anniversary and I could tell he was about to go when I left earlier in the evening. We discussed this all at length and he insisted over and over that I was not to be sad or do anything rash. We also decided that I should sell the boat, while it still has value, and go somewhere comfortable. Since I am ninety-two, it doesn't much matter where I go, as long as I get to be scattered near where I am going to scatter him, after I die. Are you interested in more work?" Matt said, "Sure, what can I do for you?"

She said, "We have been living here in the Keys, on a boat for forty years now. Not the same boat, mind you, but on a boat. Now I have to deal with that boat and since you, and your girlfriend have been extra kind to us I want you guys to get the boat." Matt said, "That's way more than we could ever afford." She said, "I am not selling it to you, but you will have to earn it. I still need care and tending, plus the boat is now twelve years old and will soon need some work too." Matt said, "Let's take care of Jim first and continue this discussion later." She agreed and they alerted the staff. Mae signed some forms that were pre-filed with the facility and Matt helped prepare Jim for the funeral home that was coming for the body. Mae insisted on taking Matt to see the boat after the funeral home attendant left. He drove because she had walked. Actually, it was not that far away. After parking and then walking down a fairly long dock, they arrived at a forty-four-foot Defever Offshore Trawler named The Dreaming Moon. Matt took this as a sign but still

couldn't figure out how he and Misha were going to pay for her. He was excited though and took the tour of the two staterooms and combined salon and galley. She was in immaculate shape, every detail had been seen to and there was not a fingerprint on any of the stainless or brass. He looked at Mae and, "She is a beauty, but we are disabled vets and working low end medical jobs so there's no way we could ever afford something this nice." Mae said, "Sometimes fate smiles on you, other days it rains. Today is a smiling day for you and for me. You see, no one helped us, Jim deteriorated so rapidly after a stroke and I struggled with caring for him here on the *Dee,* that's what we called her. When I could no longer physically do it, I had to call a medical transport to get him over to the nursing home. There was just no one in any shape to help us." Matt asked, "Don't you have children?" Mae replied, "Dead. Both died years ago. Jim, Jr. died in a car wreck and Jasmine in a plane crash. Seems Strange how death seems to stalk some families closer than others. We learned from those experiences that everything must be in order or those left behind will be thrown into chaos and misery. That's why Jim and I laid everything out. You're not going to live forever, you know. It's a fact."
They returned to the deck and as Mae stared into the sunrise she continued her lecture, "The Dee is paid for, solid and seaworthy. We haven't had her out in almost two years, but I can assure you the engines are in pristine condition and everything else is in fine working order. Jim was a boat mechanic all his life and took pride in his work. As far as money goes, I will be getting half a million dollars from Jim's life insurance and am going to move into an assisted living facility. I plan to donate a lot of the money to help preserve our reefs and the boat is yours, if you can help me." Matt said, "Okay, what do I need to do?" She said, "Help me take Jim's ashes out and up the coast off Miami Beach. He loved to cruise up there when we were younger and that's where he

wanted to be dropped off. Then you have to promise to read to me on my last day and then take my ashes up to Miami Beach and release them into the surf. That will let me meet Jim again and we can repeat our life in eternity." Matt said, "I can do all that but have never had a boat of any size, so I will have to find somebody to help me." She smiled a wrinkled smile and said, "You're looking at her! We start tomorrow at eight in the morning and bring that lovely girl of yours with you. By the way, I pay one hundred dollars a day for a deckhand." Matt began to present an argument and she cut him off, "I ain't exactly poor, so don't feel bad accepting the pay. You were kind to Jim, and he would have done this exact thing if he was alive, and I was dead." Matt felt he had no choice and said, "Thank you, and I'll see you tomorrow." She handed him a hundred and said, "Bring a bottle of single malt, we have to send Jim off with a toast, you know." Matt Luna looked at the name, Dreaming Moon, neatly stenciled on the stern of the boat and again thought it was a sign. The *Dee* he thought was a gift from heaven and he hurried to tell Misha the good news. As he got into the car, his phone rang, and Misha asked if he had forgotten her. He said that something amazing happened, that he couldn't explain it over the phone and would be there in to pick her up in less than ten minutes.

THE DREAMS OF THE MOON

Matt arrived at the hospital's employee entrance and Misha was waiting with her arms crossed. It had been an especially rough night for her. There had been an accident on US 1 involving a church van and a semi-truck that netted her four new admissions. Getting them settled, and then doing the data entry work, had taken most of her time. She had seven other patients and it was a mad rush to get everything done before the day shift arrived. She had enough experience to know that if she left the day shift work, they would return the favor, with interest, and then it would become a vicious cycle. Needless to say, she was unhappy that Matt was late. Matt was all smiles when Misha got into the car and leaned over to kiss her. She pecked him and said, "We need two cars so when you are late, I can get home from work." Matt said, "We don't have a home, yet. Don't you think we should deal with that before buying another car?" She said, "Yes, it was just a bad night and I need to get relaxed." Matt drove them to the end of a street, with a view to the east and a small piece of waterfront. They sat on the rocky piece of beach smoking a joint. He wanted to tell her all about the Dee, but she was jabbering about her night so much he couldn't get a word in edgewise. It was so bad that he finally asked her, "What's going on with you? You're jabbering like crazy this morning!" She said, "Melody, at work, gave me some speed to help me get through the night." Matt said, "Seriously? We don't have enough problems already?" She said, "It was just this once, I just couldn't keep up." Matt said, "Jim died, and I have to tell you something important." She got on a rant about how she was in charge of herself, and he didn't need to worry about her drug use because it wasn't his body in pain and trying to keep up. She then pouted and smoked a joint by herself. Matt decided to keep the news about the Dee until they woke up later in the day.

They picked up a drive-through breakfast on the way back to the motel. Matt ate while she showered and then she ate while he showered. Misha had slowed down considerably, and they curled up in bed with the air conditioner going full blast. At four in the afternoon, Matt woke up. He began looking online for information about the Dee and it wasn't long before Misha was looking over his shoulder asking why he was looking at yachts. He casually said, "Because we have one." She answered, "Been buying lottery tickets again?" He said, "No, but I did hit the jackpot." She said, "What are you talking about, already?" He said, "Jim's wife, Mae is giving us their boat because I was kind to him." She said, "Great, a piece of crap that we will have to maintain and store somewhere." He decided her attitude meant he better not try to explain things and said, "In the morning, I am taking you to see it. I think your tune will change, then." She said, "Whatever, I'm starving."

They went to the regular bar and ordered their regular fish sandwiches and fries. Misha had two beers as Matt wondered how she planned to work, they never drank before work, and he was stunned by her behavior. She said, "I can handle it, just don't worry." Matt didn't say a word and as they left, she said that she needed to get some gum at a convenience store. Matt said, "I only have a few hours of work tonight, remember. And we are going to look at our new boat in the morning." She said, "Whatever!" and he dropped her off at the hospital.

Matt had lined up a few hours relief for a man sitting with his wife and drove over to the nursing home. The man was happy to be able to leave for the four hours and the woman was conscious and alert. Matt felt that this was getting beyond what he now considered his regular job but decided to stay, since he was there already. The man was anxious to leave and as soon as the introductions were over, left Matt to sit with an older woman who was awake and very chatty. She told him all about how she and her husband had met and when their babies were born, and the four hours dragged along. Her husband reappeared on schedule, gave Matt the full hundred dollars, and asked if he would come back once a week. Matt decided it was worth working four hours for eight hours pay and agreed. That was the start of his sitting with Sally Rogers, who was one of the youngest persons in the facility at forty-eight years old.

Matt went to the motel room and organized things a little while thinking about what he had to do so that he and Misha could move onto the Dreaming Moon. He also worried about Misha's newly developed bad habit and considered getting the boat in his name only just in case she continued to flake out on him.

At seven in the morning, Matt was waiting by the employee entrance for Misha who showed up fifteen minutes later. Somehow, she already smelled like vodka. He asked her, "Are you going to be able to go see the boat?" She said, "I guess!" The tone of the day was now set. Ten minutes later, Matt got her to chew some gum and helped her down the dock. Mae was on deck and greeted them enthusiastically. Misha seemed confused and quietly asked Matt, "Why are we here? We can't afford anything like this." He cut her off and said, "I have this all under control, just look around with me." She said, "I'm already here, might as well."

Mae looked at Misha and said, "Hard night, honey?" Misha sarcastically replied, "From hell." Mae said, "I have just the thing, let's go inside." The boat seemed even cleaner than when Matt was there the day before and Mae took Misha by the arm and gave her the tour. Matt tagged along to see if there was anything new. Back in the salon, Mae asked Matt and Misha to have a seat. She sat down too and asked if they minded if she smoked. Nobody minded.

Mae reached into a cabinet, pulled out a beautiful teak box, opened it and began rolling a fat joint. She finished, lit it up and passed it to Misha. Misha took a big hit, smiled, and passed it to Matt who took a hit and passed it back to Mae. When the joint was gone, Mae said, "Relax a little, and then we'll see about business." Mae went to the galley and got a bowl of pretzels and three beers. An hour passed and Mae asked Misha if she was ready to talk business. Misha said, "I guess," and it was not in the sarcastic tone in which she had arrived. Mae said, "Did you not think marijuana was around before you were born?" Misha said, "I guess I never thought about it before."

Mae changed tone and said, "You have a great young man here, he was kind to my Jim without needing to be and then was kind enough to sign on to help me. If you're as smart as

you seem, you'll keep him interested in you." Misha started
to talk but Mae waved her off with, "Save the excuses. You
get sloppy and some twenty something will be taking him for
a ride. But you don't want advice, you want to know how
Matt can afford to let you live on this boat with him, right?"
Misha quietly said, "Yes." She was starting to wonder why
this old woman was lecturing her and what her relation to
Matt was. Mae went on, "I am going to get some money from
Jim's life insurance and go live in Key West for a while. When
I can no longer care for myself, I'll call Matt and he will come
get me, put me into the nursing home and sit with me a few
nights a week with pay. When I die and am cremated, he has
promised to take the ashes to Miami Beach and release them
into the surf. In return for this, he gets this boat." She
reached into the oversize coffee table and pulled out a guitar.
She asked, "You kids working tonight?" Both Matt and
Misha shook their heads no. Mae said good and handed the
box to Matt while saying, "Make yourself useful." Matt
began rolling a joint while Mae began playing and singing,
Hey hey, my my,
Rock and roll can never die,
There's more to the picture,
Than meets the eye.
Hey hey, my my.

Out of the blue and into the black,
You pay for this, but they give you that,
And once you're gone, you can never come back,
When you're out of the blue and into the black.

Mae finished the song and accepted the joint. She said, "You
guys know who Neil Young is?" Matt said, "Was with
Crosby, Stills and Nash for a while in the late sixties then
went off on his own with a group called Crazy Horse. Mae
added, "Came from Canada, like me." She then started
playing again but something completely different,

Mother, mother ocean I have heard your call,
Wanted to sail upon your waters since I was three feet tall
You've seen it all, you've seen it all

Watched the men who rode you, switch from sails to steam
And in your belly, you hold the treasures that few have ever seen,
Most of them dreams, most of them dreams…

Mae finished and said, "Jim and I first heard Jimmy Buffett in 1969 when he was busking in New Orleans. He wasn't famous then and hadn't brought a swell of tourism down here yet. We were on an anniversary trip up to Mardi Gras. You should go up there at least once in your life."
Mae took a toke and continued, "This was our third boat. When we were your age, we would motor out a few miles and spend the nights fishing and stargazing and the days below deck, in the cool shade. You kids have that kind of opportunity here. That is if you want to take advantage of it. You, young lady will have to learn to learn to control your habits though, or there will eventually be another woman enjoying what should have been your life."
Misha was getting upset but was too messed up to act on it.
Mae said, "The boat was named The Dreaming Moon because it's what Jim and I always joked about while we were out on the water. Jim would say something silly like, "Look, the moon is dreaming of us while it was behind a cloud." We might have been under the influence of the sixties, at that particular time. I know you kids are tired. I have the guest room ready for you and we can go out this evening and have dinner offshore, if you want to that is."
Matt and Misha wandered into the smaller stateroom and then crawled into a very comfortable bed. Neither one tried to initiate sex, both thinking that the noise would be embarrassing.

Sleep hit Matt and Misha very quickly. Matt dreamed of the star-filled nights and the Miami skyline coming into view. Misha dreamed of the moon, who was dreaming of her. They woke up at five in the evening and upon wandering out found Mae looking at the horizon listening to a symphony by Gustav Holst called *The Planets*. Mae said, "If you're going to live on a boat, you better learn to make the bed and stow your laundry as soon as your feet hit the deck." She pointed at a door and said, "Head's in there. Mind that you flush adequately."

DINNER DATE FOR THREE UNDER THE STARS

After Matt and Misha finished making the bed and using the head, Mae said it was time to learn how to properly unhook from the dock and take the boat out to sea. She called them over to a control panel and said, "First thing you do is shut down the power. You don't want any power surges or spikes frying your electronics because they are not cheap, and you need them." She showed them the primary power switch, which had three settings, Off, Shore and Ship. She said, "Always off when you need to disconnect from the dock. The Ship setting is for after the generator is running, and you turn the switch back to off before shutting it down too." She then showed them the water control valve and turned it off too. Then she continued, "Turn it on after disconnecting from the dock, and after the generator is running, because of the pump. After moving to the helm, she showed them how to start the engine and make sure that they were functioning properly by the reading gauges. They then went on deck and Mae showed the attentive couple how to disconnect the external electrical and water lines. She then said, "There is no sewer cleanout, per se, a small barge comes once a week and pumps the tank for a fee, or you release it to the sea, far offshore. That's why it's so important that you use the right kind of toilet paper and learn how to use it sparingly." She then showed them the sequence of untying the ropes and emphasized that the last stern line remained tied until the boat was fully ready to leave. She led them around the perimeter of the boat and said, "Always look for new obstacles before moving. Anything could have washed up between the boat and the pilings since you last moved and it could cause you problems, big ones."

Everything was clear and Mae asked Matt to release the last line. Mae and Misha were at the helm when Matt finished his task. There was a discussion about boat rights-of-way mainly that any vessel that was not under power had the right-of-way, period. She said, "Remember sailboats, when under sail, require lots of room to maneuver and do not stop quickly, so beware." She then showed how to engage the transmissions and slowly apply power as you maneuver out of the slip. Next, there was a lot of discussion about buoys and the hazards of not being between them. Mae guided them carefully and slowly through the channel. A thirty-six foot sport fisher passed and went to full speed right in front of them. Mae said, "There are assholes everywhere and the Marine Patrol never seems to be around when they show themselves. This is a slow speed, no wake zone. Making waves here puts a strain on every boat's ropes and the moorings of those out here on the balls. It also damages the Mangroves and who knows what else. So don't succumb to the urge to go tearing out of here. This is supposed to be enjoyable, not a competition." They rounded a piece of land and found that the Marine patrol was there and that the sport fisher that blew past them at full speed, now had an official boat tied to its side and the captain was being administered a field sobriety test by one of the officers. Mae carefully maneuvered by and waived at the officer not conducting the sobriety test. She told Matt and Misha, "Those guys are your best friends on the water. Get in trouble and they will risk

their own life to help you. If you choose to act stupid though, they will eventually bust you. You make that choice yourself, not them."
Clearing the marked channel, Mae applied a little more power. She said, "Once you pass the last marker you are clear to go as fast as you want and in any direction you want. Just remember, speed sucks the fuel and when you're empty out here, you might die." Everything must be planned, and I hope you never decide to take her out after you have started drinking." She looked at Misha and said, "Have enough respect for the sea to at least get to where you're going before starting. Even if you don't have enough respect for other people to show up sober."
Misha fired back, "I have a shoulder injury and you have no idea how bad it hurts sometimes." Mae said, "I'm old and have pains in my back that sometimes make me sit up and cry for days, but I wouldn't take it out on you by showing you disrespect. I see that Matt wears leg braces most of the time. He probably has pain, too, but he had the courtesy and respect to show up sober the first time. You ain't so special, like that. Everybody has a reason to show up drunk. Most just don't act on it." Misha went to the bow and Mae continued giving Matt lessons on operating the boat properly. Matt said to Mae, "You were a little hard on Misha." Mae said, "Somebody had to tell her that she was fucking up her life and then dragging it over onto yours. I'm going to be gone soon and she can hate me all she wants." Matt said, "She really is a nice person." Mae said, "You mean when she's not drinking excessively." Matt let the subject drop. Two hours later, they were approaching Miami Beach. Mae showed Matt the GPS markers for places to anchor where they wouldn't damage any reef structure, could catch dinner and see the lights of Miami Beach at night. She then asked him to take them to one of them. Misha came back to the cockpit and told Mae, "Sorry that I showed up to meet you drunk. I really have been having a tough time lately and

it just seemed to overflow at that moment." Mae said, "Apology accepted but I am only a temporary fixture in your life, you may want Matt around longer. He's going to get up to a place to fish for dinner and then we have the rest of the night for eating, smoking and drinking." The weather forecast is for clear skies and a full moon. The marine forecast is for flat seas through tomorrow night when we get back to Marathon."

Matt successfully navigated to the GPS coordinates and Mae showed him how the anchoring system worked. They were solidly at anchor within ten minutes, in sixty feet of water. Mae directed everyone to the fishing tackle locker and asked if they knew how to fish. They both did and Mae went to get the frozen bait, asked Matt to get the beer, and Misha to get the weed. Misha said she had some and Mae said that she should save it for another day. Soon, lines were over the sides and stern and within an hour, they were all comfortably buzzed and had enough snapper for dinner. Mae said, "We'll stock the freezer a little for you guys, so keep catching them." She filleted the fish they had saved and said that they were going into the freezer and dinner still had to be caught. By dinner, they had actually caught the legal limit and Mae gave instructions on how to change the rigs to catch something other than snapper. Mae filleted all but two of the snapper and used one to teach Misha and one to teach Matt the art of fish filleting.

The night fell and dinner was cooked on a grill that swung out over the side of the boat. Mae had ready-made Coleslaw and frozen fingerling potatoes to go with the fish. She admitted to having steak also just in case the fishing was poor. Matt prepared most of the food and they ate under the stars while drinking a bottle of Pinot Grigio. Misha felt no need for pain pills and her attitude had taken a one-eighty. Miami was beautiful in the distance and the moon came slowly over the eastern horizon as the second bottle of wine was opened. There was some small talk and then Mae announced, "I'm going to bed. I am taking out my hearing aids and having a large snort of Scotch before turning in, I won't be back out of the stateroom, guys. I promise." Matt and Misha both turned a little red, but the moonlight failed to reflect it and, if it had, they could have easily blamed it on the wine and smoke.

Once Mae was gone, Misha said, "I don't like her most of the time, and why don't you defend me?" Matt said, "I did defend you, you had just stormed off to the bow and missed it. Besides, most of the time she's right." Misha asked, "Would you really leave me for a younger woman?" He replied, "I don't plan on it. The problem is that people who drink a lot and use excessive amounts of painkillers tend to eventually make rash decisions. You'll probably eventually meet some charming guy and be gone." She said, "I wouldn't do that." He said, "No, but the drugs and alcohol might." She stormed off to bed and he eventually fell asleep in a deck chair. Somewhere in the night, he woke up and after contemplating life a few minutes, went in and got into bed with Misha.

Somewhere near ten the next morning, they fell out of bed. Misha went to the head. Matt made the bed and picked up the room. Misha came out, dressed, and left the room while Matt went to the head. Soon everyone was on deck with coffee in hand. Mae asked, "How'd you lovers sleep?" Matt said, "Fine." Misha said, "Me too." That was the end of the conversation and Mae asked Matt if he thought that he could pilot them back home. He said that he thought that he could and after finishing his coffee began preparations for departure. He and Misha both had work that evening and it was going to take several hours to get back to the slip. Matt checked the boat over, started the engines and raised the anchor while Mae and Misha sat in deck chairs drinking coffee. Matt began by taking the boat out to open water and made the south turn. He asked Misha, "Baby, can you please get me a cup of coffee?" Misha slowly got up, poured some coffee in his cup, and handed it to him. She then returned to her deck chair and looked out at the ocean. Mae asked her, "What's wrong, honey, don't like the boat?" Misha said, "You're mean to me." Mae looked at her and said, "Sorry if what can plainly be seen by an old woman offends you." The conversation ended and Mae went to check on Matt.

At the helm, Mae looked everything over and told Matt he was doing a fine job. She asked Matt, "I see no one else is concerned about you so can I get you some more coffee or something?" Misha heard this, ran into the smaller stateroom, and lay on the bed crying. Mae told Matt, "You should go see about her, she seems upset with me today. I'll take over the driving." With that, Mae took the wheel and punched some buttons and the Doors, *Riders on the Storm* began playing from speakers all over the boat.

Matt knocked on the stateroom door and didn't wait for a response before going in. He found Misha on the bed with a tear-streaked face. He asked her, "What's wrong?" She said, "I do care about you, she just doesn't see it." Matt got into the bed and put his arms around her. He said, "I know baby, you just have a unique way of expressing things." Something clicked in her mind. She said, "You think, I'm selfish. Don't you?" He said, "Well, you do think of yourself first, *all* the time." She said, "I'm sorry. I will try to improve. Will you stay with me?" He said, "I have no intentions of doing anything else, but it's your choice anyway." She asked, "How is it my choice?" He said, "I know I want to be with you and try to treat you that way and express it. Sometimes I feel you would choose your pain pills and alcohol over me without even realizing it and I would be gone from your life in a flash." She said, "But I love you and want to be with you." He said, "I guess I could always choose to be the third or fourth most important thing in your life." She said, "You are the most important thing in my life." He said, "We both know that is not true and you proved it when you came out of work already drinking and coming down from speed.

Then, last night we could have had a romantic night under the moon and stars, and you decided to come in here and drink yourself to sleep instead. That tells me alcohol and drugs are ahead of me." She got up to storm out. He said, "And, there you go again!" She stopped, looked at him and said, "You're the one who ruined the mood, I need a drink now."

Out in the salon, Misha opened the fridge and got a beer. Mae said, "Can't handle the day without a drink, huh?" Misha snarled and said, "What do you know?" Mae said, "I know if I had a good man, I'd cook him some breakfast and apologize for being a bitch to him on a regular basis. But, what do I know? Jim and I only lived and loved each other in the small confines of a boat for forty years. He was a good man and always let me have my way and I always repaid him in kindness." Misha popped the beer top and headed for the bow.

Six hours later, they arrived in Marathon and Mae asked Matt to take them into the slip. Misha had drunk three beers and was sleeping on a couch in the salon. Matt had some difficulty maneuvering the boat, but the bumpers kept the boat from sustaining any damage. Misha had managed to get up and help put the bumpers over, but only after Mae asked her. Once in the slip, Mae asked Misha to help get the stern lines attached so the engines could be shut down. Once the stern lines were fast, Matt shut down the engines and began helping with the other ropes. Mae simply said, "Fail to tie in properly and the boat will suffer from the constant motion of the sea and if a sudden storm develops, like they tend to do down here, you've got even more troubles."

Misha was mad at the world. Her shoulder hurt and she was hung over from the three beers coupled with the boat's motion. She decided to call in sick to work while they were still on the boat. Mae told Matt that tomorrow they would go to the DMV and get all the paperwork done and she wanted them to give her a ride to Key West in a few days. Misha thought, "Good, the old bitch is leaving." Goodbyes were said and Matt and Misha drove to the motel to begin getting ready for work. While Matt got ready, Misha called in and told Matt she was too sick to go to work. He asked if she needed him to stay home with her. She said, "No, I'll be fine. Can I keep the car though?" Matt said, "Sure, if you can drop me off at the nursing home." She said, "No problem."

Three hours later, Misha was in a popular Islamorada bar and being hit on by a man down from Orlando on vacation and looking for some easy ass. Three drinks, the promise of drugs and a lot of charm later, they were on the way to his hotel room. A few minutes up the road, blue lights began flashing and the man, who was driving on a suspended license from a previous DUI and was wanted for questioning in a drug operation and a bad deal, decided to run for it. The run was short as he T-boned a car at a red light.

Misha's world exploded. First, the crash jarred her and then the airbags hit her in the face and the side of the head. She was unharmed except for chemical burns and a bloody nose that was surely going to develop into two black eyes. By the time she recovered, a police officer was at her door trying to get it open and yelling for her to keep her hands where they could be seen. The man she was with ran and officers were in pursuit. Misha was being interviewed by the police officer who opened her door. She produced her retired Army identification, and it bought her a break, the officer decided to listen to her story instead of taking her directly to jail as an accessory to a felony, which would have cost her nursing license. He asked, "Did you know the driver before tonight?" She said, "No, I just met him down at the bar and he seemed like a nice guy, so I decided to take a chance on him." The officer said, "If you are lying to me, I will be knocking on your door." She said, "I was just out and had a stupid moment, that's all." She was already trying to figure out how to reconcile with Matt after this all shook out. The officer said, "You come back clean, but the man you were with is wanted in connection with a bad drug deal where a young woman died in the gunfire. His stupid driving may have actually save your life. Again, you seem clean, and I am going to give you a break, but the paramedics have to clear you before we can see what happens next." She said, "Thank you, sat down on a bus stop bench where the officer had led her right after getting her out of the car. Two paramedics came over, checked her out and asked a string of seemingly endless questions. They eventually cleared her, and the officer asked if she would submit to a sobriety test. He had purposefully waited for enough time to pass so she would have a better chance of passing. She passed but only because the officer was being lenient, and she seemed cognitive enough to act intelligently. He asked her if she needed a ride to her car and she said, "Yes." Fifteen minutes later, she was at her car and the officer asked her again if she had lied. She assured him that she had not, and he said she was free to go but might be called in for an interview in a few days.

A pink tint was beginning to blotch the eastern sky when she got into the car and cautiously drove south. The dashboard clock read 5:45 as she left Islamorada. There was no traffic, but the experience of the evening caused her to drive at the speed limit and very cautiously. It was six fifteen when she stopped in north Marathon for coffee. At seven, she was at the nursing facility and Matt came out soon after. He was bleary-eyed from reading all night to his patient but noticed Misha's burned face and swollen eyes immediately. He asked her, "What happened, are you alright?" She said, "Can this wait until we get home?" He said, "We're supposed to meet Mae soon, you know." She said, "Shit, I need to get some ice for my face and another coffee." She pulled into the first open convenience store and they both got coffee. She got a huge cup of ice and a package of zip-locks. They had a roll of paper towels in the car, and she asked Matt to drive while she made and applied an ice pack to her face. Matt said, "I could drop you at the motel and just tell Mae that you're not feeling well." She said, "That woman would immediately assume that I was hung over or something." Matt said, "I don't think she's purposely trying to pick on you." Misha said, "I really do need to go home." Matt dropped her off at the motel and left wondering what had happened to her last night while he was working.

Mae was ready when Matt arrived at the dock. She wanted him and Misha to come early so that they could all have breakfast. When Mae saw he was alone, she asked where Misha was. Matt said, "She looked so sick this morning that I told her to stay home. She wasn't drinking or anything, just sick." Mae said, "Well, I hope she feels better soon. Are you up for some breakfast and DMV time?" Matt said, "Sure, did you have any particular place in mind?" She said, "No, the IHOP would be fine." They went to the IHOP, did the boat transfer paperwork, and ate breakfast. She also asked him to sign a contract to care for her when she needed it and for what he was to do with her ashes after she died. He signed without hesitation as she was telling him about her prepaid arrangement with a funeral home. They went by the DMV. Matt hadn't thought about the taxes, but Mae had and took care of them. Matt paid the registration fee. Mae said, "You will need insurance and don't let it wait." On the way to drop her back at the boat, they arranged for him to take her to Key West in a few days.

RAIN AND PAIN

As Matt arrived at the motel room, it started raining. Misha was asleep in bed and the ice pack she had on her face had melted and was leaking on the floor. He picked it up and put it in the bathroom sink on his way to shower. After the shower, he crawled in beside Misha, and she stirred a little. She asked, "Everything go, okay?" He said, "Yeah baby. I have work tonight, so I have to get some sleep." He turned over and she snuggled up behind him, but he ignored her and thought only about going to sleep.

Matt woke up at five-thirty in the afternoon and was in bed alone. He heard the shower, so he tried to go back to sleep for a few more minutes thinking how glad he was it was only for four hours tonight. Misha came to his side of the bed, wrapped in a towel, and asked if he wanted some coffee or something. He said, "Coffee would be great," without looking at her. She said, "Okay," and he felt her leave the side of the bed. A few minutes later, she returned to bed with two cups of coffee and asked him, "Can we talk for a minute?" He had a sinking feeling in his stomach as he sat up in bed. He rubbed his eyes and looked at her offering him his coffee. "What the hell happened to you?" It just seemed to spring from his mouth. She said, "I made a big mistake." He asked, "Should I take you to the emergency room, or something?" She said, "No, I've been checked out and it's okay." Matt was confused but she started talking again before he could get a question in, "I went to a bar last night and fell on my face leaving. They insisted on calling paramedics and that's how I got checked out." Matt said, "What bar?" She said, "I drove up to Islamorada so I wouldn't run into people from work." Matt said, "Okay, but your eyes are black, and your face looks all messed up like it was burned or something. Are you going to work tonight?" She said, "I can't go in like this, can we see if Mae will let me stay with her on the boat?" Matt said, "I don't see why not. Let me get dressed and we will go over there, didn't think to get her phone number."

The rain was really coming down as they drove over to the marina. Mae was home and when she saw Misha she immediately asked, "What happened? Are you okay?" Misha blurted out, "Can I stay here with you tonight, I can't go to work like this and don't want to be alone." She said, "Sure honey, let's all get inside and sort this out." As soon as they were inside Misha said, "Matt had nothing to do with this, it was all me." Mae said, "I didn't think he would do something like that to you. But wow, something walloped you." Misha kissed Matt and said, "You should go to work, baby." Matt said, "Okay but I can come back later, it's my four-hour night." Misha said, "Why don't you leave us girls alone for the night?" Matt said, "Okay," kissed her and said goodbye as he went out the main hatch.

Misha asked Mae, "Do you have some ice?" Mae said, "Got something better," and pulled a facemask shaped ice pack from the freezer. Misha put the pack on then asked Mae, "Did you ever just mess up?" Mae said, "You don't live this long and do it perfectly. What happened?" Misha said, "I ran away from home while Matt was at work and left a bar with a man. He turned out to be wanted by the police and ran when we got blue-lighted. He hit another car and the airbag did this to me. Now you can let me have it." Mae said, "A long time ago, I ran away from Jim. Didn't take up with a man or anything but I did spend some time up in Cocoa Beach where he couldn't find me. I was just young and had no idea what I was doing. Fortunately, I came to my senses and got him to take me back. He never mentioned it again because I never gave him a reason to." Misha said, "Did you just make that up?" Mae said, "No, really happened, way back in the mid-sixties. Can't even remember what the fight was about, or even if there was one." Misha said, "I wasn't sure that I was going to do anything with the man I was with, he was just so charming, and I wanted to run away from all the rules. The police said that I was lucky because he was wanted in connection with a drug deal where a woman was killed, and I could easily have been next." Mae sighed, "All men are charmers until they slide out of you." Misha said, "Guess so, do you have a beer?" Mae said, "Yes, and get out the box and roll us one." Misha rolled while Mae got cold beers.

Soon after finishing the smoke, the conversation began again. Misha asked, "What should I do about my little outing?"

Mae answered, "I'm guessing that Matt is wondering what really happened to you and thinking everything bad that it could've been. I would say the thing he will settle on is you cheated, and the man beat you up, which ain't far from the truth." Misha protested, "I wasn't sure that I was going to cheat." Mae countered, "If you weren't going to cheat, why'd you pick a man that was obviously trying to screw you?" Misha said, "It seemed like a good idea, and I thought I needed to be rebellious for a minute." Mae said, "Okay, here's my advice. Talk to Matt about the reasoning behind your actions and then tell him exactly what happened. If you lie, then it will surely come back to bite you. If he dumps you, you'll survive. But I'm betting he won't." Misha asked, "You really think he will want to be with me after I pulled this stunt?" Mae said, "Have you noticed how he looks at you and how he treats you? I have. Apparently, he loves you and you have just been along for the ride." Misha said, "I hope you don't think too badly of me, I really have had a lot of problems." Mae said, "Problems don't make you special, everybody's got 'em, it's how you handle them that makes you different and that's solely your decision. If you think you are having significant issues, you should go to the VA and get some help. There is absolutely no shame in that, Jim went after his experience in Korea, and it made a real difference. We also supported the service organizations when we could, mostly by drinking at their bars and paying the dues, though. Probably should have done more."

It was quiet for a while and Misha asked if she could roll another joint. It was okay with Mae, and she went to get fresh beers and a bottle of aspirin. After the joint and beer was gone, Mae said, "I'm going to go to bed. You should stretch out in the other bed and decide what you really, deep down, want to happen."

Misha took two aspirins and went to bed. Morning came like a flash and Misha woke up to the smell of coffee. She got up, made the bed, dressed, and went into the salon. Matt and

Mae were talking about the cost of diesel fuel. Misha poured a cup of coffee and asked Matt to please come into the stateroom with her. Mae said, "I need to take my morning walk, so you two can sit in here. You'll soon learn that the shower house on the dock has proper flush toilets, and it beats the need to pump out the tanks so often." She left the boat and Misha sat down across from Matt.

Matt asked her, "What happened to your face, baby?" She smiled a little and said, "Matt, I think I need to go to the VA and get some help." Matt sat up and asked, "Right now? I can drive you over to the clinic as soon as they open." She said, "Not right this minute, but soon. I want you to know that I was about to leave you the other night and actually drove up to a bar in Islamorada to look for a man." Matt's stomach dropped and he tried to speak but she cut him off. "Don't worry about that, I didn't screw anybody. I might have if fate hadn't intervened though and I want to tell you that I'm sorry and if you'll let me stay with you, it won't happen again. I was just being stupid, and I think that it has to do with my abuses and injuries." Matt asked, "Did the man hit you?" She said, "No we were in a car wreck, he was possibly a murderer and the police said I was just plain lucky. I think he let me go because I have a military ID. The airbags are what hit me." Matt said, "Are you sure he didn't hurt you?" She said, "He didn't touch me, at all." Matt said, "Why would you do this? Do I not give you everything that I can and support you in every way possible? Why, baby?" She started crying and sobbed out, "I think I might be crazy sometimes and need to see someone." Matt said, "We will work this out, if that's what you want. But don't do it because you have nothing else to do, I don't want to spend a few years thinking everything's alright and then find out you are cheating on me while I am working at night. It would just be too much for me to manage." She threw her arms over his shoulders and with a trembling mouth said, "I was just stupid and won't do it again, I promise."

Matt said, "I think that we both should go to the VA and seek some counseling. I have nightmares and think maybe I'm not treating you the best, in a lot of ways because of my own issues." She said, "No, as Mae pointed out to me, you treat me so good that I just expect it and take advantage of you." Matt said, "I'm still going, too. Couldn't hurt and we have the time. We are going to take Mae to Key West tomorrow, though." Mae returned and asked if they wanted to go have some breakfast, they both declined and headed back to the motel.

It had been a half night for Matt and Misha didn't work, so they were not ready for bed when they got to the motel. Misha wanted to get Matt into bed, anyway, to help him forget she had just stepped out on him. He said, "Since we both have to work tonight and drive to Key West and back tomorrow, we should go to the clinic this morning and get some bed time this afternoon." She didn't want to agree but he didn't seem interested in sex at the moment, even though she was naked and offering. She felt rejected, even though she was trying to use the sex to manipulate him, and it caused her to want to drink or something. She chose to shower instead and felt good she had made that choice afterward.

Matt checked for a VA clinic while Misha showered and when she came out of the bathroom, he said, "We have to make a choice, Key West or Key Largo." She asked, "For what?" He said, "Those are the nearest clinics that have what we're looking for and Key West is where I think we should go." She said, "Fine with me, aren't we taking Mae down tomorrow anyway?" Matt said, "We'll try to get everything set up then, and when we go down, we can check on Mae and keep up my deal with her." She said, "I'm glad to hear you say *we*, now let's just spend the day in bed." He said, "Let me shower and relax a few minutes first, please." He was actually delaying getting into bed with her because he thought she was going to try using sex to manipulate him. He excused himself to the shower and spent a good fifteen minutes in the bathroom.

Misha got into bed but desperately wanted to drink some of the vodka that was in view on the counter. She got a glass of ice water and tried not to think about the alcohol just a few steps away. She wanted to start showing Matt she was able to control her impulses a little bit, even if he probably wouldn't notice. Matt came out of the bathroom and got into bed with her. She moved to him and gave him a kiss. He immediately noticed that she wasn't drunk, high or smelling like alcohol and liked it. He broke away and asked her, "How do you feel? I can see that the swelling is going down a little in your nose, but your eyes are beginning to turn purplish. I hope nobody thinks that I hit you or something." She said, "I will make sure no one at the clinic or work thinks that." They went back to kissing and then went all the way. Afterward, Matt said, "We've never had bad sex, but it was really nice to do it while you were sober and not even stoned. Everything just seemed to work better." She said, "It was nice, but I need to smoke or drink now." Matt wished he had kept his mouth shut as he watched her butt while she mixed a vodka drink. He said, "Why not?" and rolled a joint. She caught on and said, "I'll make an effort to be sober for you more often." He smiled and said, "Okay, baby."

HELP ME IF YOU CAN

Matt had sat with Sally Rogers again, the night before, and now lay in bed, awake, thinking about how she repeated everything she told him the first time that he sat with her almost word per word again last night. He decided to ask the nursing staff the next time he was there. Tonight, he was going to be sitting with a man who was at home and the family was all exhausted. Someone from the facility had gotten the oldest daughter in contact with him and he took the job without going to visit first. He eventually fell asleep and dreamed of Misha leaving him with a man she met at a bar and then of the rope that snapped and disabled him. The rope turned into a snake that chased him through Mangroves that came alive and tried to grab and trip him with their roots so that the rope-snake could catch him. Misha lay beside him dreaming of their future on the boat and night out on the ocean under the stars. She was sleeping peacefully while he was sweating. Soon however, her dreams turned ugly. Her dream began benign enough; they were out on the boat, under a full moon with beautiful stars all around. Then she drank too much and was sick. When she leaned over the side of the boat to throw up, she somehow fell into the water and instead of popping back to the surface, just kept going down into the blackness. She woke up choking and found a sweating Matt beside her. He looked pale to her, and she instinctively reached over and checked his pulse, it was well over one hundred and seemed to be getting faster. She shook him and he came to and immediately felt cold. She cuddled up to him and said, "Looked like you were having a nightmare." He said, "I was, a rope was chasing me through a mangrove forest and the trees were trying to help the rope catch me." She said, "I fell overboard and when I didn't come back up to the surface, woke up choking." He said, "Has that happened to you before?" She said, "Not really, I usually have no dreams. I close my eyes and there is nothing until I wake up." She thought for a second and asked, "What about you?" He said, "I have had dreams of the rope, off and on, since it took my back out." His eyes shifted for a check of the clock said it was already time to get ready for work. Misha tried to cover her black eyes and swollen nose with makeup, but it didn't work. Everyone at work asked her about her face and she simply said it was from a fender bender and everything, including the car was all right. Matt went to the address he was given and found he was to sit with an ancient man who had not been out of the house in years because of seemingly permanent confusion and an inability to walk. He liked to talk though, and Matt presented a new opportunity for conversation. Matt engaged him for hours while the family went up to Miami for the night. By two in the morning, Matt was tired of the endless banter and asked his charge if there was anything he would like to watch on television, or something that he would like to be read aloud. Matt added, "I usually get requests to read something aloud." The man thought for a long time and said he always liked the poems of Walt Whitman and was sure he had a book somewhere. Matt spotted the book on the small bookshelf in the room and picked it up. It was well worn, and some kid had used a crayon on a few of the pages, but everything was still legible. The book was called *Leaves of Grass,* and was the eighth edition, which was published in 1889. Matt looked the book over again and thought that it was possible that the book was actually from 1889 and then began reading. The rest of the night passed with him reading to a snoring man. He actually read through the poems twice and when he put down the book, he noticed he was not alone. A calico cat sat quietly watching him from under the bed. He tried to coax it out but had no luck. He noticed that his patient was extra still, so he checked for a pulse. The man was alive and had a slow steady pulse. Matt touched the man's forearm, and his thoughts went to Paris. At least he thought it was Paris, based on the Eiffel Tower being part of the landscape, it could have been Vegas for all he knew. He let the thoughts flow for a few minutes and whispers of buying bread from street vendor and wine from a hole in the wall shop wafted through his mind, which blew away the Vegas possibility. Then there was a park bench and sharing the bread with the birds while drinking the wine. Matt let go of the man and thought about the previous times that the apparent thoughts or dreams of a dying person were somehow visible to him. It was only now that he was kind of freaked out by it and decided it was something best kept to himself.

The family arrived at six thirty in the morning and asked Matt about the night. Matt said everything was quiet, he read poetry and there was a cat under the bed. The man's wife said, "It's coming up on the time, isn't it?" Matt said, "I think so." She said, "Thank you, when can you come back?" Matt said, "Day after tomorrow, I have to go down to Key West today and won't be back until then." She handed him five twenties and said, "Please come then." Matt excused himself and left to pick up Misha at the hospital. She came out the door at ten past seven. She was completely sober and very tired. Matt asked, "How'd it go?" She said, "The head nurse said I should take tonight off to let my face heal up a little, it seemed to disturb a few of the patients a little." Matt said, "Great, we'll just spend the night in Key West, then."

Mae was at the end of the dock with a rolling suitcase when Matt and Misha drove up. Matt jumped out to grab the suitcase and Misha crawled into the back seat. Mae said she would be happy to ride in the back seat, but Misha said she intended to try getting a nap in on the way and was happy to be in the back. They stopped for coffee and Misha declined, still hoping to nap. Tourist traffic made the trip half an hour longer than normal and Mae gave Matt the address where she was going. She explained that it wasn't exactly an assisted living facility, but she knew the people that came and went. She added in a sly tone that there would be lots of *assistance* for her there, if she wanted it. Matt never caught the innuendo and drove while the radio cranked out a late sixties classic rock mix. The hotel at the address was actually a collection of cottages and Matt helped Mae with her suitcase. After Mae was finished checking in, Matt got her to the cottage door and she handed him the keys to the boat, "You take good care of her, and I will call you once a week so we can keep up until it's time." Matt touched her arm and felt a sensation of the open ocean. He took his hand away and she just smiled at him and said, "I know. Just got a few things to do first, that's all." He smiled back at her and said, "Take

care, I'll call you in a few days to see that you're settled."
Matt was lost in thought, about the meaning of encounter, as
he meandered back to the car and got into the driver's seat.
Misha rose up and asked, "What's wrong?" Matt said, "We
now have a new home. But we are still going to spend the
night down here." He thought about how Mae had somehow
known what he sensed but there were more pressing matters
at hand.

They drove back toward Stock Island and found the clinic
inside a gated facility. After presenting their military IDs to
the guard, she pointed them in the right direction. Inside the
clinic, they immediately discovered that there was a high
demand for services here and joined the check-in queue. It
wasn't long until they relearned the process that they both
had been told about before being discharged. They needed to
be registered with the clinic before receiving services unless it
was an emergency. They were directed to the place they
needed to go and went there to wait their turn. Two hours
later, they left with appointments to return on different days
to see different people. The alternative was to go up to
Miami. They decided it wasn't that bad to come down here
and headed over to the tourist area to look for a hotel for the
night.

The hotel they opted for was the Southern Cross. It was right
on Duval near Eaton Street. They checked in and were direct
to park in a lot over on Whitehead Street about a block away.
They had lunch at Cheeseburger Key West and then started
drinking. Six hours later, they made it back to their room and
they both passed out.

Misha was first to stir and throw up, Matt soon followed. At
two thirty in the morning, they were awake and starving so,
they decided to venture out for food. After several false
hopes, they found that Sloppy Joe's was the only viable
option. With more cheeseburgers in them and even more
beer, they headed back to their small room and fell back into
bed. At ten in the morning, they got up cursed the alcohol

that they had consumed as they prepared to check out. Leaving town, they meandered through the streets looking for mid-day coffee and stumbled upon Sandy's Café. It was part of a Laundromat, which confused them, but gave it a shot anyway. Soon, they were back on the road with Café con Leches and Cuban sandwiches. Matt was in better shape, so he drove. By the top of Stock Island, they were both saying how that would be the last time for that drunken nonsense. Both knew it wasn't, but it made them feel better about the night before, so they repeated it.

They arrived back in Marathon and Matt asked if she wanted to go to the boat or the motel. She said, "The motel, I'm not sure my stomach could handle the boat at the moment." He agreed and drove them to the motel. It was a day of recovery and then Matt went to work while Misha stayed at the room. She was going to get things together for them to move onto the Dreaming Moon over the next couple of days.

Matt was returning to sit with the man who had given him visions of Paris, Jean Patrick Brown. Jean Patrick was especially restless when Matt arrived. Jean Patrick's wife, Ann, said she would stay for a while and maybe between the two of them, they could get Jean to settle down and rest. Jean Patrick had no intention of settling down, and asked nonsense questions steadily for the first ten minutes. Ann must have heard all this before because she answered most of the questions with a practiced precision. Matt finally got Jean to listen to him for a moment and asked the cat's name. Jean looked at him like he had just pronounced a death sentence and said, "Callie, we could never come up with a better name." All conversation paused for a minute and Ann asked Jean Patrick, "Honey, how do you feel?" He looked at her and said, "Mummer, you must have heard I was sick and come to see me off." Ann said, "Where are you going?" He replied, "Out of this world, my dear. I am at the end of the road." Ann said, "Can I get you anything?" He said, "Just stay here with me for a while." Ann kissed Jean Patrick on the forehead and said, "I'll stay as long as you need me." He said, "I always loved you," and slipped into a quiet sleep. Ann quietly said, "I have always loved you too," and kissed his head again. She turned and with teary eyes asked Matt to please read him Leaves of Grass some more. Matt read and otherwise there was silence. Callie eventually poked her head out from under the bed then curled up at his feet and began purring. Ann fell asleep in her chair and Matt read the book through three times. At six in the morning, Jean Patrick stirred, and Ann woke up and moved to his side. He mumbled something and raised his hand. Ann took his hand and he pulled her down to him. At the instant Ann's head touched Jean's chest, Matt knew his services would no longer be needed. He made sure that he touched Ann's arm before leaving and got no visions or odd feelings. Ann must have known this was Jean's last night because she had paid Matt shortly after he arrived. Matt was ready to leave when the ambulance came. Ann held his arm and said, "I hope that I can find you when my time comes." Matt said, "I think that will be quite a while and I don't plan on going anywhere anytime soon."

Matt arrived at home to find Misha had packed everything up and the only thing in the room that wasn't ready to go was the motel's property. She met him with coffee and a smile. He said, "You've been very busy." She responded, "How was work?" He said, "I will not be needed there any longer." She said, "I'm sorry." He said, "This seems to be my calling, reading to the dying." She said, "Are you okay with that?" He said, "Strangely, yes." She changed the subject and asked, "Do you want to go sleep on the boat? I've been up all night and am about ready for bed." Her smile said she was interested in more than sleep this morning and he found a little extra energy and said, "Yes, let's try it out." They loaded up their suitcases of work clothes and toiletries then drove to the marina.

They woke up at five thirty in the afternoon. Matt's phone was ringing, and he answered it cautiously, since it rarely rang, "Hello, this is Matt." The voice at the other end said, "I got your number from Mike Rogers, Sally's husband." Matt said, "Yes, I sit with her one night a week." The voice said, "Yes, and I want to hire you to sit with my wife once a week, as well." Matt said, "What night would you want me to come?" The man said, "Would it be possible for you to come tonight?" Matt said, "Sure, what's your name and room number?" Matt wrote down the information and got out of bed. Misha asked, "More work?" Matt said, "Looks like it, another once a week sitting but I don't know all the details yet." She said, "If you don't mind, I'll drop you off and start moving things over here so we can get checked out of the motel." Matt hesitated a second, she noticed, and he quickly said, "Sure, no problem."

Misha now knew that Matt no longer fully trusted her, and it bothered her. She also knew it was her own doing, but she had said she wouldn't act like that anymore and thought that should have been enough to close the matter. They were intimate and he seemed to have all the same feelings, but that slight hesitation and hint of mistrust were somehow very troubling to her. Matt was not seriously worried about Misha going out on him again, but he did think about it. His primary concern was the boxes and available space on the boat. He asked her, "How much do we want to try getting on the boat?" She said, "Maybe we should have a storage unit for a month or two, until we can determine how much we want to deal with in this space." He said, "Okay, I think you'll know what we really need here, can you drop me off a half hour early?" She drove him to the nursing home and after dropping him off headed straight to the motel.

She wanted to repack some items to get just what they needed on the boat. Since Mae had no more need for kitchenware and left all of hers, which was better than theirs, Misha sorted out all of that and put it into a box for a future yard sale. It was much the same for everything else and she found that only one box and some food items were going to the boat. She made sure that she had all of their military paperwork and headed for the marina.

Back on the Dreaming Moon, Misha quickly got bored without the motel TV and thought about going over to sit with Matt. She decided to investigate the dock instead. She walked up and down the slips and met several people who were hanging out on their boat decks. Some were cooking and drinking, others were just drinking. She accepted an older couple's invitation to have a drink with them and then went back to the Dreaming Moon. Bored, she decided to smoke a joint and go to bed.

At the nursing home, Matt checked on Sally to make sure everything was still the same and then went to his new client's room. He found Abe Smothers anxious to pay him and leave. Matt asked a few questions and Abe was off. His patient was Tina, and she was unable move her right side, the left side moved but she couldn't coordinate the movement and she couldn't speak. This was all due to a stroke. Matt decided that she was probably in her mid-thirties. It had been a bit alarming to discover Abe was probably under forty when Matt arrived, the initial thought was that he was the patient's son. Tina's condition was such that Matt didn't really have a problem sitting with her until he touched her arm.

She was cold and as Matt realized this, in his mind he suddenly was underwater exploring a reef. He moved his hand away and the underwater feeling left him. The next thing he thought about was how young Tina looked and how hard it would be to have your wife dying at this point in life. He also wondered how long Abe had been here and went to the nursing station to get some information. Since he was known to the staff, and considered a huge help, he had no trouble finding out what he wanted to know.

Tina Smothers was involved in a scuba diving accident almost a year previous. An almost unheard of equipment malfunction cut off her air through the yoke on top of the tank and after trying her backup and finding that it too, was useless, panicked at around eighty feet. She had just left Abe's side a moment earlier and was out of his sight behind a coral head. He did not see her desperately trying to get air and she shot for the surface as fast as she could. He finally saw her about fifty feet above him and began to follow. She made it to about ten feet from the surface before her panic and lack of air caught up with her and she blacked out. Abe did not stop to decompress adequately when he saw she was limp in the water and surfaced way too quickly with her in his arms. He started giving her mouth-to-mouth and the boat didn't realize that there was a problem for a few minutes because it looked like they were kissing at first. The boat was properly equipped, and the captain professionally trained, so everything was done by the book from there. They both ended up in the decompression chamber and it appeared everything was going to be okay. Three days later, he opened the car door for her. He was taking her to the hospital for an appointment. When he looked at her, she looked at him oddly. He was about to ask her what was wrong when she suddenly collapsed. He quickly picked her up, put her in the passenger seat and drove the short distance to the hospital with the thought that he could have her in the emergency room before an ambulance could even get to them. He was right, but there was still nothing that could be done to change the outcome. All the right medications were administered, and the doctors and technicians all did their absolute best without any luck. A CAT scan showed a large blood vessel had ruptured in her brain, damaging critical areas. A neurologist checked her over and more advanced scans were run with and without contrast. The rest of the vessels in her brain all were normal and the only thing possible at this point was to wait for a miracle. A month later, their insurance forced a move to the nursing home since it was the closest thing to a long-term care facility available locally. It would have been possible to move to Miami, but it simply wasn't practical, and the prognosis was just not good enough to try it. They did take her up for an evaluation, but it just confirmed what was already known.

Matt returned to Tina's room and looked around for a book or anything that he might read to her. There was nothing there. He thought that he had seen a tattered paperback at the nurses' station and went back there to look at it. It was gone when he got there, so he grabbed a magazine from the common area and went back to the room. Eventually, a nurse came by, after listening to Matt read Tina an article about how to get organized, cleared her throat and said the place had a small library for the patients and that he was welcome to use it. She said, "Can you help me for a minute here first, though?" Matt said, "Sure." She asked, "You want to roll or clean?" He realized that she meant that it was time to clean Tina up and said, "Roll, if you don't mind." The nurse said, "No problem, any help is appreciated. Just let me get some things together here."

The nurse got a pan and a package of pre-moistened washcloths. Matt asked, "Why not use the shower?" The nurse said, "Too much trouble." Tina tried to speak but the sounds were unintelligible, and Matt looked at her face to try and see if he could garner meaning from her expressions plus the noises. Tina had one eye that seemed to work, the other was fixed in place, which took a second to get used to. Matt asked her, "Please try again?" Tina's face only worked on one side, but it was obvious to Matt that it was reflecting pain. Matt looked to see what the nurse was doing and saw the condition of Tina's back and buttocks. Her skin was beginning to breakdown and bedsores would be coming soon. The nurse was carefully cleaning and then replaced the adult diaper that they kept on Tina. It disturbed Matt that Tina's skin care was failing, and he asked the nurse, "Can I

use the patient lift later?" The nurse said, "Sure, but it's very
hard to get her out of bed because her right side is
deadweight." Matt said, "The physical damage in my back
healed up, the leg braces are because some of the nerve
damage didn't. I can still lift and pull, just not like I could ten
years ago." The nurse said, "I'll bring the lift down in a few
hours and help you." Matt said, "Thank you." The cleaning
and changing was over and the nurse asked Matt into the
hallway. Matt followed her out. She closed the door and said,
"I know that her skin is breaking down but there is only so
much that can be done with the staff and resources here. You
are an immense help, just by getting the family out,
straightening up a little and assisting with the funeral home
when they come. So, we all like, and greatly appreciate, you
and will do whatever we can to help you help us." Matt said,
"No problem, it seems to be my destiny to be the comforter of
the dying." She said, "There are far worse things that you
could be. Lord knows most of us could never do it more than
a few times and that's why you will have the job for as long
as you want it."
The nurse walked Matt to the small bookshelf that was the
facilities library, as they talked, and pointed, "There used to
be more, but the television has taken over as the source of
attention for most of these people." Matt thought the
television, as a source of attention, was an odd thing as he
went to see what he could find. The pickings were slim, and
he went back to Tina's room with a torn copy of a Tim
Dorsey's *Cadillac Beach*. He was glad he found a Dorsey novel
because when he was holding Tina up for the diaper change,
he began thinking about travelling around Florida and
especially the water and beaches. Tina's left eye was open
and moved to look at Matt, so he said, "I'm sorry that I didn't
introduce myself earlier, I'm Matt and Abe hired me to sit
with you for a while so he could get some rest." Her face
took on a weird shape that Matt could only interpret as
anger, and she tried to speak again but the words came out as

garbled sounds and grunts. Matt felt bad and said, "Please let me read to you a little, it might make things a little easier for both of us." Her face relaxed a little and he began reading. Two hours later, her face took on a different expression and the sounds she produced seemed desperate. A minute or two later, Matt smelled the reason and noticed a tear seemed to come from Tina's eye. He put the book down and said, "It's okay, I do this for a living and there is no need for you to feel embarrassed or anything else. We'll get you taken care of and maybe you'll be able to sleep for a while."
Matt left the room and found the nurse that had changed Tina last time. He asked her if she had time to bring the patient lift and help him for a minute. She didn't but directed him to a female nursing assistant down the hall. Matt walked up to the nursing assistant, read her nametag, and asked her, "Sue, can you help me with Tina Smothers?" She flatly said, "What is it?" He said, "She needs to be lifted out of bed, given a good shower and her diaper needs changed." Sue was obviously not happy with the request and asked him, "Can you just change her? I have seven patients that all need attention, and it might be an hour before I can get down there." Matt looked at her in disbelief and said, "I am here to help, and there are rules about males needing a female escort to do something like that." She said, "Not here, *you're just changing a diaper*. It works just like she was three months old, the diapers are just bigger." Matt realized he had just met the reason nursing facilities sometimes had problems with patient care and walked away. He found the nurse again and asked her again. She said that a patient was sick and was being prepped to go the hospital, so she would be tied up for a while. Then she added, "The lift is in the third door to the left, just go ahead and get started and I'll check in on you in a few minutes." Matt decided this was just the way it was going to be, got the lift and went back to Tina's room. He told her, "I'm going to get you out of bed and as soon as one of the staff comes to help, you're going to get a shower. He

knew that there was a wheeled shower chair in the bathroom, so he got it and positioned it beside the bed. Next, he used the mechanical lift to carefully put Tina into the chair. She looked happy to be out of bed. He strapped her into the chair securely, and then went looking for Sue or the nurse. He found Sue first. He approached her and asked her, "Can you just come and be the escort? I'll do the actual work." Sue sighed and followed Matt back to Tina's room.

With Sue as the escort, Matt felt a little more comfortable caring for Tina and got her properly showered and even washed her hair. Matt was surprised how bad Tina's skin condition was, especially on her right side and made sure she was clean and dry before redressing her in a diaper and a hospital style gown. He then put her back into bed and positioned her on her stomach. He told her that he would roll her back over before leaving for the day and she seemed to smile a little. Sue left and Matt began reading again. He had made it through eight chapters when the nurse came in and asked him how things were going. He told Tina that they were going to look at her back and pointed out three places on her back, to the nurse, which were about to turn into decubiti, more commonly known as bedsores. The nurse said she would pass it along to the day shift that she would need to be monitored and turned more frequently. The nurse then asked him to step out into the hall and he followed her out of the room. Once the door was closed, the nurse asked, "Did Sue help you with Tina at all?" Matt said, "She was the escort, I thought that it would be appropriate for a female to be around. Tina needed a bath, badly." The nurse said, "I know, and Sue is just about worthless, so I just wanted to see if you had any better luck with her than I have had." He said, "I only take care of one person at a time, so it's easier for me to provide more personal attention. I know you guys have a heavy workload and I don't mind helping out, but I like to have an escort when I need to do things like bathe a woman." The nurse said, "I understand, and thank you for helping out but it may be that you will have to do some things without an escort. We actually consider you a family member, not a part of the staff. So, the rules are not so stringent."

He returned to the room and resumed reading. Around six, he told Tina he was going to check her and get her in a different position for the day. He quickly got her diapered and then rolled her onto her left side and propped her left leg and arm up with pillows. She made a sound that he thought was a cat purring and thought she tried to smile again. He did not have such a strong feeling while he touched her now, but it was still there. Abe did not arrive at seven. Matt decided he had been paid, so he could leave. He said goodbye to Tina and then went home hoping that the day shift would turn her and let her shin breathe a little.

CLOSE QUARTERS AND OMENS

Misha was outside the nursing home waiting for Matt. He came outside, with a woman was walking beside him asking if he would come and sit with her husband that evening. He agreed and the woman went back inside. He got into the passenger seat of the car and Misha reached over, kissed him, and asked how his night was. He told her, "New patient is a young woman who had a stroke and is close to dying." She said, "*How young?*" He said, "Thirty seven and very much dying." She said, "That's so sad, are you okay with sitting with her?" He said, "Even though she is unable to communicate, she deserves good care and not to die alone, just like anybody else." Misha said, "I wish that I could stand to do what you do. It just freaks me out that the person is definitely going to die and probably while you are there. You know, we at least have hope for the hospital patients." Matt said, "I have hope for the dying people too, just a different kind." They arrived at the marina and found a parking space.

In the evening, they found a note on the car to see the office if they planned to park in the lot again. They stopped by the office, paid for a month of parking, and found out that the slip rent would be due in three weeks. Mae must have forgotten to tell them about it, but it made perfect sense that there was rent. At least the slip rent plus the parking for an additional vehicle was less than the hotel, and all of the apartments they had considered. Neither thought anything about the extra vehicle descriptor of the parking charge.

Matt dropped Misha at work, and then went to the nursing home to meet his new patient. He checked on Sally and Tina and then to his new assignment. Bill Massey had been in the home for two weeks because his wife Ellen was no longer able to help him at home. He was at least ninety-five years old, and Ellen was not much younger. She had the added disability of not being able to drive any longer and asked Matt, "everyone tells me about the rate for you to sit overnight is a hundred dollars, if I give you an extra twenty five, will you drive me home and pick me up in the morning? We only live about two miles away." Matt said, "Sure, you can tell me about Bill on the way."

Ellen was agile but her vision had deteriorated, that was the reason she no longer drove. She explained to Matt on the short ride that Bill had lived in the Keys all his life and was a conductor on the Overseas Railroad when it carried passengers and then a brakeman when it carried only freight. He had only left the Keys once in his life and that was for a year in Europe near the end of World War II. He was lucky enough to arrive after almost all the hostilities had ceased but was with a unit that helped find and clear concentration camps. He has nightmares about that, even though it was so long ago, must have been horrible for it to stay with him this many years. Matt said, "I'll take good care of him, does he have a favorite book or something?" She said, "Give me a minute and I'll get it for you." Matt watched Ellen go into a nicely maintained mobile home that was sandwiched between two that were not so nicely tended. He wondered about how it happened that people came down here to live in paradise and promptly junked it up and ruined the character of the place. Ellen came back out of the trailer and noticed Matt was studying the neighborhood. She handed him a book and said, "It's sad but we had to sell the two lots to make it back in the nineties. Six families have cycled through that one," pointing at the worst of the two eyesores. "These particular people are fishermen and hardly ever come home these days. But, when they do, it's a continual party until they leave again. Guess there's no time to clean and maintain the place amidst all that." She smiled wryly, handed Matt money, and said, "Take good care of Bill tonight, I'll be out here in the morning." Matt droves back to the nursing home with one eye looking at the condition of every building he passed. Hurricanes had made the last tourist season a bust for a lot of people and several businesses were in a sad state of disrepair. Awnings were half torn off, roofs had blue tarps, and some had palms half-fallen or on the ground with their roots in the air. He arrived back at the nursing home and took the book inside with him. It was an older hardback, and the title and author were worn off.

He stopped by the nurses' station to review Bill's chart and a nurse that he hadn't seen before greeted him with, "So you are our very own Michael. I've heard about you." He said, "I'm actually Matt Luna and I'm here to sit with Bill Massey tonight." She said, "Michael is an angel that some say carried Adam to his grave, and sometimes called an angel of death." Matt said, "I'm definitely not an angel but I do sit with dying people, so they don't have to die alone or lonely." She said, "Hi, I'm Elizabeth, hope we didn't get off on the wrong foot." Matt said, "No, most people have a tough time with what I do. Can I see Mr. Massey's chart, please?" She said, "Sure, let me pull it up here and you can have this seat." He put down the book and began reading the entries in Bill's chart. Elizabeth picked up the book and began leafing through it. She said, "Is this your book?" Matt didn't look up and said, "No, it's Mr. Massey's, I usually try to read to my patients at night. Especially, if I can find something that they liked, it helps the time." Elizabeth said, "This is a very interesting book. Most people just watch television. We have to constantly turn them off after the patient is asleep because it can be heard three rooms away." Matt said, "The television seems to upset most of my patients and raise their blood pressure. I sit with them by myself at night and have tried to turn on television shows for them. The ones with blood pressure monitors always show an increase while the television is on. They usually calm down when I read and their blood pressure usually drops, along with their pulse rate." She said, "That's very interesting." Matt thanked Elizabeth and went to Bill's room with book in hand.

Bill was a leathery wisp of a man and looked like he had been malnourished for at least a year. He was lying on his back looking at the ceiling when Matt approached. Matt said, "Hi Bill, I'm Matt and I'll be here all night while Ellen gets some rest at home." Matt touched Bill's arm and Bill's eyes widened as he said, in a surprisingly steady and deep voice, "You've finally come for me?" Matt had a strong feeling of doom and moved his hand away as he replied, "I have not come for anyone, I'm only here to read to you so Ellen could go get some rest. Bill said, "Think whatever you want but you *are* her to see me out of this world." Matt said, "Just to keep you company and to read to you."

Matt opened the book in his hand and stared. It was a copy of Alexander Pope's translation of Homer's Odyssey. He read the first book and Bill asked him to repeat it. Matt read and repeated the sections all night and Bill stayed right with him the entire time. Matt had hoped that Bill would eventually settle down and go to sleep but it didn't happen. At seven, Matt left to go get Ellen and picked up Misha on the way. Misha didn't really want to deal with Ellen, but decided it was better if she went along for the ride. They dropped Ellen off in front of the nursing home and Matt suggested breakfast at the IHOP. That worked for Misha and after eating, they headed for the marina, talking along the way about what to do with the stuff that wasn't necessary on the boat. On the boat, Matt did a quick check, determined that a storage unit was cheaper than the motel room and called a place to arrange for a unit. He told Misha, "Tonight's my four hour night, so I can get everything into the storage unit tomorrow." She said, "Great, let's go to bed then. This boat hasn't been rocking enough lately." He closed the laptop and joined her in bed.

After sex, Matt asked Misha, "How was your night last night?" She said, "Same old string of endless messes to clean and beds to change. There were no admissions or discharges, so the in between times were extra boring. I saw an opening was available in the emergency room and think I might want to try it for a while." He said, "Go for it!" She said, "I think I will, and it will allow me to continue to work at night, like you." He said, "That's important. Remember how we were just crossing paths for the two weeks you were in outpatient rehab?" She replied, "Yeah, let's not repeat any part of that experience." He said, "I love you, let's get some sleep." She said, "I love you, too," and thought about how long it had been since they last made that exchange.

Matt had a restless sleep, and his moving around must have caused her to begin having her own desperate dreams. He was dreaming that the rope snake was chasing him across the ocean, and he was getting too tired to swim. She was dreaming of him leaving her for a younger woman. She woke up first and watched him for a minute. She nudged him and he woke up with a start. She hugged him and after a second, he returned the hug. She asked, "What were you dreaming about?" He said, "The rope snake that chases me across the ocean. What about you?" She said, "You, leaving me for a younger woman." He said, "Why are you so worried about that these days?" She replied, "I don't know, it just happens."

He said, "I love you, things are going to be all right." She said, "I hope so, you know I have been trying to stay off the pain pills and other stuff. I hope you keep giving me chances." He wondered if she was about go on a binge and asked her, "Are you having any problems that we can deal with together?" She said, "Not really, we have appointments next week and that might help. I am also going to try working in the emergency room to see if a change at work helps any." He said, "Sounds good. I have a short night and we need to get going to make the storage place before they close. Do you want drive-through or are you going to eat at the hospital?" She said, "What are you going to do?" He said, "The home has no cafeteria, so drive-through for me." She said, "Me too then."

They hurriedly got ready to go and barely made the storage place before they closed. Next, they got some fried chicken and ate it in the car while sitting at the end of a street watching the sunset. Matt said, "We need to go to the fish-fry this week. What days do you think you'll be off?" She said, "I think we can go on Saturday and if not, we can always go on Sunday afternoon." Matt said, "I miss those people." She said, "It is fun!" They finished eating and he dropped her off at the hospital.

He arrived at the nursing home and checked on Abe and Tina before going to Sally's room. Mike was ready to go and handed Matt a hundred dollar bill as he almost ran from the room. Matt wondered about this behavior for a second but noticed Sally was not looking very well this evening and immediately went to check on her, which meant Mike's behavior was no longer relevant.

Sally was not telling her story over and over again. Instead, was very pale and quiet. When Matt checked, her breathing was shallow and faster than normal. He decided to check her pulse and, when he touched her arm, went on a trip to

somewhere with very high mountains and then driving to a
ski lodge. He pulled his hand back and went to check her
chart and get a nurse. He read the nursing notes in Sally's
chart while Elizabeth looked over his shoulder. He said, "She
hasn't eaten in two days, and she has a low grade fever."
Elizabeth said, "Not too uncommon around here." He said,
"I guess not, but she is about to die." Elizabeth said, "I
reckon you would know that." He said, "I am not the angel
of death, you know." She said, "No, I do not know. Let's go
see about Sally though."
Sally was mumbling something indecipherable when they
entered the room and had broken out in a sweat. Elizabeth
said she wanted to get a thermometer to check Sally's
temperature and left the room. Matt went over and took
Sally's hand. He was now at a ski lodge, and everybody was
having a good time, he let go a second later and saw
Elizabeth smiling at him. She said, "Her temperature has
gone up to 103 degrees, I'm going to call the doctor and see if
we can get some antibiotics delivered." Matt asked, "What
do you think it might be?" Elizabeth motioned him into the
hallway. Once the door was closed, she said, "She most likely
has a systemic infection, you know it's very common in
places like this. You get a small cut or something and then it
blossoms into this. I'm going to go call her doctor, can you
start sponging her down?" He said, "I need an escort." She
said, "No, you don't, this is an emergency and there is no one
else to help. I'll come as soon as possible." He sighed and
said, "Okay." She went to call, and he went back into the
room.
Sally was very warm to the touch as he rolled her onto her
stomach and began sponging her back off. He decided this
was the best he could do to cool the largest surface area and
not expose her too much. Elizabeth arrived a few minutes
later and said, "We have a limited amount of medicine here,
you know, so this is all I have, at the moment," she held up a
suppository. She purposefully said, "Sally, I have to give you

a suppository, it's going to be cold and wet on your bottom for a second." Elizabeth uncovered Sally's bottom, spread her cheeks, and stopped. She asked Matt to look, and he reluctantly did. There, between her cheeks was a large sore, oozing puss. Elizabeth carefully avoided it and inserted the suppository. She told Sally, "Try to keep that in there for a while." Elizabeth then washed her hands, put on a clean glove, and checked the sore. When she touched it, it spewed a pale greenish substance that looked like moldy cottage cheese and a stench filled the room. Matt and Elizabeth then spent the next ten minutes cleaning Sally and changing the bed. Elizabeth said that she was going to go call the doctor again and would be right back. Matt returned to sponging Sally's back. The air had cleared in the room and Matt was certainly happy about that. He ran his hands through Sally's hair to separate it and help it dry a little. When he touched her scalp, he was on the beach basking in the warm sunshine. It was a perfect day, and the rays didn't feel like they would ever burn him. Matt was disturbed by the thoughts, took his hand from her head and the thoughts stopped. He was surprised how strong the thoughts were and wondered if it meant she would be dead soon. He didn't have long to wonder because there was a doctor making a visit to a patient in the facility and the nurse had convinced him to come take a look at Sally. Doctor Art Waldbaum was ancient, but you wouldn't know it unless you could see his face to help determine his age. He had been a surgeon for forty plus years and when he looked at the open wound and the drainage sample said, "I will look at the chart and write a prescription for antibiotics and some packing. We also need to wash out the wound with saline and then pack it with iodine impregnated gauze." The nurse said, "I think there is gauze here, but don't know about the saline." He asked if there were any IV bags stocked and the nurse went to look. Meanwhile, Matt continued to sponge Sally's back. Art said, "What's her temp now and Matt said, "I don't know, I am a private duty sitter and don't have access to a thermometer." Art looked at him and said, "How long have you been doing this?" Matt said, "Less than a year, why?" Art asked, "How did you start?" Matt thought a second and replied, "Just sort of happened, nothing intentional." Art quickly asked, "Do you sense when?" Matt looked directly into Art's eyes and said, "Yes." Art maintained eye contact and asked, "Every time?" Matt said, "Yes, so far." The nurse returned with an IV setup, a jar of packing gauze and a sterile suture kit. Art knew that the kit had scissors and tweezers in it and didn't ask her what it was for. She said, "This is the best I could do." Art said, "No problem," and asked if sterile gloves were available, they weren't so he had to use non-sterile ones. Absorbent pads were layered under Sally's bottom and Art used the sterile end of the IV tubing to washout the hollow area left when the cyst burst open. He then carefully packed the gauze in with the sterile tweezers. He said to leave the area exposed to the air, and keep it as clean as possible. He looked at Matt and his expression asked the question. Matt said, "Yes, very strong." Art asked Matt for his number, explaining that he knew of a few home care cases that needed his unique kind of services.

It was only nine o'clock and Matt was already feeling tired. The nurse checked Sally's temperature, it was down to 101 degrees, and she excused herself to catch up with Art to get the necessary prescriptions and his entry into the chart. Matt stopped the sponging, cleaned out the pan and put the disposable washcloth in the trash. He left Sally's back uncovered so she could continue to cool down. He sat down and began reading a magazine that was in the room, *Southern Living*.

An hour passed and he checked on Sally, she was quiet and didn't feel as hot but touching her immediately sent him into a strange place. In this place, he was in bed with her and that disturbed him enough to keep him from touching her again until it was time to go. At two in the morning, he covered her lightly and softly said he was leaving. She said, "Thank you, I love you." He just thought that she believed he was Mike, touched her shoulder and slipped out of the room. The touch was quick, on purpose but it carried a message to him that didn't register to him until he was driving to the motel. Matt didn't want the message he received from Sally and tried to forget it as he shuttled boxes from the motel to the storage. It took five trips to get everything moved. He finished at five thirty in the morning and wondered what he was going to do for the next hour and a half until Misha got off work.

The answer soon came to him, and he went to the boat, got a fishing rod, some bait and fished off the end of the pier for a while. He landed a couple of mangrove snapper, but they were too small to keep. It kept him from thinking about Sally for a while though. He picked up Misha on time and said that they should go by the motel and check out so that they could stop paying for an unused room. She said, "Can we get coffee on the way?" He said, "Certainly."

REVELATION

Matt had three appointments scheduled over the week, all from Art's referrals. Misha took the position in the hospital emergency room. They made the Sunday fish fry, but the character of the group seemed to be changing to less than desirable. They soon figured out it was people filtering in from a nearby campground. Further inquiry told that it would all clear up again in a few weeks, happened every year. They ate and left without too much interaction.

The following Tuesday, Misha had an appointment at the VA and Matt had one on the next day, which meant an overnight stay made sense. When Matt had talked to Mae, she said she was doing fine and planned to stay in Key West for a while longer but wanted to take a boat trip to Biscayne Bay in a few weeks for a day, though. Matt asked if she wanted to have dinner while they were in Key West.

Tuesday came, and Matt drove Misha to her appointment at the VA and waited in the lobby for her. Her appointment was at two in the afternoon, and they left the clinic at a quarter to six. As they drove to dinner with Mae, she told him about her psychiatrist, how he asked her to join a group that meets every two weeks and includes three other women. He said, maybe I'll get the same group. She said, probably, doesn't seem like there is a lot of choice down here.

They met Mae at The Flaming Buoy for dinner, after checking into the cheapest hotel they could find. The meal was excellent, and Mae seemed energized from living here. She was dressed colorfully, and her eyes had a new light in them. Matt purposely touched her arm and still got a strange feeling. Then, he asked her, "How are things going?" She said, "You guys first, you have to tell me how you've adapted to the boat." Misha spoke up, "I like it because it forced me to change some unhealthy habits like not cleaning up after myself and cleaning as I go." Matt said, "Same for me, and we are about to have a yard sale to get rid of all the crap we found out that we didn't really need." Mae said, "Oh, I remember that feeling. And, that was over forty years ago. I felt so free after getting rid of the excess baggage we had carried from apartment to apartment, kept in the trunk of the car and every other possible place. Of course, we probably had less to start with than you guys did." Matt said, "Now, how are you doing here?" She said, "Can't you see? I am having a blast, just like I always knew I would. We do have a job to do, though. The full moon is coming, and Jim's ashes need to go up to Biscayne Bay." Matt said, "We can arrange to do that." Misha joined in, "At sea, or on the beach?" Mae said, "He needs to be left at sea, I need to be left just off the beach. It's symbolic. We will be rejoined by the wind and tide. We left Jim, Jr. off Lauderdale by the Sea, and Jasmine off Indialantic. Those were their favorite places to go to when we left the Keys. Once we all are back in the ocean, we will meet somewhere up off Cape May or something." Misha said, "That's sad." Mae said, "Not really, we all get to be together out at sea again, that's all.

There was a lull in the conversation and suddenly Mae looked straight at Matt and said, "I guess you're wondering about the visions?" Matt said, "Yea, they are disturbing sometimes." Misha looked at Matt and said, "What visions?" Matt said, "I haven't told you because I don't understand them, and they only happen sometimes." Mae interrupted, "He didn't tell me either, honey. Don't get upset. It's something I know about from Jim and knew Matt had them as soon as we met, and I learned his name." Misha was confused and said, "What is this all about?" Matt added, "Yea, which would be nice to know." Mae said, "There's a little bar down the street, let's go there and I'll let you know everything." Mae insisted on paying for dinner and then they drove a few blocks and went into a bar without a sign. It was probably the only bar in Key West that wasn't geared toward parting tourists with their money. Six older people were scattered between the bar and one of the three booths on the wall. Two tables sat empty and there was no television. Mae ushered them into a booth and waved at the bartender. A second later, a bottle of light beer sat in front of Mae and the bartender asked Matt and Misha what they were having. After all, three had a cold beer, Mae looked at Matt and said, "I knew that you were coming, way back in the early seventies." He said, "Are you feeling okay, you seem to be drifting?"

Mae did not allow him to talk again and said, "You are one of the ones that our ancestors called 'can wape Hiha, which is as close as I can get to the Lakota name given to people like you and Jim, it means owl of the falling leaves, which is in October. The affliction usually runs in families and that might have something to do with your family name being Luna." Matt answered this with his immediate thought of, "Our meeting was just a coincidence." She smiled a little Mona Lisa smile and said, "Who were Ernest and Edith?" Matt's eyes widened and he said, "My great grandparents. I barely remember them. How do *you* know about them?" She said, "Met them in Pompano Beach in the early seventies. We had driven up there to look at a boat and had a flat tire on the bridge going over to the marina. Back then, people always tried to help each other and of course, your grandfather went out of his way to help. When the two men shook hands, they saw each other's thoughts, we spent a week with them up there and the next year they spent time down here, in the Keys, with us." Matt just stood there looking at her with his mouth open. She said, "It is your destiny to comfort those who are on their final trip in this world. It won't be everybody, but it will happen often. I don't have this, and I bet Misha doesn't either. Jim told me everything and tried to deny it his whole life because it scared him. Didn't stop it from happening though, people would seemingly involuntarily reach out and touch him in stores and other places to pass their thoughts along to him. That's one of the reasons living on a boat helps, not so many people can do that to you by surprise." Misha said, "Mae, are you sure you feel, okay?" Matt jumped in and said, "This is all true. It happens to me when I sit with the dying people and touch them. It's like I can see what they're thinking, in some weird way." Misha said, "What about when you touch me, then?" Matt said, "I can't see your thoughts or anything, don't worry." Mae butted in, "Misha, honey, it is almost only people who are dying, and their consciousness is trying to escape their dying body. Kind of like people getting off a sinking boat by getting into a life raft." Misha asked Mae, "Can you see these things?" Mae answered, "No, I can just feel the power when I touch someone who has it. I never noticed it with Jim until after meeting Ernest and Edith up in Pompano that day. I knew that there was something special about Jim. I saw it in his eyes and when he touched me, I could feel something. I just called it love before I knew what it really was. Oh, and I didn't believe it for over a year but when I started paying attention and seeing the people react to Jim in public places, it started sinking in. The clincher came years later. Jim, Jr. had an appendectomy and when Jim walked down the hall of the hospital, there was a man on a gurney being wheeled to surgery. When Jim passed, the man reached out and touched him for no apparent reason. They had never met before, or anything. A few hours later, we learned that the man had died while in surgery of a previously unknown aneurism. After that, I saw things like that happen all the time." Matt said, "Does it go away?" She said, "No, it gets stronger before it starts to fade. It will never leave you, though."

Misha said, "I'm not sure that I believe this. Did you two put this together to freak me out?" Mae said, "There are plenty of things that are true whether you believe them or not." Misha said, "I guess, but this all sounds a little *too* far out there." Matt asked her, "Is this a problem?" Misha said, "No, not a problem. I just have trouble believing it, that's all." Mae said, "I did too at first. Don't let it bother you. He's the one who has to deal with it on a daily basis." Misha said, "Okay, can we talk about something besides people dying?" Mae asked her, "What do you suggest?" Misha held up her empty and said, "How about more beer, for starters." The bartender saw her gesture and brought fresh, cold beers for all of them.

Mae said, "This will be it for me, gotta get my beauty rest." Matt said, "No problem, we'll drop you off." Misha said, "The VA wore me out today, or maybe it's because I'm off schedule." Beers were empty in a matter of minutes and Matt insisted on paying here. They dropped Mae off, and Misha said, "I think we should get a six pack and I want to soak in the tub for a while. Can you buy champagne at the convenience store?" Matt said, "Don't know, let's find out," and pulled into a store lot. They found out that you actually can buy champagne at a convenience store and left with a six-pack of beer and a bottle of bubbly.

At the hotel, Matt watched television while Misha enjoyed a long bath. While soaking, she drank Champagne from a motel water glass and when it was gone, drank beer. There was a lot of sex and then it seemed to be time to check out. Matt drove them up to Stock Island, where they had breakfast and headed home. On the way, they drove to a secluded place on No Name Key, and they smoked a joint. They had decided it was not a good idea to smoke on the boat so much, unless they were offshore somewhere. Back at the boat, they slept most of the afternoon. They microwaved potpies for dinner and then went to work. Misha was eager for a new adventure in the emergency room and Matt was going to one of the private home appointments that were the result of meeting Dr. Waldbaum. The full moon was in four days and the day coincided with Matt's appointment at the VA Clinic.

The next morning, Misha was babbling about all the things that happened overnight in the emergency room. Matt encouraged her and asked questions to keep her talking about her new experiences. She was especially happy that the cases came and went quickly, and you were mostly busy all night. Matt asked if she wanted breakfast and noticed she had fallen asleep in her seat. He drove to the marina and gently woke her up. She asked, "We didn't stop for coffee?" Matt said, "I didn't want to wake you up until you could just go straight to bed." She said, "Thank you, guess I was more tired than I thought." They went to the boat and straight to bed.

CLIVE

Evening came too fast, and Matt dropped Misha off at the hospital on the way to yet another new patient's home. He was amazed at the size of the house and the bareness of the rooms. A young woman introduced herself as Sarah Willow and said, "We've sold most everything to help pay for dad's home care." She led him through the rather large house to a bedroom suite and before entering called out, "Dad, the man is here to look after you. Can we come in?" A small voice answered, "Come on in." Matt followed her into the room and found a man in a hospital style bed, with the head cranked up, looking out a huge window at the bay. The man said, "I'm Clive Willow and I'll be dead soon. Sorry my daughter failed to properly introduce us." Sarah spoke up, "You've been dying now for ten years, we stopped believing you after the first two." Matt said, "Hello Clive, I am here for the night to help out." Sarah said, "I'm out of here, see you guys in the morning!" Clive said, "Go on, get out of here. Go have some fun somewhere." Sarah left without further comment, leaving Matt and Clive alone in the house. Matt immediately wondered about Clive's condition. Clive was not shy and said, "Prostrate cancer. I was shot three times in Vietnam, and I end up dying a horribly slow death fifty years later." Matt asked, "How long have you known?" Clive said, "I maintained my reserve status after leaving active duty, it seemed like the thing to do. When retirement time came, about twelve years ago, I had a discharge physical, and the doctor found that I had a very large prostate. After testing, I was handed the sentence and now it is about to happen." Matt said, "What service?" Clive replied, "Active duty was Army, reserve was Air Force, did drills up in Homestead. Thought about the Navy but figured that sharks don't eat you as you fall, the Army already tried to kill me, so that left the Air Force. Back then the Coast Guard didn't have any viable options for me." Matt said, "So, tell me what I can do for you." Clive said, "Shoot me, right here," and pointed between his eyes. Matt said, "Didn't bring a gun tonight." Clive went on, "I just need to unload all the stuff buzzing around in my head to someone and you drew the short straw." Matt said, "No problem for me, just let me check your pulse." He picked up Clive's arm and there was a disturbing sensation, not a dream like the others, just a feeling of distress. Matt didn't like this new development in his gift and dropped Clive's hand after only a few seconds.

Clive asked Matt, "How long do you think?" Matt stared at him blankly and Clive continued, "Art told me that you could sometimes tell by touch." Matt said, "Can't say right now. I didn't get a good feel for anything, we'll just have to wait and see what develops." Clive said, "I'm still not sure about all this but Art said he knew it was real, and in the past several years stranger things have become known to me. So, why not this too?" Matt said, "What are you talking about?" Clive said, "You, and things that become evident to you when you are old and dying." Matt played along and said, "Like what?"

Clive went into story telling mode and began a tale of how he was shot three times while serving in Vietnam. He started with how he decided to leave Lily Bay, Maine. He explained that his family had a place there that had a dock on Moosehead Lake, and he spent most of his early life on the water, when it was warm enough. And so, the story of Clive Willow began.

Clive seemed to be in a dream as he talked, and Matt listened. "I was born in the middle of winter, at home because there was so much snow that year that my father said he had to shovel in front of the door twice a day to keep from being trapped in the house. The snow was over the first floor windows and it was evidentially lucky that the house had a basement and that's where the coal and cord wood for the heat and cooking was stored. I didn't know anything about all this, of course, I was just born, you know. Anyway, I fished in the lake, worked in the garden, and read every book I could find until I figured out the joys of the female anatomy. After that, I was bound to leave the backwoods existence for city life and scores of beautiful women. Of course, like all greener pasture dreams, it didn't quite work out that way. I ended up in an Army recruiter's office and on my way to boot camp. It was nineteen sixty-one and America really hadn't gotten that involved in Vietnam yet. Some advisors were there, and the French had only been evacuated from the north six or seven years earlier. We didn't follow politics closely back in Lily Bay and I was clueless that the whole thing was about to become explosive, and I would end up fighting in a jungle. I was in the Army for three years and thinking it wasn't too bad. I was a radio operator stationed in Hawaii and it all seemed too easy. I was six months from discharge, thinking about reenlistment when the Gulf of Tonkin incident occurred, and patriotism motivated me to re-up and volunteer. I was a corporal and had dreams of making it to sergeant major."

Clive paused and asked if Matt would please make him a gin and tonic while pointing at the wet bar beside the large window. Matt hesitated and Clive said, "I'm already dying, what's a few drinks going to do?" Matt fixed the drink and Clive said, "Make yourself one too." Matt said, "I'm working, wouldn't be right." Clive said, "Suit yourself, then!" When Matt handed Clive the drink, he noticed Clive was shaky and maybe not as strong as he first appeared to be. It wasn't heavy shakes like in an Alzheimer's patient but fine shakes like someone shivering from the cold. Matt asked Clive about his medications and Clive said, "I take fifty pills a day, and they aren't going to save me, so we don't need to concern ourselves with them here." Matt said, "Okay, just didn't want to forget to remind you about any medication you needed to take." Clive said, "Good point, but I'm not due any more pills until morning."

Clive took on a dreamy air as he sipped his drink and began his story again, "For the first six months, we sat around the airfield at DaNang. In Nineteen Sixty-five Marines arrived to reinforce us from an impending attack and the war was on. Patrols began and by the end of the year, there were around two hundred thousand troops on the ground. I was a Staff Sergeant then and was sent to some place north near a hell-hole called Deo A Yen, they thought that the north Vietnamese were coming across the border from Laos near there because there was a road, of sorts, through part of the jungle there. Turns out there were a lot of North Vietnamese there, don't know where they came from, but they were certainly there. We had a company-sized firebase and did rotating patrols. After two weeks, we got a little lax and walked into an ambush. Fortunately, it was squad against squad. They heard us first and were half set up before we got up to them. It was really just a coincidence that we were all in the same place at the same time. It's a big jungle out there and most of the time you couldn't see over a hundred feet from where you stood. Anyway, there was an intense exchange of fire, and I was out front. Turns out I was hit by three bullets. One hit my left thigh, one my right side and one in my right arm." He raised his arm and pointed out the scar and continued, "I went down like a sack of stones, nothing I could do but lay there and wonder if I was going to make it. Bullets whizzed by and grenades went off, but it was the artillery that scared the crap out of me. The explosions were all around and I had no idea whose were whose and thought that I was in the middle, the no man's land and would be hit at any moment. We had not seen a lot of artillery casualties at that time, mostly because it was our guns doing the shelling. We had seen a couple of NVAs, and they were in a lot of pieces. I tried to crawl somewhere for cover but with a leg on one side out of commission and an arm on the other, it was not happening. The effort also seemed to make the bleeding worse. It all seemed like hours, but it must have just been minutes. The gunfire ended and someone found me. Soon, a medic was working on me. I remember he was a PFC but not his name. I just kept thinking to myself, that an E3 was now the only thing between me and certain death. He did exactly the right things and a helicopter arrived half an hour later in the clearing, where I had been carried.

As the bird came in, a second squad of NVAs arrived and began a new firefight. The medevac pulled up to let two troop carriers land and once they were gone, the medevac came back in. The NVAs knew it was an important thing to us, so they were making a special effort to shoot it down. I was quickly placed in the bottom rack and a second man in the upper. Three walking wounded jumped in, and I felt us going up. A few seconds passed and I felt the helicopter shake. It was already shaking but this was different. I didn't know what happened until a week later, the on-board medic had started an IV on me and after determining that the worse part of my injuries consisted of a broken arm and leg, gave me morphine. I slept the remainder of the ride. The helicopter had been hit with machine gun fire and the pilot actually flew us out of there with a bullet in his left thigh, the co-pilot was hit in his right arm but luckily, it was just a flesh wound." That was the war for me. I spent six months healing up and teaching myself how to walk again. From there, I decided to go to medical school and when that didn't work out, I went to be an accountant. Turns out it was a pretty good choice. Passed the CPA exam in Nineteen seventy-two and retired with a little bit of money thanks to some very lucky breaks in the eighties. I always wanted to find the medic and the medevac pilot that saved me, and repay them somehow, but never was able to track them down. By the time I had the maturity to realize how much I actually owed them, it was all too late."

There was a pause and Matt said, "Is that what you wanted to get off your chest?" Clive said, "No. While I was in Vietnam, I did some other things. I shot at least four men and may have left a girl pregnant. The men haunt me. I have had thirty years of nightmares about the firefight where I shot the men and the one where I was shot. The pregnant woman always seems to make an appearance in them and sometimes they intertwine. The nightmares come almost every night now and I try to stay awake as much as possible." Matt said, "I can understand that." Clive threw back in a sharp voice, "What happened to you that was so bad?"

Matt was thrown off by Clive's sudden change in demeanor and thought before answering him. "Clive, I sit with the dead, every death is a trauma to me and chips away at my being. And, you may not have noticed the leg braces. They came from losing an encounter with a two-inch hawser. It snapped in the middle of an underway resupply and made me its whipping boy. We were three days from port, and I had to be strapped face down to a backboard during the trip. Had a good captain though and he made flank speed for Bahrain, the nearest port with medical facilities that could help me. It's probably not as bad as being shot, but it'll do for me." Clive said, "So, you're a squid too!" Matt almost went off but caught the jovial tone in Clive's voice just in time and saw him smile a little. Matt did say, "That's usually an invitation to throw down and usually comes from a Marine, you know." Clive said, "I know, and back before I was injured, I went out for the throw down regularly. There's nothing like a good brawl to make you feel alive!" Matt said, "I guess it gives the medics something to do." The atmosphere in the room lightened up a little and Clive eventually fell asleep. Matt read some of a book he brought, *Complete Stories and Poems of Edgar Allen Poe,* and waited for the morning.

At the hospital, Misha was too busy to think and working on pure training and reflex. There had been a code blue and three car wrecks in the first half of the shift. She was currently in the middle of cutting off a woman's clothes so that doctors could examine her while she was still strapped to a backboard. The woman had been sleeping in the back of a pickup truck and when the driver hit a concrete bridge abutment, she was thrown across the creek and into some mangroves. It took two hours to get a boat and cut enough of the trees away for paramedics to get her strapped to the backboard and carried out. The three paramedics were all soaked to the waist and left a water trail to the room where Misha was now working.

Fortunately, Misha's patient was going to survive, with the worst injury being a broken ankle and a lot of bruising. Once Misha finished her task, she was called to a trauma room to assist with the driver of the pickup. The pair had been returning from the very bar where Misha had tried to go astray, and the driver was not wearing a seatbelt. Two of the paramedics were talking to the doctor and Misha heard most of the conversation as she worked to remove clothing and begin to clean blood away so that assessments could be made. The paramedics said that there were no skid marks, and the truck engine was in the cab. Misha had a little trouble with trying to figure out how the engine could end up in the cab of a pickup truck but was too busy to contemplate it at the moment. Another nurse had asked her to hold pressure on the man's femoral artery because after cleaning the area near it, it had begun spurting blood. Misha held down tight and felt something hard under her fingers. She called the doctor over and told her that there was something very hard where she was holding. The Doctor asked her to take her hand and the gauze away for a second. When Misha moved her hands, blood began spurting again and the doctor began feeling around. A second later, the doctor asked Misha to resume pressure and said, "It's a piece of bone." A technician delivered four units of blood and a nurse got two of them attached to the current IV lines and flowing. A surgical resident was installing a sub-clavicular main line to help replace blood and fluids faster and was having a little difficulty due to the amount of blood the patient had already lost. The floor was becoming sticky with blood and Misha's white nursing tennis shoes were now mostly red, along with the lower left leg of her pants. She was wearing a protective gown, but it just wasn't long enough.

Alarms went off and the assortment of people in the room
changed gears into code blue mode. The doctor shocked the
patient and got some response but had to administer a
second shock to get a decent rhythm. Everyone went back to
their assigned tasks and after a few seconds, the alarms went
off again. This time the shocks were only effective for a few
seconds each and the doctor called for a chest tray.
Epinephrine was injected directly to the heart and still it
wouldn't cooperate, so she cut open the patient's chest to
begin manual stimulation. More blood and then after five
minutes everything was quiet. The doctor said, "Call it at 2:03
AM," and left the room. Misha and the two other nurses in
the room began the cleanup and preparation to take the body
to the morgue. When Misha finished and asked the
technician from the morgue to sign the transfer paperwork, it
was almost four o'clock. Three hours to go, she went to get a
cup of coffee and as she finished pouring her cup and turned
to leave, the doctor came in to get a cup.
Doctor Kim Chang had been an emergency medicine
specialist for five years, three of them at this hospital. She
asked Misha, "Are you new?" Misha said, "I just transferred
from acute medical." Dr. Kim said, "What an introduction to
the emergency room, huh." Misha said, "It has been busy
tonight, but the time is passing quickly." Dr. Kim said, "You
handled the blood and gore very well, you'll probably do fine
here." Misha continued out into the hall and saw a new
gurney being wheeled into the main trauma room.
The night was speeding by for Misha and dragging for Matt.
Matt was deep into reading when Sarah arrived home at
around five in the morning and startled him. He came out of
the bedroom and closed the door behind him to see what was
happening. Sarah had been in Miami Beach and appeared
was thoroughly stoned, she studied Matt up and down and
asked, "How's dad?" Matt said, "Sleeping soundly." She
casually said, "Good, wanna fuck?" Matt was not sure he
heard what she said quite right, and, in the pause, she threw

it out there again, "I am buzzed and horny, you look good, so let's fuck." Matt was having a tough time resisting Sarah because she had thrown off her clothes and was trying to pull him to a couch. She was a good-looking girl, naked and willing but he managed to say, "No, this can't happen. I am getting paid to take care of your father and this wouldn't be right." She said "Ah, c'mon," and jerked him as hard as she could as she went down on the couch." Matt landed on top of Sarah and lucked out. She ran out of energy, all at once, and went limp as she passed out. He recovered, looked at what he was passing up for a few minutes and then got a blanket to cover her. She was snoring loudly as he placed the cover over her and returned to Clive's room. Clive woke up and asked what time it was. Matt said, "Six thirty." Clive asked, "Did Sarah come home?" Matt said, "Yes, a while ago." Clive then asked, "Did she pay you?" Matt said, "No." Clive went on, "Would you like to come back regularly? Sarah needs to get out and have a life and I will pay you cash." Matt said, "I have some regulars, but can come two or three nights a week." Clive said, "Deal, call and work the schedule out with Sarah this evening and here's your money for last night." Clive pulled a hundred dollar bill from his pajama shirt pocket and handed it to him. Clive shook Matt's hand and said, "We're going to get along just fine." Matt got that dark unnerving sensation and said, "I have to run pick up my girlfriend from her shift at the hospital. I'll call Sarah later today." Clive said, "See you soon!"

ROUTINES AND RITUALS

Matt picked up Misha on time. She looked, and felt, like she was crawling uphill, as she made her way to the car. She was in scrubs and Matt asked, "What happened?" She yawned and said, "Everything, let's just get home and into bed. Wake me when we get there." Matt was ready for sex and realized as she slumped in her seat that it was unlikely, she was going to want anything to do with his desires this morning. By the time he was out on US 1, she was snoring, and he was certain sex was off the table, at least until evening.

On the Dreaming Moon, Matt got Misha settled in bed then did a little Internet research on Clive and Vietnam before crawling into bed. He was nudged awake at five in the evening with Misha wanting attention. He was happy to provide her with a little more than she planned on getting. After showers and dressing, it was a close call getting to work on time.

A few days later, it was the full moon and time to take Jim to sea. Matt drove to Key West by himself for his appointment at the VA, and also to get Mae. On the way back to the boat, they stopped by the mortuary to get Jim's ashes and then, at Mae's insistence, Publix. Mae bought an assortment of groceries and then they went on to the boat. Misha had stayed to manage the pump-out barge and was waiting impatiently for them to arrive. Both Matt and Misha were off work for two days and Mae had no specific schedule. The Dreaming Moon was checked over, untied and Matt slowly took her out the channel. He felt more nervous than before because he was now taking his and Misha's home out into the unpredictable, and unforgiving, ocean.

All went well out to the Gulf Stream, which was very active today because of the moon's phase and the current provided them with a roller coaster ride north. A brief rainsquall hit them off Key Largo and visibility was reduced to a few feet. The Dreaming Moon had basic radar, so Matt was able to see that there were no boats in near proximity. It was a leap of faith though because the radar was mostly returning storm clutter. After five minutes, Matt asked Mae if she would take the helm while he went to the bow to watch for obstructions. Mae said, "We're drifting north in the Stream, so anything out here with us is almost certainly doing the same, relax a little, watch the radar and blow the horn every minute or so if you're worried." Matt did as suggested and the storm passed after about twenty minutes. The surprise was how far they were up the coast when the tempest subsided. Mae said, "Sometimes that happens. The winds push you faster, and further than you realize because you are busy with the storm and the speed increase doesn't always register on the speedometer." The GPS now said they were only ten miles from the desired coordinates. The storm was long gone, and the sky was now clear and blue. The storm could be seen, far out on the horizon, heading northeast and out to sea along the Gulf Stream.

They arrived at the coordinates Mae had provided and it appeared to put them over a reef. Matt carefully anchored them in bottom sand, so as not to damage the reef and shut the boat down. Mae suggested a few hours of fishing to stock up the freezer. They spent the evening catching, cleaning, and putting snapper and grouper into the freezer. The smoking and drinking created intense hunger and Misha volunteered to cook the steaks Mae brought. They ate dinner as the sun provided a full-spectrum color show to the west out over the Everglades. The sun had what appeared to be a smaller sun above it and Mae said, "Always thought that was a Sun Dog, but have been corrected. Sun Dogs appear to the sides of the sun. This is likely something akin to *Joule's last glimpse*." The bright ball of light slid completely over the horizon. Once the bright ball was gone, there was an explosion of colors that shifted from oranges to yellows, pinks and finally shades of deepening blues. Stars appeared from east to west, as if chasing the daylight. It was probably the most spectacular sunset that any on the boat had ever seen, and they all stood agape for a few minutes until the show was over.

It was half an hour later when the moon finally made its appearance. A little yellow light to the southeast followed by the familiar shadowed face slowly climbing from its bed somewhere over the sea. It was an apogee moon, more often called a super moon, and Mae remarked, "Matt, this is your moon, the moon of the falling leaves. It was also once Jim's moon and now we have to send him off on the next step of his journey." Mae got up and wobbled into the cabin to get the urn. She asked Misha to get the paper bag of separated grocery items. She asked and Matt to go ahead and dump the remains of the filleted fish over the sides and back of the boat. Inside the cabin, Mae flipped a switch located on the cockpit panel that Matt and Misha had not noticed before. Lights came on under the waterline on the sides and stern. Matt marveled at the life on the bottom, thirty-five feet below and quite plainly visible in the clear tropical water.

Mae and Misha returned on deck to find Matt staring intently over the stern. Mae asked, "Is it crowded down there yet?" Matt said, "Very!" Misha looked over the gunwale and was instantly under the ocean's spell. Mae returned to the cabin and several minutes passed before she returned on deck. Matt looked up as Mae came to the stern and froze. She was nude and had a large, long-stemmed pipe in her hand. Misha turned and had much the same reaction as Matt. Mae said, "Sorry for the view but it is how we always did this. We were naked and unashamed when we arrived here in the world, and we leave the same way. This was our way of paying respect to that." She handed Matt the pipe and a pack of wooden matches.

Matt accepted the stone pipe and lit it. As the smoke came up the stem, he instantly knew that this was not the same thing they had been smoking all afternoon. He handed the pipe to Misha, as Mae directed, and she took a long drag. Her eyes widened as she held the smoke in and handed the pipe to Mae. It was Misha who decided that if Mae was naked, she could be too and threw her dress off, revealing her lack of anything under it. Matt reluctantly joined in. Fortunately, Mae had maintained herself well over the years and was not unpleasant to see nude. The pipe had a large bowl and made five rounds before there was no more smoke from it. Mae said, "Now it's time to return Jim to the sea."

Mae picked up the urn and went to the stern, Matt and Misha followed. Mae began speaking in a muffled voice, "While we live, we feast on the animals and fishes of the world. When we die, it is only fair that we give them the same courtesy" She threw handfuls of frozen peas over the stern and the water came alive she then checked the wind, went as far astern as possible, asked Matt and Misha to throw peas and began dumping Jim's ashes overboard. Tropical fish leapt from the water to get the mixture of ashes and peas. When Mae finished with Jim's ashes, she grabbed a filet knife from its place on the stern and raised it toward her head. Matt and Misha both stopped what they were doing and were about to yell out but saw that Mae was only cutting a lock of braided hair off. Mae threw the hair overboard and said, "I'll damn well mourn you if I want to, please come back to haunt me over it. I'd welcome it."

Mae came forward, picked up the pipe, refilled it and lit it herself this time. Matt was next, then Misha. This mixture was supremely potent and also must have contained some kind of hallucinogenic agent because both Matt and Misha soon found themselves transfixed on the moon. Some minutes later, there was another pipe and then time melted. The three unlikely nude figures lay on the deck watching the moon and stars as fish made periodic splashes around the boat. They were over a mile from shore and no other boats were within sight. This left them alone in the universe with only the moon's movement tracking time. A pre-morning chill woke Matt and Misha simultaneously and they found themselves alone on the deck. Nature took over and soon they were engaged in very quiet and slow sex. After the climax, they stood up and looked at the water off the stern. There was Mae, floating in a pool of luminous algae. Matt almost dove in but realized that she was in a floating chair that was tethered to a stern cleat, before committing to the jump. Mae saw their shadows and said, "Come in and join me for a minute." They did and found that the water was actually warmer than the air.

The action of Matt and Misha entering the water and swimming over to Mae caused the glowing creatures to brighten into a show of lightning like flashes and some clung to their skin, especially where they had been attached just previously. There was something magical about the moment and somehow it was not strange that they were sharing it with a very old woman, in the middle of the night, in the middle of the ocean. The moment passed too quickly for all of them, and it was back onto the boat, a freshwater spray off and time for bed. Mae said, "You two go on, I'm going to smoke and stay on deck a while longer. You are both welcome to have a few puffs before bed though." Everyone was wrapped in a towel now and they watched the last of the moon disappear over the horizon. The sun was still an hour away, so the stars were all that lit the ocean. Several falling stars streaked across the sky and seemed to be headed directly for them. Matt realized that the pipe mix was probably at fault and asked Misha if she would like to accompany him to a nice comfortable bed. She agreed, and they disappeared into the cabin. Matt grabbed two beers from the fridge and handed one to Misha saying, "I'm so thirsty all of a sudden." She said, "Me too!" They drank the beer as they dropped the towels and then snuggled in bed. Once the beer was gone, nature seemed to take over again and they made love in what seemed like a dream space. They woke up, well after noon, to Mae's call of, "Foods ready!"

BILL AND ELLEN

Arriving back in Marathon, they stopped at the fuel dock and then secured the boat into her slip. It was early evening, and a thunderstorm was passing on the eastern horizon. The sunset had trouble competing with the storm show in the colored clouds, glowing lightning and periodic bolts dancing about the colored puffs and folds. Misha asked Matt, "How was your appointment? With all the funeral and travel, I didn't have a chance to ask." Matt said, "We are going to be in the same therapy group, that's about it." There was a ten minute pause for thunderstorm and sunset watching. Matt said, to Mae, "I will take you back down tomorrow, if you don't mind." She said, "No problem and I have something else for you guys. Now mind you, it's just a loan until I'm dead." She motioned them to follow her off the boat.

In the parking lot, the extra car fee for parking that they had paid without question, made sudden sense. Mae uncovered a 1988 Alfa Romeo Spider that appeared to be in excellent condition. She said, "Jim and I had a lot of good times in this car, cruising up and down US 1 and up on Miami Beach. Everything should be good on her, but I don't think she's been moved in six months or more." Matt said, "You've given us way too much already, how will we ever repay you." Mae said, "How many people would have taken me up to place Jim in the sea, and participate in all the mixed-up ceremonies with me? You two, I'd say that's about the total count. I think you have already proven your worth and taking care of me, and then my ashes, will pay everything in full. Don't you worry about it one bit."

Mae held out the key, "See if she starts, Matt." Matt did and they discovered that the car was dead. Mae said, "There's a solar charger on the Dreaming Moon, we'll hook it up and by noon tomorrow we should be ready to go. Jim always said there was a little trick to get into second gear, a hook or something. You'll probably grind the gears for a while before you figure it out, just like he did." They covered the car and went back down the dock.

Mae motioned for Matt and Misha to follow her as they passed the boat. She said, "You will need a good supplier after I 'm gone, so I'll introduce you." A fifty-five Bertram sat in a slip four down, on the opposite side. Mae called out,

"Sam, you in there?" A sixtyish man wobbled out the hatch and said, "Mae! Sorry to hear about Jim, how are you doing?" Mae said, "Took care of him last night, thanks to these two. Can we come aboard?" Sam and Mae exchanged looks and he said, "Sure, come on in!" The boat was spotless, and everything shined like it was brand new. Matt noticed that the galley seemed to have never been used. Sam saw the interest and said, "I'm a single man, no need to cook, ever!" Mae broke in and said, "Sam, this is Misha and Matt, they will be taking over the Dreaming Moon and are good people. Can you make sure they get what they need?" Sam said, "Anything for friends of yours." Mae said, "Good, they will need some of the special mix you got me for Jim's funeral, it kept good even though we got it six months early." She handed him three-hundred-dollar bills and said, "You guys can work everything else out." Sam said, "You'll explain delivery to them?" She said, "No problem, same as it always was. See you later, Sam." He said, "Where you staying? She said, "Depends on the offer?" They both smiled and she said, "Stop by and get me when you're ready."

Back on the Dreaming Moon, Matt and Misha drank beer and Mae got ready to go out. It seemed strange to Matt and Misha to think about the two of them going out together. Mae answered the unasked questions for them. She came from the stateroom in a short, form fitting dress and it was obvious there was nothing under it. She said, "How do I look?" Misha said, "I hope that I look half that good when I get older." Matt said, "Lookin' good, where you guys going?" Mae said, "Sam has let it be known over the years that he wanted to bed me, so I'm thinking a drive through for take-out and then his boat. Actually, that's my plan; I have no idea what he's planning." She added a pair of high heels and checked the mirror. Matt and Misha just stared at each other, trying not to think about what Sam and Mae would look like having sex. Mae said, "I'm old, not worn out. Besides, I haven't had a full treatment in almost a year." Sam called out from the dock and Mae left saying, "Don't expect me home tonight!" She purposely said it with enough volume to allow Sam to hear.

Matt slept soundly but Misha had dreams of being blown into pieces and, after the pieces were gathered up, they were scattered over the ocean with fishes swallowing up the chunks of her. It seemed odd to her that she was in a million pieces yet was still thinking and feeling as a whole person. That dream faded and she was helping a soldier with an injured foot beside a Humvee. After a second, she knew what was about to happen and as it did, she jerked awake. Matt stirred and said, "You okay, baby?" She snuggled against him and said, "No, the nightmares are back." He said, "We go to group in two days, that'll probably help. But, what can I do for you now?" She rolled on top of him and said, "Help me think about something else."

At seven in the morning, Matt got up, dressed, and looked around to see if Mae was on the boat. She wasn't. He went on deck to check the weather and, after deciding it was going to be clear, got the battery charger and went to hook it up to the Alfa. On his return to the boat, Mae joined him and asked if he had coffee going yet. Matt said, "Next thing on the list." Mae said, "Mind if I join you guys?" He said, "Never a problem!" Misha was up before the pot finished brewing and they all enjoyed coffee on the deck. Misha asked Mae, "How'd the date go?" Mae said, "Don't kiss and tell but you might assume that I slept with him since I didn't come back here." She looked around and lowered her voice, "Kind of a long wait for a quick ride on a short bus, if you know what I mean." Misha was fairly sure that meant that more than the length of the ride was unfulfilling but didn't want the imagery in her mind. Especially since, she was already certain that Mae was in better physical shape than she was, and that really bugged her. Not enough to cause a sudden change in lifestyle and habits, just a thought burr in the back of her mind that stuck a sensitive spot now and then. Matt was desperately trying to stay completely out of the conversation and getting uncomfortable.

An hour later, Matt checked the Alfa and it started right up. Mae suggested that he take it for a spin to make sure everything was okay. Half an hour later he returned and said things appeared fine. Mae said, "We'll hit the DMV in Key West before you drop me off, then." A quick conversation resulted in all three going south in the Toyota. The Key West DMV was not that busy just before lunch and Mae offered to buy lunch, if they were willing to eat where she wanted to go. Neither Matt nor Misha had plans and work was still just over six hours away, so they agreed to lunch. Mae said, "Great, let's go over to Havana 1 and see if we can get seated." Matt followed Mae's directions to Truman Avenue. Getting seated took fifteen minutes but was well worth the wait. Mae said she was going to stay at the restaurant for a while after lunch and Matt and Misha drove north so that they could rest for an hour or so before work.

Matt was sitting with Bill Massey tonight and Misha was in the emergency room. Misha arrived and there was very little going on, so she began cleaning and checking stock. In the emergency room, there is often no time for missing or expired items. When someone's life is on the line and a doctor reaches for a chest tray, it had better be there, complete and within the expiration date. Otherwise, somebody gets to go out, look some husband, wife, mother, or father in the eyes and tell them that that their loved one didn't make it. The emotions, on both sides, are more than anyone should be dealing with at any given time. This is something that no one in the emergency room wants to do, even when it was unavoidable, or the person was dead when they arrived, and nothing could have been done to save them. The failures of the emergency room staff weigh far heavier than the successes and often the workers have to transfer permanently, sometimes in as little as a shift, to remain sane.

Matt arrived at the nursing home and found Bill in bad shape. Bill looked at Matt and weakly said, "I guess this time I'm not getting away." Ellen was nowhere to be found and there was no evidence that she had been there recently. Matt went out to the Nurse's Station and found Elizabeth working. She saw him and said, "The reaper is here, who is slated for a special visit this fine evening?" Matt smiled wryly and said, "Mr. Massey. Has anyone seen his wife, Ellen lately?" Elizabeth said, "I've been off for three days, so not me. I'll ask around though." Matt called her closer and softly said, "I think there is a problem with Mr. Massey, can you come help me check him out?" She said she would be down to the room in a few minutes.

Matt returned to Bill's room, walked up to the bed, and hesitantly touched Bill's arm. The tension was intense, and no focused images came. Matt decided that there was a bigger problem because Bill was catatonic. His arms and legs seemed frozen in place and his face was locked into an expression that Matt interpreted as severe anxiety. Matt quietly said, "Bill, how are you doing in there?" There was a slight change in Bill's breathing and a small grunt-like noise came out. Matt checked vital signs and found Bill's pulse and blood pressure were both too high. He looked into Bill's blue eyes and then waved his hand close to see if there was a reaction, there was not. Matt decided to see if he really could read things from someone else and grabbed Bill's forearm. A few seconds passed and Matt began getting a sensation of running and desperation. He felt like something was missing but there was no indication of what it might be. This went on for a few seconds, it seemed like an hour to Matt and then it was clear. A vision of Ellen came into focus, in the distance, so far away, but still clearly distinguishable and apparently very slowly moving further away.

Matt was trying to decide what the vision meant when Elizabeth came in and asked what she could do to help. Matt said, "Can you help me turn Mr. Massey?" Elizabeth was unsure why this required her time but agreed and went to assist. She quickly saw what Matt was trying to impart to her and after getting Bill turned, she asked Matt into the hall. Once the door closed, she asked, "Is he going to die tonight?" Matt said, "I don't know that." She quickly said, "I'm not sure that I quite believe you but think I will call his doctor." Matt said, "Can we call his wife, Ellen?" Elizabeth said, "Only if he is dying or there is an emergency. Phone numbers and stuff like that are all protected information, you know." Matt said, "I am going to go to their house to check on Ellen, I get the feeling something is wrong." Elizabeth smiled and said, "I knew it." Matt rolled his eyes and said, "I am not the reaper!" She said, "That's merely your opinion." Matt had no idea what that comment actually meant, and quickly forgot about it, as he walked out of the facility.

Matt drove to the Massey's trailer and knocked on the door. There was no answer, he tried the knob, and the door was unlocked. Very slowly and cautiously, he opened the door a crack and called out, "Ellen, are you home?" There was nothing; he opened the door a little further, went to call out but stopped and closed the door instead. A second later, he was on his cell with the police department asking for a unit to come by. The dispatcher insisted on knowing why and he said, "Mrs. Massey hasn't been seen in days and there is an overpowering odor coming from her trailer. Matt was certain of what he smelled and was not willing to go in and make the discovery himself.

A patrol car arrived five minutes later and after Matt introduced himself and explained how he was connected with the Masseys. It was decided that the officers would check things out. One of the officers, Ed, said, "My wife works at the nursing home and has mentioned you before. You sit with people when they die or something." Matt said, "Something like that." The other officer knocked, called out and checked the door. A few neighbors had showed up now and Matt heard someone say that they hadn't seen Ellen in a long time. The officer at the door opened it a little and called out, a few second later he opened the door further and had an obvious reaction to the smell. He closed the door and both officers walked around the trailer to check for any signs of forced entry or anything else. They also called EMS to come, once they were out of the neighbor's earshot.

Twenty minutes later two police officers and two paramedics announced their intention to enter the trailer. Matt waited outside for what he was sure the news would be. Seconds later, an officer came out and asked Matt to come in. He forced his feet to work and went inside. The stench was almost overwhelming, and Matt fought the urge to gag. He followed the officer into the back bedroom and was instantly relieved and more worried at the same time. There, on the bed was a large dog that had been dead for a few days without air conditioning. That left the question, where was Ellen?

A Senior Alert went out and Matt tried to recall if there was anything in his vision that would provide any clue as to where to look. He immediately thought about the hospital and called the admissions desk. They were not much help other than to say that no one named Ellen Massey was listed as a patient. That was not good enough for him, so he drove over to the hospital to see Misha.

Matt waited at the Emergency Room nursing station for ten minutes before Misha could come see him. He explained what was happening and asked if she could check for unknown females over the past week. She said she would, but it would have to be later in the night when she got a break. They kissed and she said she would call him later. It was a busy night in the emergency room and one of the nurses had called in sick to add to the workload. Matt left and tried to think about where an old woman without a car could have gone. The vision of her getting further away was clear but nothing about it gave any indication of place. Matt returned to the nursing home to revisit Bill and possibly get a better image. He felt strange believing he actually saw things but figured it was worth a try.

Bill was in the same catatonic state when Matt arrived and grabbed his forearm. This time there was no vision of Ellen, it was a peaceful beach and sunset. Matt didn't know how to interpret this, so he let go and sat down. An hour passed before Misha called and told him that there were no elderly women admitted without identification in the past week. He went out to find Elizabeth. He did not find her but found a nurse he had not met before at the desk. He explained who he was and asked if Mrs. Massey had been around. The nurse said, "I have no idea, I'm just part-time and haven't worked here in two weeks. Matt went out into the parking lot and then began walking toward Bill and Ellen's to see what he came across on the way. He realized after a few minutes that the Greyhound stop was on US1 and turned around. One of the officers at the trailer had given him his card and Matt called the cell number listed on it. After introductions, Matt said he had been back to the nursing home and had called the hospital without luck. The officer said that they had not had any luck either so Matt suggested that Ellen might have been confused and boarded the Greyhound or something. The officer said, "Why not, I'll check it out." Matt returned to the nursing home and sat with Bill.

At six in the morning, Matt felt strange and checked on Bill, within seconds of Matt standing up, Bill went silent, and Matt knew it was over. He checked and sure enough, no pulse or breathing so he pressed the call button and Elizabeth came in the door a second later. She knew that the call could only mean one thing since Matt was the only person in the room capable of pushing the button. Matt was more upset that Ellen was missing than about Bill dying. He left to get Misha as soon as he finished getting Bill prepped for the funeral home.

While Matt was waiting at the hospital, he thought that he saw Ellen being wheeled in the door on a stretcher. He went inside to see, and it was definitely her. He asked the paramedic if she was alive since it was not apparent. She was, but just barely. The paramedic asked how Matt knew her. Matt waved him aside and told him very quietly that he had been taking care of her husband, Bill Massey, and that he had died at the nursing home a few hours ago and that there was a Silver Alert out for her. He added that she had not been to the nursing home in a few days and a dead dog had been found in their house. The paramedic called in the Silver Alert information in on his radio. Misha was ready to go, and the new shift leader arrived to tell the paramedics which room to put Ellen into. Matt told Misha that he wanted to stay and see if he could help, she said, "I have to get out of here, can you walk home or something." He said, "I'll drop you off and come back."

Half an hour later, Matt was back in the emergency room at Ellen's side. When he was asked who he was, he said that he was her home health aide and came as soon as she was found. Since she was unresponsive and he knew a lot about her, he became the de facto decision maker for Ellen because it was the best, and easiest, thing possible. Tests quickly determined she was suffering from dehydration, malnourishment and was in a diabetic coma. The police officers eventually arrived, and Matt asked where she had been found. They said he was right, she had gotten onto a Greyhound and by the time the driver realized she had no ticket and no money to buy one, they were up at Duck Key, and he just let her off. She had made it quite a ways but evidently took a wrong turn and was found at the end of a street unconscious. We just got it all pieced together from several calls and interviews. Matt said, "Guess she was lucky." The officer said, "Very."

After IVs and medication, Ellen was ready to be released and Matt was all she had. She had regained enough faculties to realize that if he was at the hospital with her there was no reason for him to be at the nursing home with Bill. Matt got a nurse to come in and slowly began, "Ellen, Bill died this morning. I was with him, and he was peacefully sleeping when it happened. I took care of what I agreed to do regarding getting him to the funeral home." Ellen was speechless for a few minutes and finally uttered a crackling and weak, "Thank you, Matt," out of her trembling lips. He replied, "No problem, things had to be done, you know. There is something else though. Did you guys have a dog?" She said, "No, but there was a stray Bill used to feed and talk to once in a while." Matt said, "When you were missing, I went by your trailer. It was unlocked and you didn't answer, so I called the cops, and they came to check things out. We found a dead dog in your bed. Animal control removed it, but you might need to think about staying somewhere else tonight. Can I take you somewhere?"

Ellen was overwhelmed and the change in her heart rate and blood pressure signaled that she was likely going to be a guest of the hospital for a while. She began crying and said, "I must have forgotten that Max got in the house and left him locked in there. I killed him, poor dog. He didn't deserve to die because an old woman forgot about him." Matt said, "It looked to me like he was just trying to be close to Bill. That's why I think he was curled up in the bed, it probably still had a scent" Ellen said, "You really think so?" Matt reached over, touched her wrist and after a second said, "Yes, it was apparent. Do you have any children I can call or anybody that you want to come?" She looked at him and said, "Kim, our daughter lives up in New York. Her number is on the corkboard in the kitchen, at the trailer. Haven't heard from her in over a month, she had a lot of trouble with her father's decline. She was a daddy's girl." Matt said, "I'll call her today, anything else I can do?" She said, "Hand me my purse." He did and she dug out an ATM card. "Take this and go get five hundred dollars out that ought to square us up." Matt said, "Too much, my fee is one hundred a shift and this is only my second shift." She said, "Suit yourself but Bill had insurance and I will be getting quite a bit of money in the near future so I can be generous if I want to." Matt said, "Okay, five it is but I will also clean up the mess from the dog." She said, "Max, that's what Bill called him. Max, and I killed him." Matt said, "No, I really don't think you had much to do with it. He just wanted to go be with someone who was kind to him." Ellen closed her eyes and said, "The card code is two, four, six, eight it's the only thing I could ever remember." Matt said, "I'll bring it back later and I will call Kim, as soon as I get to the trailer." Ellen drifted off and the nurse came by to check on her and tell Matt that she was being admitted for observation. Matt said, "Thank you, I'll be back later." The nurse said, "Check at the visitor's desk for her room number, I don't have it yet."

Matt went straight to the trailer and evaluated the cleaning needs. He then called Kim as he drove to Kmart to get the things he needed. Kim said she would be there as soon as she could get a flight to Miami, rent a car, and drive down. Matt told her about Ellen's insistence that he withdraw money from the bank because he felt strange doing it. She said for him to go ahead, and they would work anything else out after she got there.

Matt arrived at the boat around three in the afternoon, showered and crawled into bed with a vodka scented Misha. She stirred and said that she was calling in sick to work because she needed a mental health break. Matt didn't understand but was too tired to give it any great thought. He did think, "Thank goodness the group therapy was starting tomorrow." Two hours later, he got up and went to sit with Sally for the four-hour shift. It was an uneventful night, and he was home with Misha before midnight. She was stoned and drunk which irritated him because it was becoming a little too common an occurrence again. He again thought that the group session might help matters and convinced her to come to bed with him and have some needed together time.

In the morning, he went by the hospital to check on Ellen and found that Kim had arrived an hour or so before him. Kim was a nice woman and met Matt with a hug. She said, "Mom told me that you were a savior to her and dad." Matt answered, "It's my job." Kim said, "You went way beyond, thank you." He said, "I have to go to Key West today, call me if you need anything and a new mattress will definitely be needed at the trailer." More thanks and then he was off to get Misha and drive to Key West.

SESSION ONE

At two o'clock, in a typical government style conference room, at the Key West VA Clinic, Matt and Misha met the other four members of their assigned group and the leader. Douglas McArthur was a research psychologist doing doctoral clinical work under a grant to find ways to help veterans deal with post-traumatic stress disorder, commonly called PTSD. He would be leading the therapy group. This was his second group, and the sessions were scheduled for six months. He had a supporting psychiatrist to help evaluate the need for, and to prescribe, any needed medications. He also had an assistant, who would not be present until half an hour after the session began, for some reason that was not explained to the group.
Doug began the session at five after two and began by saying, "My name is Douglas McArthur, no relation to the great general in blood, or deeds. Please call me Doug and all future sessions *will* begin on time. My roster shows six people in the group please nod or wave when I call your name, Matt Luna, Michelle Pomeroy, Eli Cesar, Leanne Booker, Jose Melendez, Judy Bond, Ryan Shackles, looks like we're all here. Now, can we go around the room and make introductions? Please?" Matt went first, then Misha. After that, there was another couple.

Eli Cesar began his story with his decision to enter the Marines as soon as he finished college. He had been an All-State football player and started every year that he was in college at the University of Florida. He said, "I knew that I loved the Marines as soon as I arrived onboard Parris Island and it only got better from there. Once I finished boot camp, I was accepted into the officer program. Six months later, I was commissioned a second lieutenant and sent to the Middle East as a platoon leader. Everything went perfectly for six weeks and then my truck hit an IED which resulted in my new bionic leg," he pulled up his pants leg to reveal the flesh-colored plastic, for effect. He continued, "Goes up to mid-thigh. Everything is intact after that. Took me a month to learn how to walk on my new leg and I recently did a half marathon. I actually finished in the upper half, for my age group, and plan to do better next time." Doug broke in and said, "What brings you here Eli?" Eli said, "I lost my leg, my driver lost his head and pieces of his skull ended up embedded in my face. I get to relive this at least three times a week, in full color and slow motion. I also have episodes where I am sure that I am going to die at any second and have logged way too much ER time." Doug cut in again and said, "We're going to work on getting you to a better place, Eli. Next Please."

Leanne Booker spoke so softly that no one could hear her. Doug coaxed a few more decibels out of her and she gained a little confidence as she spoke. She looked at Eli and said, "I am Leanne, and I was shot in the head by a sniper. Sounds like I should be dead, I know. I just happened to have turned my head a split second before the impact and the bullet ripped off the back of my skull instead of simply killing me. I was in a coma for two months and the doctors did bone grafts and plastic surgery to close everything back up. I lost most of my childhood memories and sometimes have trouble with loud noises. I am a Marine like Eli, and we have been together for two years now. My biggest issues are open spaces and night terrors." Doug was steadily writing, and the silence hung in the air a second too long. He looked up and said, "Thank you, Leanne. We will be addressing a lot of fears here and hopefully we can help with the night terrors also. Who's next?"

Jose Melendez stood up and said, "I was Army Special Forces and got hit by shrapnel from a suicide bomber while in garrison. I lost my left eye and have metal plates in my arm from when I threw up my arm to shield my face. The metal broke my arm and drove the bone into my eye, damaging the optic nerve and destroying the eyeball. I don't have nightmares like others. I just can't function without drugs. It took all the prescription meds I normally take, plus two Xanax just to get here for this meeting." Doug said, "Thank You Jose, we'll work on that agoraphobia. Next, please."

The third female in the group, Judy Bond, spoke in a slower and very clearly southern accent, "I followed my father's footsteps into law enforcement. He was a beat cop and I specialized in disarming bombs. The Army is one of the best trainers in the field, so I joined up. Just let me get right to it, here. My partner pulled the wrong wire and vaporized as I was coming up to help. Lost my right arm, shrapnel took out my ability to have children, and mangled my right breast. If you do choose to talk to me, I can't hear anything out of my right ear. I no longer dream of anything much." Doug asked, "Are you functional with your prosthesis, Judy?" She said, "Almost, I was right-handed so it's still a challenge." Doug quickly added, "Who is next?"

Ryan Shackles spoke slowly, like he had to think about each word before sending it out into the world, "I was on patrol with my unit when we encountered small arms fire and I took four rounds. One hit me in the neck, one in my left hip and two in my left thigh. Luckily, there was a medic in the platoon that day and he got the bleeding stopped. A helicopter took me to the field hospital, and they really came through for me. I was just lucky that everything lined up that day for me, I thank God every day for my life but have trouble sleeping and that's causing me to have trouble keeping a job." Doug said, "Thanks Ryan, sounds like you have a good attitude and that's a very good start. Does anyone have any questions for me?"

Ryan raised his hand and asked, "How long is this experiment scheduled for?" Doug said, "It's not really an experiment, it's a mixture of things that have worked for other groups. What we want to do is improve the outcome for everybody." Jose asked, "What does that mean, improve the outcome?" Doug started to speak but a knock at the door, followed by it slowly opening, interrupted him. The light in the open door silhouetted an obviously female form and Ami Serrano walked into the room. All eyes followed her form until she took the seat beside Doug. He said, "Guys this is Dr. Serrano, a psychiatrist, who will be helping out with any medication needs or anything else we need, Ami…"

Ami spoke with a slight European accent, "I am here to help and will be observing and even participating in the discussions sometimes. I am not a source for drugs to feed any addictions you might have, but I will prescribe needed medications for you. Our goal is to get you to a place where you feel better and can once again do the things that you want to do. My entire practice here is to take care of groups like this, so I have time to see you, if you feel the need to see me. Doug will give you all the information that you need to schedule an appointment." She got up and everyone watched her leave the room. Doug recovered and said, "Okay, now that you have met Ami, which leaves RJ, and she should be coming in at any second. While we wait, who wants to throw something out for discussion?"

Matt said, "Why was I chosen for this group, everyone else was shot in an explosion. I have the only non-combat injury here." Doug answered like he had the answer rehearsed, "You have an injury as a result of your military duties that is directly related to combat. I read your records and see that your ship provided fire missions for several operations. Clinically, there is very little difference between you being almost killed by a snapping rope while moving the supplies needed to provide support to ground operations than being hit by sniper fire or walking into an explosion. All are events that are sudden and could have been fatal if the circumstances were only slightly different. In fact, all of you were chosen for this group because your injuries were the result of a single definitive act. You all also had to endure extensive rehab and have shown great determination to recover and have a somewhat normal life." RJ knocked and entered, all eyes followed her matronly form to the chair beside Doug, who introduced her, "Everyone, this is RJ. She knows everything and if you have any problems or questions, she is the one to see. RJ…"

RJ was all business, "I am RJ Steele, Colonel, U.S. Army, Retired. I served in Vietnam from 1969-70 and was on active duty from 1967 to 1995. I would still be on active duty, but time is sometimes cruel and now I look like somebody's grandma instead of a lean, mean machine. I can still kick ass with the best of them though, so don't cross me up. On the other hand, no one will deny any member of this group anything he, or she, needs or is entitled to without feeling my sting. If you have any problems with anything about this clinic, tell me so that they can get fixed. Nothing improves without someone taking the initiative to identify the problems and then to fix them. Are there any questions?"

The group unanimously chanted, "No ma'am!"

Doug said, "Thank you RJ. Now, let's cover your assignment for the next session. Before you leave today, you will get a disposable video camera. Your task is to record a nightmare related to your condition. That is to say, if you happen to wake from a nightmare turn the camera on and record yourself describing the dream in as much detail as possible. If you don't have a dream issue, try giving a detailed description of the event that got you here. We will be watching the video as a group, so dress before you hit record." There was a nervous chuckle in the group and Doug said, "Everyone here has a similar story, so just let it go." RJ said, "Who's nervous?" Everyone's hand went up and she said, "Just give it a try, I did it and my video will be the first one shown. By the way, keep them to around five minutes please." This stopped a lot of the worry, but not all of it. Doug said, "We have half an hour to discuss any topic, any suggestions?" It was quiet so he said, "Okay, Jose, you were hit by a suicide bomber while eating lunch at an outdoor restaurant. Have you been able to eat at an outdoor restaurant since then?" Jose said, "I tried one in Miami but had to leave before I could order, had a major panic attack." Doug asked, "Were you alone?" Jose said, "Yes." Doug asked, "Were you alone because you didn't want to expose anyone else to a possible attack or some other reason?" Jose said, "Never thought about it, just didn't have anyone to go with, at that particular time." Doug, "Has anybody else tried exposing themselves to a situation similar to the one that got them here?" Everyone's hand went up. Doug said, "That's a good sign that you want to deal with your situation and move on. If you feel up to it, do a second video of you visiting a place where you feel exposed to what injured you. Keep it to about five minutes also, and we'll discuss them in the next few sessions."

Matt and Misha left the session, each of them with a video camera. They talked about how neither of them wanted to do the assignment and about just dropping the whole group therapy thing. It was the same thoughts that every other member of the group thought as they made their way back home, or the bar where they habituated most of their waking hours. By the time Matt and Misha were back aboard the Dreaming Moon, they had decided that they would give it a try because they had to get rid of the nightmares before they completely took over, and ruined, their lives. The bottom line that they arrived at was that this was no better or worse than anything else they had been exposed to and it might have some benefit or, it would just keep them engaged in some kind of outside activity. The enthusiasm for the whole thing was pretty low.

Matt sat with Tina Smothers and Misha worked her regular shift in the emergency room. Tina's stroke related paralysis and inability to communicate was the same as before. He checked her for bedsores and found that none had developed yet. He said, "Hello," to her and got her on her stomach, left her diaper unhooked so her skin could breathe and tidied up the room a little. After a while, he walked down to check on Sally. He found her in fair shape and alone. He decided to test his visions and put his hand on her arm, she still had a fever. A second later, he got a cold, dark feeling and let go before a vision fully developed. Back in Tina's room, he read a few chapters from *Cadillac Beach* to her and thought about how long Sally might have. He was still not getting a sensation from Tina, so he wasn't that concerned about her. The night passed slowly, and he almost fell asleep around five.

Seven finally came, and he went to pick up Misha from work. They talked about the group, and they were both still not fully enthused about the video discussion business. It didn't take long for them to fall asleep once they got into bed. They were both awake by noon and Matt thought about making the first video. Misha was thinking about making a video and volunteered to film him if he would return the favor. They got everything set up and as soon as Matt began to speak, the electric kicked off and thunder shook the boat. This had happened before, and it normally only lasted a few seconds before everything returned to normal. This time, however, the power did not come back on right away. Matt looked outside, saw the reason, and yelled for Misha to hold onto something.

Matt ran to Misha and held her as he pulled her to the floor. There was a loud roaring sound, quiet and then the roar returned. The boat heaved violently, and Matt began to worry that the ropes would not hold and how he had not checked them in a few days. The sound of hailstones pelting the topside came and went in a matter of seconds and then it seemed to be over. Misha said, "What was that?" Matt gave a sigh of relief, and answered, "Waterspout!" He went to a portside porthole and pulled the curtain aside to see what was going on. Hailstones blanketed the dock like snow, and a sailboat looked like it had been torn from its mooring and was aground with its mast tilted at a forty-five-degree angle. The people who lived on it were on deck and frantically trying to get it unstuck. The sun reappeared and Matt went topside for a damage assessment. All seemed well on the Dreaming Moon. Matt walked down the dock and yelled to the sailboat occupants.

The couple on the boat said that they needed to get the boat back a few feet and then they could get back in position. Matt decided he would take the Dreaming Moon over to help and as he walked back down the dock, a man on a thirty-six-foot sport fisher said, "If you'll help, we'll get Lou and Savannah over there ungrounded. I'm untied, except for the stern, c'mon! Let's go sailor." Matt untied the boat and jumped aboard. Misha was outside now and had one of the video cameras. She thought that she would take a short video of the hail and Matt. She spotted Matt on a boat, which normally was tied up four slips down, headed for a sailboat that looked like it was sinking. She began filming him.

On the sport fisher, the captain stuck out his hand and said, "Captain William Shartner, welcome aboard. And yes, my mother had a Star Trek thing, call me Capt. Will." It took a second for Matt to put William Shartner together with Star Trek before he got it. By then, Captain Will, as he was normally called, said get a hawser from the rope locker on the bow and make ready to tow the vessel in distress with the stern cleats." Matt did as he was told, got a thick nylon rope from the locker, and headed for the stern. He measured out about ten feet of line and attached the rope with a figure eight to the port cleat at that point. Then he attached the longer portion of the line to the starboard cleat in the same manner. The loose end from the port cleat was then tied to the main line forming a triangle that would allow for the force of the pull to be distributed across both cleats and lessen the chances of damaging the sport fisher. Captain Will had them in position now and a twenty-eight Bertram was coming alongside to help. The Bertram captain yelled, "Hey, Captain Will, I'll take the stern if you take the bow!" Captain Will called back, "Get it moving then!"

On the sailboat, Lou and Savannah were in a near state of panic. The tide was changing, and the water level would drop six to eight inches very soon and may cause the boat to capsize. Neither Ken, nor Savannah was an experienced sailor and Captain Will was aware of it, he yelled for them to go to the bow and check the water level as the boat moved. He mostly wanted them out of the way. Misha was on the bow of the Dreaming Moon and had a particularly good view of the unfolding events.

Captain Will yelled to Matt, "Secure out line to the bow and get Captain Drew's line on the stern." Matt jumped over the transom and onto the sailboat, secured the rope in his hand and then caught Captain Drew's thrown line and attached it. Captain Will yelled to Captain Drew, "Ready?" The thumbs-up signal was given, and the two boats slowly began applying power. Captain Will yelled at Matt, "Man the lines!" Matt checked the ropes and gave the thumbs-up. Captain Will's rope was first to tauten and then Captain Drew's. Matt noticed that the two men seemed to know what they were doing and watched the tight ropes begin to stretch and move the sailboat. Matt knew that counter balance was needed to help right the boat and called out to Lou and Savannah to move to the highest point on the rail and he turned to join them. A chill ran up Matt's spine as he realized the position, he had just put himself in, it did not stop him for one second though. He knew that the boat had to be ungrounded and moved straight to the rail along with Ken and Savannah. A second later, the boat bobbed upright in the water and Matt returned to the lines. Captain Will yelled for Matt and Lou to get the sailboat secured to prevent any bumping. They were now ten feet from the mooring ball and would drift to it. Matt called for the two towboats to slow up, to allow for the movement. Ten minutes later, the sailboat was secured and thank you was being exchanged.

Captain Will backed his boat back into its slip and asked Matt to help secure it. When they finished Captain Will said, "Thanks, son. I see you guys bought Jim and Mae's boat," and stuck out his hand. Matt shook the outstretched hand and said, "I'm Matt and my girlfriend is Misha. We are both medically retired from the military and now work in the medical field." Captain Will immediately commented, "You were Navy, she?" Matt said, "She's Army, how'd you know?" Captain Will replied, "The captain title means Captain, US Navy retired. I could see by how you handled yourself that you had deck training at Great Lakes or San Diego. What happened to you?" Matt said, "Hawser snapped during underway resupply, caught me mid-back. Rouge wave counter listed the ships." Captain Will thought a second and said, "You were with Captain James, then. I heard about the accident because they wanted me to activate for the accident report study. I turned them down though. I think that I deserve to relax after my twenty-six years. How are you doing now?" Matt said, "Some nightmares and some pain every now and then. I am functional to a great extent and doing okay by all accounts." Captain Will said, "And your lady friend?" Matt said, "Mortar attack on her unit. She took shrapnel to the shoulder and face, really messed up her shoulder." Captain Will said, "You two are welcome to have a drink on my boat anytime. Thanks for the help getting Lou and Savannah ungrounded." Matt said, "No problem, happy to do it." The two shook hands again and Matt headed back down the dock. Misha was on deck and as he approached said, "I got it." He said, "Got what?" She said, "You doing what caused your injury. You did get hurt by a rope between two boats, right?" He said, "I guess that you could say that, and I did think about it for a split second when I turned my back to the ropes but knew that I had to keep functioning. So, thank you!" She said, "I don't know if I'm going to get mine done." Matt said, "I'll help any way that I can, you know that baby." She asked, "Who was that man you went over with?" He said, Captain Will, he's actually a retired Navy Captain." She raised her eyebrows and he said, "Nice guy, said we are welcome to have a drink on his boat anytime." Matt began checking the Dreaming Moon's lines.

It was a working night and Matt's night to sit with Sally. He dropped Misha off at work and drove to the nursing home with a sense of dread, because he somehow knew it was going to be Sally's last night. He arrived, Mike handed him a hundred and disappeared like a scared rabbit. Elizabeth came by and said, "Hi," and pulled him into the hallway. She said, "Sally has not been doing well and Mike has been gone more and more when you aren't here. Even I can tell she is sliding out." Matt said, "I kind of knew that when I came to check her while I was sitting with Tina. Come by often tonight if you can." She said, "Often as I can," and was off to do her duties.

Matt went back into Sally's room and found her twisted in her sheets and crying. He went to the bed and touched her arm and it felt warm. The next sensation was overwhelmingly sad, empty, and lonely all at the same time. He let go of her arm and tried tugging on the sheets to get her untangled but had to touch her again to get her back in what looked like a comfortable position. The longer that he touched her, the more the feeling he got from her abated. The feeling actually began turning warmer and less empty. Since the feeling was less and less dark, he maintained contact with her arm and said, "Hi Sally, it's Matt. I'm here for a few hours to take care of you." She seemed to respond with her eyes but nothing else. The feeling improved even more, and he decided that he could let go. As he sat in the chair, he began looking for something to read; he suddenly got an odd sensation and decided that he needed to hold Sally's hand. The sensation was cold and empty again but immediately began improving. Elizabeth looked in the open door and watched for a minute. Matt's eyes were closed, Sally's were open, and he was holding her hand as he sat by the bed. She quietly stepped into the room and decided to watch for a minute. Several visions passed through Matt's mind in quick succession, kids playing, boating, at the beach, dancing and then nothing. He opened his eyes and found Sally's lifeless eyes and Elizabeth's very live eyes looking at him from the other side of the bed. Elizabeth spoke first, "She's probably much better off now. The Alzheimer's had taken her mind and life away. It's always hard to see it happen to someone so young." Matt added, "She went out dancing."

It took an hour to get Sally's body prepped and for the funeral home technician to arrive. Elizabeth helped Matt and all the while wanted to ask him a sting of questions, but his look seemed to indicate he was not receptive to being interviewed. Mike arrived in time to say goodbye to Sally's body. Matt thought how useless that was for Sally, how Mike could have done things differently but that it was not his business. Mike thanked Elizabeth and then Matt before leaving with the funeral home gurney. Elizabeth seemed to be very upset, and Matt reached over and touched her arm. He immediately pulled away and she said, "Ovarian cancer, they give me six months. This is the last shift for me here because I have to get things in order and try to have a few more good times before the real sickness catches up to me. What did you feel?" Matt said, "The sensation was not strong, just barely there really. The thing is that sometimes I get the sensation from someone who just lost someone that they cared about." She said, "Touch me again, please." Matt lightly grasped her forearm and said, "Not very strong at all." She said, "When you touch me, it makes me tingle, not sexually just a tingling sensation." Matt said, "No one has ever told me that before." She said, "Maybe it's just the stress." Matt left the facility wondering about the encounter with Elizabeth and went home, it was just after midnight and it seemed to be a big sky night, so he decided to sit on the deck and stargaze for a while.

NEXT SESSION

A few days later, Matt and Misha drove to Key West for the next group session. She and Matt had each recorded a dream tape, but she had not had an opportunity to recreate any kind of reenactment scenario yet. Matt suggested she see if it was possible to do a ride along with an EMS unit but there hadn't been time to orchestrate that yet.

Just as Doug had said, the session began right on time. After everyone said hello, RJ turned on a sixty inch HDTV and started her video. The first thing about the video was the background. There seemed to be nothing but jungle and swamp. She also looked a few years younger when she appeared and the narration began, "I outfitted myself for a little excursion out here in the Everglades to recreate the hot, wet, sticky and remoteness of where I was when I was first injured. It could have been a self-fulfilling prophecy but the set up and sleeping in a tent triggered the recurring nightmares. We were set up at a forward operating base as the second-tier medical support unit and since we were two clicks from the area where an infantry battalion was going to clear, we felt pretty safe. A few casualties had come in, mostly accidents, then a few booby-trap victims, then the trickle turned into a steady stream. We patched and got about a hundred injured out and sent more of the walking wounded in deuce-and-a-half transports to the rear. About midnight, the casualties stopped coming and we had no idea why. The assumption was that the firefights were over, or the VC were on the run. That assumption was the first mistake. The second was not to have a fully manned perimeter. Along about one in the morning, the firefight reached us. We were the ones retreating, not the VC, it took ten minutes for us to realize that we were being overrun and had to high tail it out of there. I caught a bullet in the ass as I jumped into a moving jeep and held on for dear life. Fortunately, it was essentially a flesh wound and the biggest physical effect was not being able to sit down for a month. I was back on duty in ten days though."

RJ turned off the television and said, "That's the first time I was shot, we'll save the second for another day." Doug quickly took over and said, "Any discussion?" Several questions about the effect of purposely setting up the scenario were asked, and Doug said, "If you know something will trigger an episode and you feel comfortable doing it, give it a try. Of course, don't try anything with live ammo or that would actually endanger you, or anyone else. This is an excellent example of a therapeutic release tape, and I will let RJ tell you if it had any value." RJ picked up the cue and said, "I had a hell of a time getting myself out into the Glades, I had a panic attack just planning it. Fortunately, I have an incredibly supportive husband and son. They helped me every step of the way and even though I was panicked and had an AR-15 clenched tightly for most of the time we were there, I had decided that this was not going to defeat me and rode it out. The simple act of making the tape the first morning we were there, made me feel ten pounds lighter. The second night was bad, but not unbearable. We now have a floating cabin out there and go regularly. I would say that it triggers a nightmare every tenth or twelfth time now." Doug asked if anyone else wanted to ask RJ anything. No one responded so he asked for a volunteer to go next, no one did. He then asked, "Anyone get a video about a dream or recreation scenario." Misha nudged Matt and he raised his hand.

Matt's video was queued up and started. Matt was unaware he was being filmed so there was no acting going on. Once the sailboat was righted, and the lines detached, the film stopped. Doug asked Matt to provide what happened. Matt stood up, as he had been taught in the military, and began to speak. Doug immediately interrupted and said the standing wasn't required. Matt said, "If it's all the same to you, I am more comfortable standing and began. There was a waterspout that crossed the marina, where we live, and a sailboat moored on a ball was torn loose from its mooring and was in immediate danger of sinking. Well, sinking might be a strong word, but it would have ruined everything the couple had plus the damage to the boat. We were lucky that our boat, the Dreaming Moon was unscathed in the storm, and I was out doing a check to be sure. Since we were in good shape, I walked down the dock to see if everyone else was okay. When I spotted the sailboat, I was going to go back to our boat to assist when a retired Navy Captain named Will called for me to help him get over to the sailboat. I followed his orders and secured lines to the sailboat, as you saw in the video. As I said last week, it was a rope between two boats that snapped and broke my back, I never thought about that though. It wasn't until I had to turn my back to the stretched ropes that I realized what I was doing. You can see the slight hesitation as I look back in the video. The good thing is that I knew that I had to be on that rail to help right the boat or someone's home and belongings were probably going to be destroyed. I forced myself to do what was necessary and now realize that I don't have to be afraid of a dangerous situation anymore. The nightmares of being chased across the ocean by a rope snake have gone away for now and I do feel lighter in that sense."

Doug said, "Excellent job, Matt. Who wants to discuss this?" Hands went up. Jose asked, "Matt, what was the possibility of one of the ropes snapping?" Matt said, "Don't know. The ropes belonged to the boats that were doing the pull. I had no knowledge of them beforehand and didn't have time to inspect the ropes before using them. I would say that there was a fifty-fifty chance that one of them could have snapped. What I don't know is if one of them did snap if it would have injured me." Jose asked Doug now, "Doug, there is an extremely low chance that a suicide bomber is going to strike a café I am having lunch at in Key West. Is it of any value for me to purposefully go to one if I know that the probability of a repeat scenario is close to zero?" Doug answered with, "You know this, do you go to those restaurants now?" Jose answered, "No." Doug said, "Well there you have it, you are not going because of fear it will happen, even though you are almost certain it won't." Doug added, "Jose, do you want to go to an outdoor café?" Jose said, "I believe that it would help me feel more normal."

Matt looked at Misha and she gave both a knowing and an approving look. He said, "Jose, Misha and I were planning to have dinner at Sarabeth's, care to join us?" Everyone in the group was soon on board and Jose finally said, "I'll try guys. No guarantees and no pressure please." Everyone said that it was no problem. Doug said, "There's going to be a few hours between the end of this session and when Sarabeth's begins serving dinner. How do all of you plan to spend that time?" Matt said, "We're flexible and will go somewhere else if it works out better." The consensus was very quickly that Sarabeth's was the place to go. This was mostly because it was an excuse to eat in a nice restaurant and most of the group could only do that on a special occasion. Soon, it was agreed that everyone would meet at the restaurant at six. Matt called for a reservation to make sure they had an outdoor seating for them.

Doug said, "That was a good start to the session, who else has something to share?" Eli spoke up for the first time, "Leanne was kind enough to take me for a drive. We don't own a car, so we rented a Humvee and headed up to Three Lakes Wildlife Area near a town called Holopaw. There are miles of sand roads there, very few people, some gunfire, and a lot of it is wide-open spaces. I drove up the Turnpike and then she took over for the back roads. It was hard being out there on the country roads without being in control. We purposely chose the Humvee because it was close to the vehicle I was in when we hit the IED. It actually turned into a fun day, after I had two panic attacks where we had to stop." RJ took the camera he offered and got the video started. The first scene was Eli getting into the passenger seat. The camera was secured on the dash, so it showed his face as they drove. You could see the color flush out of his face as the light brightened. "He said, here is the first open spot and then we go under the turnpike. Next, we turned left and went out a sand road that seemed to lead to nowhere." Eli's pale face took on a level of terror and the audio kicked in, "Stop! Please, God, stop!" The vehicle stopped and Eli bolted out the door. Leanne picked up the camera and followed him. He was heaving up his breakfast and she handed him a paper towel and asked, "Do you want to go on?" He said, "I have to, have to kick this thing out of me!" She said, "Okay, whenever you're ready." The video skipped a frame and now they were back in the Humvee and moving again. Eli was still obviously terrified and said, this looks a lot like where we hit the IED and after a second, he was frantically moving and saying, "Have to stop, stop now please. Stop please!" The vehicle stopped again, and he flew out the door again.

The camera left the Humvee and after going around the vehicle, showed Eli pacing nervously back and forth. He then walked a ways ahead, after arriving back at the Humvee, got in, and said, "Let's do it." The vehicle began moving and Eli's face scrunched up and then relaxed. He said, "Speed up a little for this part, please." A few seconds later his face regained some pallor as shadows began crossing the scene.

On the tape, he said, "Made it, let's go around again." The video skipped a frame and now Eli was tense and watching carefully out the side window. After about three seconds, he said, "Okay, let's see how many of these roads we can travel," and unfolded a map. The video ended and Eli said, "Didn't cure me but did make me face up to a major fear. Had a nightmare in the hotel we stayed at but didn't want to wake Leanne, she looked so peaceful. For anybody who doesn't know we have been together as a couple for around two years now. Just didn't want anyone to think we were just hooking up for the trip." He gave Leanne a one armed, seated, hug and said, "Thanks honey." She said, "Anytime." Doug took control again and said, "Who wants to discuss?" Leanne spoke up first, "I had some serious doubts about this video reenactment having any effect, but I can tell you it relaxed Eli a few notches and improved his overall mood." Eli said, "You really think so?" She said, "Vastly!" He said, "I'm sorry if I was an ass to you or anything." She said, "You weren't an ass to me, just edgy and irritable a lot of the time. I had no problem with it, other that it was eating you up." Eli smiled and said, "Thank you," again.

RJ spoke up, "It took a lot of guts to get out there and do that Eli. Leanne, you are a great friend to lend that level of support. But, did you not worry about being shot while out filming Eli. I heard gunfire in the background, and you held steady." Leanne gasped, "I didn't really think about it, I was more worried about Eli." Doug looked up from his notes and said, "When you introduced yourself last week, you said you had problems with open spaces, loud noises, and got night terrors. Did you have any nightmares after this trip?" Leanne said, "Not especially, but I did have a sleepless night once we were home, but I think that might have just been normal stress." Doug said, "Is it possible that the stress was from exposing yourself in an open space where there was sporadic gunfire?" She said, "No, it is what is almost always about, money matters. The trip wasn't that big a deal, we just don't ever seem to have enough money to be comfortable. There's always an edge and it wears on you." Eli had a nervous grin and quickly took over, "I have had a very hard time getting steady work that pays decently and the few times that I have, I had to leave the job because of lack of sleep or severe pain from standing all day." Doug said, "First of all, we can talk about anything in this room. Everyone here has problems, and we all know them because we either have them ourselves or, in my case, it's my job to help people with them. Please feel free to talk freely about anything. But, as with all freedoms, there is a cost. You, and I mean everyone in this room, may not judge the person talking or take it out of this room. Can everyone deal with this? We all have to be honest here." The general consensus was almost immediate. Doug added, "We also have a financial counselor here, and it's no shame to use her services. Remember, we're in the helping, not the judging business."

There were no other videos, and the rest of the session was general talk about the effect of stress on the nervous and cardiovascular system. As they were all getting ready to go, RJ said, "Those who did not make a video, make one. Everyone else, you need to make the second one, try to get one of your nightmares on tape for us." The group was set unofficially to reconvene at the restaurant in two hours. Doug called Eli and Leanne back but only Misha saw it because the room had cleared rather quickly. She and Matt had no place to run to before dinner, so she was in no hurry and Matt had headed for the men's room.

By six, everyone was at the restaurant and within a few minutes they were all seated outside. Judy volunteered to video Jose. They were both single, but it seemed apparent that there wasn't chemistry between them. But who knows how these things work? They did have the commonality of being disabled veterans and relationships based on flimsier things have been known to develop and flourish. There was one thing working in Jose's favor and he was unaware of it.

He was a macho man and there was no way he was going to let Judy film him being anything else. False bravado was his best friend, at the moment. Everyone secretly wondered how he could look so calm and so terrified at the same time. Drinks were ordered and Matt said, "I am paying for three rounds, after that you're on your own." He and Misha had discussed this, so she was not surprised. They knew that they were probably doing the best financially of anybody in the group.

Jose made it through the drinks, the appetizers and dinner. Everyone tried very discretely to check his status all through the meal. Once the grumbling about the long hospital stays started, Jose relaxed without realizing it. It was his pride, he knew that everyone was watching, and refused to fail in front of the group. A round of special coffees ended the evening and everyone dispersed. There was a decision to find a cheaper place and do this after every meeting, if possible. Matt said he had the place and would announce it at the next meeting. Jose was proud to have made it through this test and trembling inside, all at the same time.

RIDE ALONG

Since Matt had spent two hundred dollars, on the drinks alone, at the group dinner, he decided to take two shifts with Clive along with his other remaining regular patient, Tina. Misha had five straight nights of emergency room shifts and the first one coincided with his night with Tina. They had decided that the Alfa Romeo was best left under its cover for now because they were actually doing okay with the Toyota. Matt dropped Misha off at the hospital and headed to the nursing home. On the way, his phone rang, and it was the third referral from Dr. Waldbaum. He set up a shift for two days later, because Clive was already on for the next night. When Matt arrived, Abe paid him and practically ran out of the room. Tina seemed okay but when he touched her arm to say hello, he got a cold sensation. She felt warm, physically, but the cold sensation was almost overwhelming. Her eyes seemed to have no luster in them, and her general muscle tone was poor. She seemed to know he was there, and a little blush crossed her face. Then, just as the blush passed, it was as if all the blood drained from her face, and she was pale white. Matt sensed a feeling of panic and then he was underwater looking at a reef. Seconds later, there was panic, and he had to let go of her arm.

Matt found *Cadillac Beach* and began reading aloud. Ten pages later, Tina seemed calm, so he decided it was time to chance touching her to check her diaper. It was disgusting and he wondered if Abe was doing anything to take care of her. He walked down the hall looking for help and ran into a nurse he didn't know. He introduced himself and she replied, "Agatha Jones, glad to meet you, I have heard about you, of course. You are with Tina Smothers tonight, right?" He nodded and she continued, "Poor thing, he stopped doing anything for her once he found that little whore, Zell, on the day shift had the hots for him. Anyway, what's up?" Matt explained that Tina hadn't been changed in a while and she said, "It's just me and Sue tonight and I haven't seen her in over an hour. Medical transport is taking a patient over to the hospital and they just arrived for the pickup. You can use the lift, if you could just, please deal with it." Matt said, "Makes me uncomfortable." Agatha said, "You can handle it, Elizabeth told me." Matt nodded and got the lift.

Over at the ER, Misha was thankful that the night was going along at a slow pace, not too busy and not so slow as to make the time drag. EMS came in with a non-emergency and she began chatting with the two male paramedics; the fact that they were quite appealing to the eye probably helped. After ten minutes, she had numbers and an invitation to ride along with them on her next night off from the hospital. Her only intention was to get her therapy group assignment taken care of; doing it with two good-looking hunks was just a bonus.

At the nursing home, Matt had Tina clean and back in bed. He knew she was about to go and decided to stay longer. He moved where he could look at her face periodically as he read. Agatha came by and checked on him around ten thirty. He walked out into the hall with her and said, "She is fading out, fast." Agatha said, "I hope not on my shift." Matt said, "I'm going to stay until midnight or so and will help, if it happens." They went back into the room and Tina was convulsing. They both ran over to check her and as soon as Matt touched her, she stopped jerking about. He was very unhappy at the vision, even though it was pleasant. Agatha stood transfixed on Matt and after a minute, Matt let go of Tina and said, "She's gone." Agatha checked and found no pulse or breathing. There was a *Do Not Resuscitate* order, commonly called a DNR, and Agatha almost cried, she and Tina were the same age.

By one in the morning, Abe still had not answered his phone. Finally, Agatha left a message that she was calling the funeral home indicted in Tina's medical record. The funeral home technician arrived and left with still no Abe. Matt said goodnight to Agatha and went to fish off the dock until it was time to pick up Misha. He thought about Tina's last dream and wondered why he had to be the keeper of it. By seven, he decided that he had to talk to Ami, the group psychiatrist, about it.

Misha was in a good mood when she left work and suggested breakfast at IHOP. Matt took her up on it. She was giddy about the upcoming ride along and he was sad because Tina died. Their individual news seemed to cancel each other's out. Matt said, "I have Clive for tonight and then possibly a new patient tomorrow night." She said, "Hopefully, I have a couple of boring nights coming up." They went to the boat and slept soundly during the rainy, overcast day. They both seemed to wake up at around two and since they were awake and close, they had a very sensuous encounter before sleeping another three hours. Dinner was drive through chicken, eaten at the end of a road looking out over the Gulf. It was not time for sunset, so they just leaned on the front of the car and looked at the water. He tried to think of something interesting to discuss but since they were so immersed in work, trying to get in some sleep and group therapy, nothing else could come to mind. She had the same problem, so they just leaned on the hood and ate the chicken and fries.

Matt had some trepidation about seeing Sarah when he arrived at Clive's. He hoped that she had decided to find a boyfriend, and that it wasn't him, or did he? He thought that having sex with her would be nice, if it didn't come with all the trappings of cheating on Misha and having a crazy woman hanging on the periphery, waiting to pounce on an opportunity to make his life miserable. Misha hoped the EMS guys would be by with something not too serious. That didn't happen; her shift was in full madness mode by the time Matt got to Clive's.

Matt arrived at Clive's and nervously rang the doorbell. Sarah opened the door in a bikini and said, "Glad you got here, dad's being a pain in the ass." She led Matt to the bedroom door, and he wondered if the thong part of her bottoms actually covered anything. She smiled and tweaked his cheek as she wandered off at the bedroom door. Matt saw that Clive was looking out the large window from his cranked-up bed.

Clive said, "Hey, glad you made it. Sarah's been a pain in the ass today." Matt said, "she said the same thing about you. So, how's it going?" Clive said, "You tell me," And held out his hand for Matt to shake. As they shook hands, Matt had a gray sensation. It was like a day that was supposed to be sunny but didn't quite materialize and your plans were ruined as a result. It wasn't dreadful, just a gray kind of feeling. He said, "Appears you're still kickin'" Clive said, "Not very high and not very often." Matt said, "So what's been going on with you." Clive said, "You're looking at it. What about you?"

Matt didn't know if he wanted to tell Clive that he was down to two patients, plus one possible new one, because of the previous invitation to sit as often as possible with him. He did need the money, though and it would be a nice, steady gig for a while. He pretended to be looking out the window as he thought and Clive said, "At least the view is good." Matt refocused and saw a woman on a sailboat, moored about a hundred feet away. She was showering on a platform attached to the back of the boat, fully nude. Clive said, "Can you hand me the binoculars, there?" Matt did and paid no attention to Clive's description of the woman's beauty and his desires for her. Matt walked around the room and found that if he sat at a certain angle that he could watch Sarah at the house's pool. She was basking in the last rays of the sun, minus the bikini that she had on earlier. Matt's mind wandered to the same places that Clive's had, and it wasn't until the sky's dark pinks faded into blue blacks, that they both regained their faculties.

Clive was the first to speak as the room darkened slightly meaning that a light was going to be needed very shortly, "I like to look but since nothing works anymore, that's the extent of it. Sometimes, I think she knows the torment she wields and uses it like a sword to cut me to pieces." Matt said, "I guess that is something women do." Clive said, "Amen brother. Have I told you about my trip to Thailand?" Matt said, "Maybe we ought to save that one for another night. Would it bother you too much if we talk about your experiences with nightmares after Vietnam for a while?" Clive said, "Having some yourself?" Matt said, "Not me so often, but Misha seems to have a lot of them." Clive said, "Freshen me up on Misha, please?"

Matt said, "I think I've told you before how we met in the transition unit and ended up down here after a series of near tragedies and misfortunes." Clive interrupted, "Isn't so bad that you got here, is it?" Matt said, "Not at all, seems like we belong here. Anyway, I wake up often and she always seems to look like she is in a state of panic while she sleeps. She hasn't said a lot about it but I'm sure the nightmares are there." Clive said, "My first wife, after Vietnam, said I would kick and fight at night while I was asleep to the point that she often had to sleep on the couch. I had no idea it was happening and denied it. But it was happening, and the subconscious effects tore us apart. I really loved her, but she just couldn't deal with my inability to do something about the problem, or really to even admit it was a problem." In the pause, Matt said, "So, what you're saying is that the nightmares might be happening, and she doesn't remember them?" Clive said, "Not quite, in my case they were happening, and I was subconsciously repressing them. That seems to be the mind's main defense mechanism, doesn't work forever though." Matt said, "Is that common?" Clive said, "Based on the number of guys I know having issues, at this stage in their life and my experience, yes." Matt said, "Do you know of any studies, or anything?" Clive said maybe ten years ago, I don't get out much these days and the Internet is not of great interest to me. I guess that I just want to get a little older and die in peace." Matt said, "And you will get older, I'm pretty sure of that. Clive said, "Mix me a drink?" Matt said, "Sure, why not." Clive had a large swallow and meekly asked Matt. "Can you help me into the shower?" Matt said, "No problem. Let me just get it all set up for you in there first." Once Clive was in the shower seat, Matt left him to change the bed. He found that there were no clean sheets in the room. He went out into the main house to see if he could find a linen closet. He found nothing and returned to Clive's room to do the best he could with what he had. Sarah poked her head in and seductively said, "You need something?" Matt answered in monotone, "Clean sheets." She said, "Come on, I'll show you where they are." He checked on Clive and then went to follow Sarah. She was in the hallway in a short lightweight translucent bathrobe that hid nothing. Matt followed her to a laundry room off the kitchen where she bent over to get sheets and Matt was presented with a view generally reserved for Hugh Hefner. He didn't look away and when she turned and caught him said, "When are you going to take me up on my offer. I can plainly see it interests you." Matt adjusted his pants and said, "It's certainly an interesting offer," and took the sheets from her. She followed close behind him and whispered, "I know how to keep my mouth shut, unless you want to fill it." Matt tried to ignore her but finally had to say, "Gotta gets your father out of the shower soon and need to make the bed first. I can't be neglecting my job." She wandered off after saying, "I'll just leave my door open, in case you come to your senses and change your mind, it's the second one upstairs." Matt thought about the offer for the rest of the night, considered taking the trip upstairs several times, but concluded that he had enough craziness in his life and acting on this would put it into a state of total chaos.

Misha was happy when Matt picked her up and immediately upon hitting the passenger seat said, "I want to go home, smoke, drink and get very personal. What do you think?" Matt said, "Sounds like a plan, baby!" They woke up at five in the evening, looked at each other and at the same time said, "I don't remember going to bed." Matt asked, "Sex or dinner?" The answer, "I can eat at work."

Matt had a new at-home care patient that night and drove to the address. It was a marina and the patient, Desi Almani, and his wife, Vicki, lived on an eighty-foot yacht. It appeared the vessel had not been to sea in a quite a while but looked in good repair and quite nice. Boarding was amidships so the name on the stern was not readily visible. As Matt approached the boarding bridge, Vicki came out and greeted him. She was younger than expected, and instantly alluring but, at the same time, seemed to exude an unavailable air and therefore garnered little more than a passing look before other factors overshadowed her physical form. If Matt had been fully appreciative of her, he would have seen her black hair was in a large bun towards the back of her head, that she had hauntingly beautiful blue-green eyes, a stunning physical form and was a completely natural beauty. He missed all this because he was lost in thoughts about Misha's issues. Vicki introduced herself in a wickedly exotic accent that snapped him back to the moment and led him to the salon. This is where Desi was set up, and introductions were made. Vicki asked if Matt was comfortable on a boat. Matt smiled and mentioned that he actually lived on a Defever Forty-four and had also been in the Navy. This seemed to perk up Desi a little, but it was clear he was not completely in charge of his faculties anymore. Vicki said, "I will be back in the morning," and gave Matt her cell number. Matt unconsciously watched her walk away and after she was gone realized he was still staring at the door after her. He spent another split-second wondering how that happened. Matt was almost startled when Desi said, "Beautiful, isn't she?" His voice was a low mechanical growl that seemed very fragile. Matt looked down to see that Desi was smiling up at him. Matt wondered if that verbal observation was purposefully designed to get him to pay attention to Vicki, because he hadn't at first and now wondered if he missed something. Desi continued, "I've been watching her come and go for five years now. Can't get enough of it but she married me for the money, you know." Matt remained quiet and after he was sure that Desi was not going to continue said, "Can I just check your pulse?" Desi held up his arm a little and it immediately began to quiver. When Matt checked, he had a cold stormy sensation, like the few minutes before a heavy storm suddenly rolls in when you're on a boat out in the open sea, and the temperature suddenly drops ten degrees in the downdraft. Matt actually felt chilly. Then he realized that the air conditioner had just kicked on and couldn't decide if that was the cause of the chill. Desi forced words out, "Throat cancer, going downhill fast." Matt said, "How long have you been down?" Desi thought and said, "Six months or so, it hit hard and fast." The speech pattern was slow and raspy. Matt did all he could to understand the words the first time and not ask Desi to repeat himself. Desi continued, "Cigars, they say. Smoked several a day for forty years. You'd think that if they were that bad, they'd have killed me long ago. I miss the days of heading out to the islands to re-stock, enjoy the freedom of the sea and lack of governmental controls on my life" He faded into a dreamlike state and seemed lost in memories of long past sojourns in the tropics.

Matt was still evaluating the set up and trying to figure out the chair/bed device that Desi was in. It appeared to be a chair that hydraulically turned into a bed and was the same size as a regular full-sized bed. Desi could discern what Matt was pondering and said, "Custom designed, did it myself as soon as I knew I would need it. Drew out the plans in a day and sent them to a shop in Miami. Works like a dream but costs too much for it to be commercially viable. Excuse me but I will have to stop talking for a while now." Matt said, "No problem, I just want to check the pulse in your other arm." When Matt touched Desi's other arm, he got the same cold, stormy feeling.

Matt sat down and Desi used a remote control to turn on the television. After flipping through a few channels, Desi settled on a Spanish language version of *Breakfast at Tiffany's*. Desi seemed to like Audrey Hepburn and when she appeared, got the word, "beautiful," out. Matt really didn't like the television, but this was more like a Spanish lesson, so he was not upset that it was the night's entertainment. Fortunately, Desi was snoring in five minutes and Matt began reading the book he brought with him.

In the ER, Misha was having a rough night and had pulled her shoulder the wrong way while handling an unruly and combative overdose patient. It was not something Misha thought would turn into anything and immediately forgot the little catch in her shoulder as the patient threw up all over her from the ipecac syrup that the doctor had forced in while Misha held the woman's arms down. The patient was admitted and transferred to a room. While cleaning and restocking, Misha began to feel a dull ache in her bad shoulder. She was going out to get some aspirin, or something, for pain when a car wreck victim arrived by ambulance and the whole place went into overdrive.

The victim was a woman in her mid-twenties and as the paramedics came in a second victim was added, a three-month-old baby still in her car seat. Misha assumed the baby was female based on the pink blanket and outfit. The car seat was on the foot of the ambulance gurney and both patients were wheeled into the main trauma room. The on-duty doctor and Misha began removing the sheets to make an assessment, an EMT sat the car seat with the screaming baby in it, to the side. The woman was unconscious and as Misha was cutting off the last remnants of clothing, stopped breathing. The doctor got a plastic airway in, a nurse took over with a bag respirator and the doctor returned to doing the assessment. More doctors arrived and there was an intense effort to find the source of blood that was beginning to drip off the table. IVs were attached to pumps and blood was drawn for type and cross match. There were several minutes of furious activity and then Misha was assigned the baby by the RN who had taken over the nursing functions lead.

Misha, unaware that her shoes were bloody, picked up the child seat with her right hand and felt another little catch in her shoulder. She ignored the pain and got the baby to an exam room, grabbing a doctor on the way to order an x-ray so the little girl could be extracted from the car seat after the clearing procedure. She carried the baby to the x-ray department, which was just down the hall, and asked the unit clerk to put her in next, so that a portable wouldn't be necessary. Less than five minutes later, Misha was back in the emergency room with the x-ray in her hand. She got the doctor to check the film and then do the physical exam. Everything checked out and Misha took the baby out of the car seat and held her up close to her shoulder. The crying stopped, for a minute, and then began again. Misha paced and patted the baby for a few minutes and then when the crying stopped again, went looking for a diaper. She ended up in the pediatric care unit and got a diaper and a bottle of formula.

Back in the emergency room, Misha changed the baby's diaper then sat down and began feeding her the bottle. Ten minutes passed and the father arrived. Once he knew the baby was okay, he began asking Misha questions about the mother. Misha had no idea of the mother's status. She offered to keep the baby and referred him to the desk. He said, "Thank You," and headed for the desk. Misha walked around to burp the baby and as she walked past the trauma room, the door opened and, from the glimpse of the activity, knew that the baby she was comforting no longer had a mother. The father came back and panicked when he saw Misha's face. He took his daughter from her and holding her close and protective asked Misha if she knew anything. Misha said, "No, I've been with the baby for some time," and excused herself. She quickly ducked into an empty exam room and grabbed a tissue to stifle the tears forming in her eyes. The doctor prepared to tell the man his wife was gone forever. Misha was asked to escort the man and baby to the family conference room. The man was not eager to follow, and it was all Misha could do to get him seated in the room without breaking down herself. She managed to keep a professional air and said she would be happy to help him with the baby later, if necessary. He didn't know how to interpret this and fortunately, for Misha, the doctor arrived before he could ask for any clarification. Misha tried to excuse herself, but the doctor asked her to remain and close the door.

Misha almost panicked when she looked down and saw she had some blood on her pants leg and shoe. The doctor was as tactful and straightforward as possible and after the announcement, tried to get out of the room as fast as possible. The man was shattered and looked like he was going to pass out. Misha readied one of the ammonia inhalers ever present in the emergency room personnel's pockets. The man did not faint but turned ashen and sat silently holding the baby as close as he could. She just stood there with no idea what to say or do. Almost instinctively, after the silence became overwhelming, and in her most caring and sympathetic voice, she uttered, "I can take care of the baby, if you need to call anyone or would like a moment before going in." He said, "I want to take her in with me, but can you just please take her and let me have a few minutes here first?" Misha gently took the baby from her father's arms and walked out into the waiting area. The other people who were sharing the waiting room with him earlier had a realization of what had just happened, and many were visibly shaken. Misha made her way back into the emergency room area and to the nursing station. There was a general sense of unease among all the personnel and Misha tried to entertain and keep the baby happy. A short while later, that seemed like an eternity to Misha, the man came out of the counseling room. He asked for the baby through tearful eyes. Misha said, "I'm sorry," as she handed him his daughter. At that time his mother, the baby's grandmother, arrived and gave Misha the chance to duck out before she broke down.

Misha barely made it to the break room before it hit her, and she joined two other nurses who were already in there crying. The worst part was yet to come, though. Misha was the junior nurse and therefore the one that was getting the job of helping the morgue tech with the body. She had weak knees the entire time and as the stress of the situation eased, her shoulder pain increased dramatically. She had two hours to go on the shift and the ride along with the paramedics was coming up.

Matt picked up Misha and asked her what was wrong. She said, "A young woman died from a horrible car wreck. It was so sad, and her three-month-old daughter was with her. That little baby must have seen everything that happened. It was awful, I took care of the baby while they worked on the mother for almost an hour." Matt said, "Must have been the Jeep that I saw being loaded onto a wrecker. It was bent down on the driver's side and the seat was hanging out. Makes sense now, there was a huge pickup there too and it looked like the passenger side front had some damage." Misha said, "All I know is it was the worst thing that I have ever had to deal with." Matt said, "I'm sorry, baby. What can I do?" She said, "Let's have a baby." He said, "Okay, can we start working on that as soon as we get home?" She said, "Maybe."

That night, Matt went to Clive's and Misha went to her EMS ride along. Matt was relieved that Sarah had gone on a trip, and it was just him and Clive in the house. Misha was ready for some ambulance time and walked into the station in a good mood, pushing away the depression of the last night's events. Her new partners, Guillermo, and Lee were ready for her and asked if she wanted to wear scrubs to keep her street clothes clean. She changed and then they all watched television. It wasn't long until a call came in and the three were off. It turned out to be an old man that had passed out in the shower and took up the first hour and a half of the shift. When they arrived back at the station, they all cleaned and restocked the ambulance for the next run.

They all returned to the squad room and sat back on the couch. It was not quite big enough for the three of them, but no one seemed to mind; Misha sat between the men and liked it. The men seemed indifferent, and they didn't make conversation before the next call came in. It was a car wreck and there were three people and two cars involved. On the way, Misha asked Guillermo, "Can we handle three victims?" He said, "My friends call me Guy. We will evaluate the victims and call the other unit that's co-located with the Fire Department. They are cross-trained and only respond if we are already on another response." He smiled at her and she blushed. Her thoughts were not exactly pure, they are *only* thoughts she kept telling herself.

The accident was slightly more than a fender-bender and one of the victims had possibly broken their nose from the airbag. The other two were checked over and were just shaken up. Misha got to experience how it was to deliver a patient to the emergency room and interact with her normal co-workers. She got a wink, wink, nudge, nudge from a couple of the nurses but shrugged them off by saying, "It's part of my VA treatment and I'll tell you all about it next time we work together." By the time they got back to the station, it was just after eleven. Lee said he was going to stretch out until the next call and went into another room. Guy said to Misha, "There are two beds in there, if you want to get some rest." Misha said, "I'm okay, for now." They sat on the couch and watched reruns of old shows on the television. Misha wasn't used to watching television. She and Matt had never even discussed buying one, so she was interested in the shows. Guy was not, and he soon drifted into sleep. Misha watched the television until she was sure he was sleeping and then took the opportunity to look him over. She noticed that his scrubs were tight across his crotch and soon saw the reason. He must have been having an erotic dream because he was growing as she watched, and it looked like he was going to bust through the seams after a few seconds. Misha had a thought about taking a ride on his lap and it caused her nipples to poke into her scrubs top.

The alarm went off and all of the sexual tension that Misha had built up flew out the window. Guy was up answering the radio with a huge projection in the front of his scrubs that was gone by the time Lee was out of the sleeping room. The call was a single car wreck that was close the station. Less than five minutes passed before the ambulance was at the accident scene. Lee was the first to arrive at the car. His sudden change in demeanor made it obvious to Guy that their services were not going to be sufficient here. The police on the scene already knew and the *jaws* were on their way. Misha went to the car to look and almost threw up. The car had careened into a bridge abutment without any skid marks and the highway speed limit here was fifty-five. The man may have had a chance of survival, but he had made a bad decision and had folded down the driver's side back seat and slid his water skis in there. The impact caused one of the skis to decapitate him and his head was hanging to the side, held only by some skin and tissue. Blood was everywhere and dripped from the crunched roof back onto the body. Guy had the coroner's office on the radio. They would be at least half an hour because the only doctor there was in the final stages of an autopsy and couldn't leave the body open. Misha stayed close to the ambulance. One of the police officers on the scene came over and said, "Passenger side had a cooler with three beers in it and there were nine empties on the floorboard area. Virginia plates. Fucking drunk tourists." Guy said, "If the people at bars had to come see this once in a while, it would probably stop most of it." The cop said, "If only," and everyone began walking over to the fire rescue truck that just pulled up.

The crumpled car was an older, full-size, model and it took half an hour just to get the top removed. Then it took until the coroner arrived to get the door and steering column removed. The man had a wedding ring on, and the police officer sighed. The coroner officially pronounced the man dead. Guy and Lee helped the coroner's assistant to carefully get the body out of the car and loaded onto the gurney. Misha stayed out of the way and thought about how bad Eli, from the VA group, must be messed up from having this kind of thing happen to the guy beside him. They left the scene in the empty ambulance.

Guy was driving now and asked if anybody else wanted to go by Taco Bell before it closed. Everybody did and they arrived back at the station with two dozen tacos. It was more television while tacos were eaten. Guy said he was going to stretch out while he could. Misha said, "Let me look at the set up in there and maybe I'll rest also." She looked in the room and saw two single sized beds. The one Lee had been in when they left, remained unmade. She asked, "How often do you guys change the sheets?" Lee said, "Every shift." She said, "I think I'll stay on the couch a while." Lee said, "Suit yourself. I'm going to stretch out then, too." The two men went into the room and closed the door.

Misha settled on the couch and as she was about to fall asleep when the call alarm went off again. It was another car wreck. Seven minutes later, they were on the scene. This was the one for Misha. A car had hit a motorcycle and the biker had a broken ankle. She asked Guy and Lee to please let her do the immobilization. They agreed and she treated the man, on the side of the road, beside a car. When she was finished, they put him on the gurney. Them after much assurance by the tow truck operator that the motorcycle was being taken to right place, the ambulance headed off to the hospital. It was becoming a long night for Misha now that she had accomplished her goal of treating a patient in the field. Back at the station there was cleaning and restocking of the ambulance. Misha happened to look into the sleeping room as they went back into the station room. Only the one bed was still unmade.

Morning found Misha asleep on the couch in the station room with Guy and Lee in the sleeping room with the door closed. An alarm clock went off and Lee came out and began making coffee, Guy soon followed. Misha rose up and the movement caused her to have to stifle a scream. There was something wrong with her shoulder. She went to the bathroom and took a pain pill. It was only thirty minutes until the end of the shift, and she hoped Matt was right on time this morning.

Matt arrived at the EMS station and since Misha was not outside, went inside to get her. Lee met him at the desk, after introductions he called Guy over, and said, "Here's Mr. Lucky, come to get Misha." Matt thought he had just figured out why Misha wanted to work this particular shift. She came out of the bathroom and looked like she had had a rough night. Guy said, "I think she saw her first decapitation, last night." Misha said, "Ooh, don't remind me." On the way home Matt said, "I think I figured out why you wanted to work that shift so badly." She responded, "There are two beds in the sleeping room and when we got called out, they were both in there and I saw that only one bed was messed up." Matt said, "Okay, I don't know what that means." She said, "I have serious doubts that they were interested in me. Maybe if you had worked the shift, it would have been a different story." Matt felt that she had dodged his first observation pretty well. This was a group therapy day, and they went to the boat to get some rest before heading down to Key West.

SESSION 3

Matt told Misha that he wanted to talk to Ami before the session because he was having a problem with the whole having visions thing. Misha said, "No problem for me, are we going to stay the night?" Matt answered, "We can but we need to start saving money if you still want to have a baby." Then he thought about the Naval Air Station and said, "I have to check the boat lines, can you check to see if there is a room at the Navy lodge on the air station?" She said, "Good Idea!"

When Matt came back inside, she said, "Got us the cheapest room in Key West!" He said, "Great, let's pack a bag and get going so we can check in before the session." She threw back, "What about Ami?" He said, "Next time, maybe." There was no more talk about visiting Ami. Instead, the drive down was discussion of baby possibilities and if it would work on the boat. Matt thought about the money that he had been stuffing into a jar and that he should probably get it into a bank, or maybe even actually go ahead and count it. His mind then flashed a rope, with a laughing lion's head and serpent's tail, wrapped tightly around a pale blue, motionless baby. It startled him back into the moment.

Everyone arrived before the session began and Matt explained directions to the bar where they were going to after the session. Only Jose had heard of it, but he hadn't been there. Doug arrived and the session began. RJ came in a few minutes after the initial chatter died down and showed her second video. It was not as dramatic as the first one and the discussion was sparse.

Misha said, "I went out with EMS and got to repeat my scenario. I didn't get to video it because there were actual patients involved and privacy laws make things like that complicated." She went through the whole scenario and then said, "I thought that the opportunity to repeat the situation where I was injured was something, but it was overshadowed by when we went to a car wreck and the guy had his head taken off by a water ski. That really bothered me, and I thought about Eli and his situation. It really made me think about how good I actually have it. I have a loving partner in my life, live in paradise, have a roof over my head and eat fairly well. I think that there are people so much worse off than me that should be getting this care and maybe I am taking their spot."

Doug broke in and answered Misha's comment, "First off, and this applies to all of you, you are not taking up space that could be used by someone that you feel might be in more dire need. The entire VA exists to serve you, no matter what level of service you need. If you are concerned that there are people not here who should be here, help them find their way to here. We will expand groups, hold more sessions, find more moderators or anything else that we have to do to provide help and assistance to veterans. The key to success here is that the people coming here have to actually want the help we offer and take on some personal responsibility about their own care. Sorry for the soapbox speech but you have to understand that not all veterans who need help seek it, or even want it. You can help change that because veterans listen to veterans."

Eli went next and opened with, "Thanks for thinking about me, Misha. I really appreciate it and I also appreciate the fact that we are all doing things together to help each other out, it just seems right." He handed his nightmare video to RJ and said, "Leanne filmed me, I just want to publicly thank her for the support." The group sat in silence as Eli described how he was riding along talking to the corporal driving. The corporal had just told him that his wife was nine months pregnant, and he was going to get leave in a week to go home. He then got quiet and said, "I looked at him, looked out the window and there was a loud noise and when I looked back his head was gone and pieces of it were everywhere. The blood was spraying and then it all went black. My nightmare is exactly what happened, over and over, sometimes three times a night. In reality, I woke up being transported to the rear. In the nightmare I never wake up, there is just blackness until the dream starts over."

The discussion was brief about Eli's nightmare and then Leanne said she wanted to go next. She handed her video to RJ, who played it. She said, "Eli was kind enough to film this for me." The video was dark, and she was sitting up in bed with a sheet draped over her. In the video, she said, "I was just crossing between two buildings in a small town. Something caught my eye and then my head felt like someone was both ripping it off and smashing it with a baseball bat, at the same time. The last thing I remember was

the burning sensation and the smell. I have never smelled
anything like that, so I can't tell you what it was like, or even
compare it to anything I know. I have no idea what happened
after that, but the medics must have gotten to me. One of the
guys, Sergeant Daly, I think, had a grenade launcher, and
later told me that he had dropped three rounds in rapid
succession on the sniper while another man poured fifty-
caliber fire into the spot. Sergeant Daly actually said, "If we
didn't have this damned embedded reporter, that sniper
would have been sorry he was born before sucking in his
final breath." I think Sergeant Daly really liked me. Anyway,
there is absolutely no doubt the man who shot me died very
soon after firing the shot. He may have been the lucky one. I
just woke up from a repeat of being shot. Except in the
dream, I am a still a kid and my mother is with me.
The troubling thing is that I can't remember being a kid or
my mother, she died when I was three and, in the dream, she
never comes into focus. I see my mother get hit and go down.
When I turn to look at her, I clearly see a bullet about to enter
my head. It looks as big as a car and would surely going to
rip my head completely off on impact. In reality, I survive
but, in the dream, I don't. I just fall into blackness and it's
strange because I know that I am falling into blackness but
have no body and there is no sensation of time. After a while,
I panic and that's when I usually wake up. Tonight, I finally
hit the bottom. It was suddenly light, I was back with my
mother and the whole dream repeated itself. I panicked the
second time and woke up. This is the first time that I made
the full cycle."
Doug said, "Anyone care to comment?" Matt asked Misha,
"Is this the only dream you have?" She said, "Unfortunately,
no. I have dreams that I can't remember and just wake up
drenched in sweat felling terrified." There was a general
agreement to this and almost everyone in the group reported
this also happened to them several times in a month. Matt
was not having these night terrors, but Misha was, he knew

this because she usually thrashed about just before waking up and it always took a minute for her to realize he was there with her and not someone or something coming to kill her. Doug took over and commented, "Leanne, what do you know about your mother's death?" Leanne answered, "Just what my aunt has told me. She was raped and killed by a man she had gone out with a few times." Doug said, "What about your father?" Martha said, "Never knew him, he was never there and was never discussed." Doug asked, "Do you ever dream of your father?" She said, "Not that I know of but sometimes there is a presence in my dreams that I can't identify. It's not somebody, just a disturbing place that has no physical body." Doug asked, "Anyone have anything further?" Judy spoke up, louder than normal, "I have a similar mother daughter nightmare. In mine we get blown up by a bomb on the sidewalk. We are just walking down the street and then we are pieces flying through the air and our body parts intermingle in the air somehow and come out as one person whose sole purpose is to kill whoever planted the bomb."

Everyone looked at Judy, remembering that she was so quiet normally and had said she didn't dream of anything much. Doug said, "Are you able to find the person who planted the bomb?" Judy replied, "No, the hunt just seems endless and futile. I normally wake up feeling like I am lost and have to look around carefully to decide where I am and if it's where I should be." Doug asked, "Do you live alone?" She hesitated and said, "I have a cat." Misha asked, "Is the other person in your dream always your mother?" Judy said, "Always, and she is alive and well just as my father is, so I don't know why she is always with me when the bomb goes off." Doug said, "Wow, our time is up already. Everybody is making an earnest effort to participate, let's keep it up. Are you guys all going out today?" There was a general yes from the group and Doug asked where. He had not heard of the bar either but thought that the group interaction was good no matter

where it happened. He added, "Remember, if you know or
meet a veteran who needs help, steer him or her to the clinic.
We have to get everyone with a need into the system. Tape
something to share if you haven't already, please." As the
group left, Judy was asked to stay a minute and RJ said, "You
should make an appointment with Ami and talk to her one
on one about your situation and dreams." Judy agreed and
left to catch up to the group.

The bar was happy to see the six vets come in, after Matt and
Misha were recognized and introduced everybody. They took
up half of the mostly empty room and talked about general
life in the Keys until a few empty bottles were on the tables.
The talk turned to war stories, and it was like everyone was
competing to tell the biggest one. Three hours passed and
everyone checked out everyone else for ability to drive or get
home and the only concern was Judy. She had gone heavy on
martinis, instead of beer, and was inebriated. Matt and Misha
offered to drive her home and she turned them down and
asked Jose if he would. He was reluctant and suggested that
he, along with Matt and Misha should do it. They drove her
to her rented camper trailer on Stock Island and she insisted
that they all come in and meet her cat. They did and ended
up staying for over an hour because Judy was obviously
having an issue. Eventually, Judy asked Jose if he would stay
with her, as a friend, and Matt and Misha excused
themselves. Jose was still apprehensive about the situation
when Matt and Misha said goodnight.

Matt and Misha arrived back at the Naval Air Station and
took a nap, they were going to go back out and hit some
touristy places on and near Duval, just because. No more
thought was given to Jose and Judy. They had discussed it a
few minutes on the ride from Judy's place and decided that
they were adults and could act as they pleased. It was
midnight before they woke up. They decided that it was nice
just having nothing to worry about where they were and
began baby making practice.

The next morning, they had breakfast at a place on US 1, and returned to the boat for some smoking and lazing about for the day. Misha had the night off and was experiencing increasing pain in her shoulder. It had subsided some while they were in Key West, and she had hoped that meant it was just a passing thing. She offered to drive Matt over to Desi's, and Matt said that the weather looked fine and that he would take the Alfa tonight. He thought it was time to get some use out of it and keep the battery alive.

At six fifteen, Matt left, and Misha tried to occupy herself; that didn't work, so she took a few pain pills to dull the growing pain in her shoulder. She then drank vodka and passed out. She slept through the night. Matt sat with Desi until he went to sleep, then turned off the television and began reading a new Tim Dorsey book. Vickie had left soon after his arrival. She told him that she would not be back until after he was gone because she was visiting her mother in Fort Lauderdale for the day.

Before Matt left in the morning, Desi asked him to come twice a week so that he could have someone on the boat with him more often. Matt almost asked a question, but Desi answered it first, "Vickie is younger than me and needs the company of a man who can still appreciate her body in a manner more than just looking. She is increasing the frequency of her outings and I'm almost certain she has a steady boyfriend now. I don't have a problem with it because she gave me great happiness for the years that I was able to participate physically. She still curls up with me some nights, like a cat. And, like a cat, she comes and goes as she wishes. It really is okay. You'll come twice now, right?" Matt said, "I'll come twice a week, no problem." Desi said, "One fifty a shift then, no less." Matt said, "If you insist."

At the boat, Matt found Misha asleep on floor in the salon. He panicked and ran inside as soon as he saw her and tried to wake her. She came to after a few seconds and was in excruciating pain from sleeping in a bad position on the floor.

She slowly got to her knees and then Matt helped her stand up as she told him about the pains. He was sympathetic and said, "Maybe we should smoke some of the special mix stuff and then you can take a pain pill and see if sleeping in the bed helps." She said, "Sounds like a plan and sat down on the couch." The smoke was accompanied with vodka and then the pain pills put Misha into a sound sleep in the bed. Matt tossed and turned as a new kind of nightmare crept into his psyche.

Inside Matt's mind, he was driving through a dark area and as he passed through intersections, he could see vehicle accidents that must have occurred at the crossroads and had deaths involved. The road entered a city he wasn't readily familiar with, and the number of visions increased as pedestrians, motorcycles and pedestrians joined in. He wanted to wake up, but the dream would not let go of him until he started seeing himself in the wrecks and then he woke up with a very uneasy feeling. The only good thing, he thought, was that Misha seemed to be sleeping peacefully. It was one thirty and now he had to decide if he was going to try for some more sleep or just get up. He tried for more sleep and succeeded.

Once Matt entered dream phase sleep again, he found himself on a small boat and as he travelled down a river, he could see all the deaths that had ever occurred along its course. He saw boating accidents, heart attacks, fights, and an execution style shooting. It was not as disturbing as the driving dream. He still just wanted to wake up and was fighting fervently to do so when Misha shook him. She was feeling a little better and asked if he wanted her to record the nightmare that he was obviously having. He said that it wasn't relevant to the group and declined. He asked how she had slept, and she said that she could probably make it through her shift, so they got up and began getting ready to go.

They drove separate cars and Matt had a few visions on the way to Clive's. When he arrived at the house, Sarah was waiting to leave. He asked her, "How's your father been?" She said, "He's still the same and I still have needs. Since you won't take care of them, I'm going down to Key West to find a tourist to bang for the night." Matt said, "Sorry, I really want to but just can't deal with the complications." She said, "What complications? You fuck me, we don't talk about it, and nobody gets attached or anything like that. Simple and fun!" Matt thought about the offer some more and in the delay, she said, "I can easily stay home and leave my door open." He finally said, "Sorry, I just can't do it. You are beautiful though and I think about you a lot." She growled out, "Whatever!" Then she stormed off to her Mercedes convertible and patched out as she left the driveway.

OVER AND OUT

Misha arrived at a full-fledged mad house in the emergency room. While helping to roll a large patient over, she passed out from sudden pain and hit the floor. She was sent to get an MRI, along with an incident report to fill out. She was getting better at writing with her non-dominant left hand, but it was still a struggle to fill out all the required paperwork. The MRI showed that a significant amount of damage had re-occurred and she was given pain pills and sent home with an appointment to see an orthopedic specialist and ordered ten days of no lifting. She took a pain pill in the parking lot and drove to the marina. Her right arm was in a sling, she was both in pain and under the influence of a very strong pain pill. Parking was a challenge and as she was pulling into the assigned spot, hit the accelerator instead of the brake, and ran into a large wooden post aptly placed to keep cars from inadvertently going into the water. The post was twice the size of a telephone pole, about three feet tall, and very solidly embedded into the ground. The car crumpled and Misha was oblivious to all that had actually happened. No one was around at the time and after the shock of the impact passed, she stumbled to the Dreaming Moon, and went to bed. Matt arrived at the marina and immediately saw Misha's car wrapped around the post. He looked inside it and then all around. It was probably a goner, the engine seemed to have been pushed off its mounts and most of the front end was simply smashed. He had not panicked about Misha yet, but it was rapidly building. He ran to the boat, rushed in, and found her asleep in the bed. She had a small goose-egg shape on her forehead. He checked for a pulse and breathing and then tried to wake her up. She did not wake, and he panicked as he dialed the phone. Since he only had a cell phone, he had to tell the operator where he was, and she had to make a second call to EMS.

Lee and Guy were working a double shift and arrived thinking it was probably one of the older residents who had fallen and hit their head, or something similar. When they saw it was Misha, they immediately went into a flurry of activity and asked Matt questions as they worked. Ten minutes later, Matt was following the ambulance to the hospital wondering about the real relationship between Misha, Lee, and Guy. At the hospital, she was checked by the neurosurgeon on call and admitted for observation and tests. Matt stayed in the room with her and slept in a chair while she was getting a CAT scan and other tests. He called Desi and said he had to take the night off and told him the reason. Desi said, "No problem, Vickie has decided to stay in tonight, for some reason." Matt said, "Alright then, I'll call you in a day or two." Misha did not wake up that day.

Misha regained consciousness the following day at one thirty in the afternoon. She had no recollection of wrecking the car or of taking the pain pills. Her shoulder was in tremendous pain though and she started asking for pain medication very soon after waking up. Matt filled her in, on what had happened, while they waited for the doctor to show up and decide what to do. Matt told her not to worry about the car. It was probably going to die soon, anyway. It had over a hundred fifty thousand miles on it and wasn't really valuable as a trade in. She was not concerned about the car because her shoulder pain had taken over her existence and Matt was background noise.

When the doctor, a neurosurgeon, finally arrived, he decided that an orthopedic surgeon was needed for a complete evaluation. The neurosurgeon completed his exam and said everything was fine as far as he was concerned, and the orthopedic surgeon would be the primary doctor now. It meant that there would be no pain medicine for Misha until the new doctor arrived and made an assessment. This took another half an hour, plus a ten-minute question and answer session and exam. He finally ordered an IV pain medication and an MRI of Misha's shoulder to help decide on a course of action.

Misha's MRI showed what Matt already figured. Her shoulder needed complete reconstructive surgery. After consultation and evaluation by the hospital team, it was decided that she would get a better rehab program at the Miami Veteran's Center and arrangements were made. Matt took Misha home for the night with plans to drive up to Miami in the morning. He had her smoke some of the special mix and went down the dock to Sam's to get more. As he walked back up the dock, he noticed that there was a ring around the moon and coupled with the nagging ache in his back and legs, knew that meant a storm was coming. He was used to the pain and had stopped taking anything for it, particularly after seeing how bad the addictive power was on Misha, putting her in and out of rehab. The cure seemed worse than the pain.

The wrecked car was still in the parking space and the marina manager wanted it moved immediately before there was an oil leak or something. Matt looked on the Internet and found a scrap company who he called to pick up the car and

made a deal with them to stop by in a week or so to collect
the fifty to one hundred dollars they offered for the junk car.
He checked the trunk and glove box, gathered everything of
value, took pictures and left the signed title with the marina
manager. The marina manager was sympathetic to Matt and
Misha because he knew she was in bad shape after the
accident and thought that she was pretty.

The Alfa performed perfectly on the trip up US 1. Matt knew
that he wasn't driving on the Turnpike in it because it was so
low and open that it scared him to pass large vehicles. Misha
smoked dope for almost the entire trip and arrived at the VA
Center in less pain than normal but needing assistance
walking. Matt was able to help her get checked in but was
restricted in some ways because they were not married, and
he was not a relative. Eventually, she got to the orthopedic
ward and was given a private room because the population
was overwhelmingly male, and it was the only solution that
fit privacy standards and normal practices. She was not
happy being an inpatient and that set a sour mood in the
room. Nurses and doctors came and then a new battery of
tests was performed. The consensus was the same as in
Marathon and surgery was scheduled for two days later.
Misha didn't want to wait for two days and was a terrible
patient. That is, until she was given IV pain medicine which
put her into a dream-like state for hours at a time. She had
visions of being out on the open blue water, flying through a
clear azure sky, making love at a waterfall on a mountaintop
with an actor from a movie she liked, and things seemed to
be perfect. Then the pain returned and whatever dream she
was in the middle of turned into a nightmare. She was
drowning in the blue water while large billowing black
clouds swallowed her from the perfect sky. Then the man she
was making love with turned into a demon. She always
seemed to wake up with a jerking movement that made the
pain worsen.

Matt was there for the two days and was beginning to need a shower and change of clothes. He synchronized the time for a trip to a nearby store and the cheapest hotel that he could find with one of Misha's pain medicine administrations. He hadn't thought to bring extra clothes and ended up buying shorts and a shirt from a Dollar General. He then checked into the hotel, took a long, hot shower and while washing his hair began having thoughts of Sarah, for some reason. He arrived back at the hospital as Misha was beginning to experience pain and she begged him to take her somewhere to smoke a joint. He had no way to do that and sponged her forehead. When he touched her arm, he got a far-off feeling that was just barely there and his stomach seemed to drop a foot. He didn't say anything to her and when she asked what was wrong, he said, "I guess this is just a lot to deal with." She said, in a slurred response, "You should try it from this angle." He kissed her forehead and said, "I have, and I liked it even less."

Misha's surgery was scheduled for the morning and that meant she was unable to eat or drink anything at this point. She was still able to get out of bed and asked Matt to help her get into the bathroom. It was ten o'clock at night and the hospital was quiet and had very little activity. Nurses were doing their administrative chores and doctors had finished rounds at least half an hour ago. Misha had just gotten a dose of pain medicine and wanted to take a shower before being confined to a bed for who knows how long and getting only the minimal sponging. She also wanted something else that wasn't going to happen for a while and asked Matt to close the door and help her get a shower. He closed the door and she said, "I need to get a little dirtier before my shower, you game?" Matt did not hesitate, and she sat on his lap and moved the best she could until she went off and then continued until he was unable to remain inside her. She then asked him to stay while she took a shower.

During the intimate contact, Matt didn't feel the intense sensation of Misha's coming demise he had feared earlier and thought that maybe the whole thing was just a mixed message from the vast amount of suffering going on in this building. He cleaned himself up and a second after getting his shoes back on, a nurse knocked on the door. He opened it and she said, "Just checking, she wasn't in bed." He said, "She's getting a last shower in before the surgery." The nurse winked and said, "I believe it's at least four hours before anybody has to come into the room again." Matt smiled and said, "Thank you." The nurse closed the door and put a sign on the door that said a procedure was being performed in the room and no one was to enter. Matt got Misha out of the shower, dried and into bed naked. He then joined her. Her inhibitions were just dulled enough to want every minute, and everything, that he could give her. He was gentler than normal and concentrated on how she was doing, with the activity level, more than anything else. This change of focus made things last far longer than normal and increased her pleasure immensely. Afterward, he got a washcloth to clean her up and she asked him to leave it alone. He then covered her with a hospital gown and snapped only the neck to keep it from sliding off. He didn't want to move her bad arm and he knew that the gown would be coming off in the operating room anyway.

The next pain medicine contained the pre-op drugs and then it was time for her to go to the OR. Matt walked by the gurney and held her hand to the automatic door where he kissed her, said he loved her and would be there as soon as he was allowed. He didn't detect any special sensations while holding her hand and was greatly relieved by their absence. As he walked toward the hospital exit a gurney went by and an old man reached out and grabbed his hand. Matt had an immediate sensation and, as the nursing assistant pried the man's hands open, Matt could see a dark storm and an odd presence. The man said, "Keep that, I don't need it anymore." As he walked out of the hospital, there was a strange feeling that seemed to infiltrate his being. The interior automatic door didn't respond to his presence, he stopped and tried waving and still got nothing. As soon as another person walked up, the door opened immediately. This seemed odd, but not weird enough to stand there and contemplate, so he continued behind the other person through the outside door. The wind howled across the parking lot and there was an odd yellowish-gray sky. He studied the billowy clouds that seemed to be moving faster than any he had ever seen before and there was a blinding flash of light about fifty feet in front of him as lightning struck a tall, concrete power pole. He watched the blue-white light travel down the pole and into the ground, unable to move for cover. The pavement under his feet seemed to come alive and his feet tingled like he had sat in a bad position too long. Then it was over, the odd sensation from the man on the gurney, that is. He suddenly felt released from a spell and ran for the car as he saw a thick sheet of rain coming toward him.

The Alfa was not the best foul weather automobile; the top had a couple of leaks and seemed flimsy against the maelstrom that had seemed to settle over top of it. Matt decided to stay in place until the rain slacked. Lightning struck the parking lot area three more times and interrupted his worry about Misha each time. An hour passed and he finally felt safe driving back to the hotel. Once in the soft bed, sleep came over him like a tidal wave. For the four hours before the alarm went off, dreams of places he had never been to before came and went and the rope snake seemed always to be the transition. After the alarm, he cleaned up and returned to the hospital. The surgeons had said for him to expect six hours and that was his target time to return to the hospital.

At the hospital, he checked in with the nursing staff at the recovery area and found that Misha was still in surgery. He sat in the waiting area and read until one of the surgeons came out to talk to him. The surgeon looked neutral, and Matt was having trouble reading what to expect. He was also struck by the delicateness of the female form that called his name and spoke in an Indian accent, "Mr. Luna, we finished the surgery for your wife, and she is doing well. The operation took longer than planned because we had to find more bone graft material and the metal plates had to be custom shaped. With this, we think that the pain will be greatly reduced, and she should regain a good amount of normal function over the next six months." Matt asked, "When can I see her?" The doctor said," She will still be asleep for maybe four hours, you should give your cell number to the desk and go get some rest." Matt did as suggested and went back to the hotel to sleep some more. Six hours passed before he got the call to come back to the hospital. He was actually getting ready to go on his own because he worried that something had gone wrong, or that they had lost his number. When he arrived at the hospital, the nurse at the recovery room directed him to SICU, the surgical intensive care unit. The nurse at SICU walked him to Misha's bedside where he became immediately concerned to find how puffy she looked and her inability to speak. The nurse said it was all a function of the amount of time in surgery and the airway being in her throat so long. Matt accepted this and gently grasped Misha's hand and said, "I'm here baby." She squeezed a little and there were no odd sensations, which was a big relief. An hour later the nurse returned and said that he was going to give her some pain medication and that she would likely be out until morning. He suggested Matt go home and relax. Matt took that advice and drove to Marathon. His initial plan was to return to Miami in the Dreaming Moon. By the time he was down to Islamorada he realized that taking the boat back to Miami would leave him with no car. He tried to formulate a new plan during the rest of the way to Marathon.

On the boat, he looked up dockage costs in Miami and quickly decided against every marina that he looked at. He then thought about buying a scooter and using it to come and go from a marina. He then looked for a marina that offered dock space without any amenities and came up empty. He decided to go around in person during the times Misha was out from medication or having a procedure to find something because he knew that a hotel was going to leave them broke very quickly since he was unable to work steadily. He decided to count his available cash. He counted twice and found that there was fifty-three hundred dollars. He then thought of going to the bank, but the cell phone interrupted him. He looked at the number and knew it was a key's area code, but not familiar one, and answered with caution.

UNBALANCED AND OVERLOADED

Matt slowly said, "Hello," into his cell phone and Mae said, "You need help?" He had forty-seven thoughts at once and said, "Probably." She said, "I'm over at Herbie's, come get me." He secured the boat and walked to the Alfa. He noticed that the Toyota was still there and walked over to read the note plastered on it. It was a notice that the vehicle would be towed, at the owner's expense, if not moved by today. He decided to deal with that after getting Mae. He wondered how she knew he might need help as he drove over to the restaurant on US 1.

Mae was sitting at the counter when Matt arrived and there was a fish sandwich and fries on a plate beside her. She was eating her own sandwich and when she saw Matt said, "I know you haven't eaten right, so sit and eat," indicating that the plate beside her was for him. He suddenly realized that she was right, and he was starving. Over lunch, Mae told him, "I saw Capt. Will in Key West yesterday, and he told me that the car was wrecked, and Misha was in the hospital." Matt said, "I was wondering how you knew." She said, "I knew something was up when you didn't answer your phone." He said, "Have to turn it off in the intensive care unit." She quickly asked, "Is she alright?" Matt said, "Had major surgery to reconstruct her shoulder, for the second time. Doctors say it looks like she may get back a lot of use and the pain should be less of an issue." Mae said, "Was she drunk when she destroyed the car?" He thought about his response for a second too long and she started talking again, "Pills and booze, I bet. That woman is going to drag you down to the bottom if you're not careful. I know that you love her, and she loves you but that doesn't always mean things work out." Matt was hit hard by her words and said, "She's down right now, and I have to take care of her." She said, "Yes, you do. And soon, you will need to help me." She reached over and lightly grabbed his arm and he instantly knew the feeling was stronger than before.

Matt asked Mae, "How are you feeling?" She said, "Not bad, got a few prescriptions now and can probably make it a few months before I'm down." Matt presented an idea to her, "Can you pilot the Dreaming Moon to Miami for me? I'm trying to find a transient space without services, to save money." She said, "I have a better idea, "You pilot the boat, I'll drive the car, we'll borrow a dinghy and take up a mooring spot that I know of. I will stay on the boat, and you can spend as much time as needed at the hospital. I might even help you there because sometimes there are things that only a woman can do for another woman." Matt said, "I still need a car up there." She said, "You don't think I'm too far gone to drive, do you?" He jokingly asked, "Are you?" She said, "At least you smiled and, seriously, you'd trust me with the boat before the car?"

At the marina, Mae asked to borrow a dinghy from a couple who had never taken their boat out. They offered to sell it to her, and she asked the price. It was a good price and she said that Matt would come to pay them and get the paperwork. Since the dinghy was actually a fourteen-foot skiff with a small outboard, it had a title and had to be registered. On the drive from the restaurant, she asked Matt if he had notified his insurance company about the car, and he hadn't. The insurance company instructed him to call a certain shop and they would take it from there, Matt made the call, and the shop sent a flatbed to get the car. Mae found Matt and told him, "Go pay the $400 for the dingy, it's the best deal you'll get this month." He did and came back to prepare for departure to Miami. The flatbed arrived and he signed a paper for them to take the car. Mae checked to make sure he had what he needed from the car and then took off.

Matt decided to get out in open water before calling the hospital. He did the pre-operational checks on the boat that Mae had taught him, untied all but one rope on the stern, got the engines going, quickly untied the last rope and ran to the helm. He eased out of the slip without bumping the sides and idled out through the channel. The sea was like glass and there was an inversion going on that created a Flying Dutchman effect on a larger boat to the south past a small island. The sky had some wispy cirrus formations sweeping across it and the surface winds were almost non-existent. Matt was both happy and sad as he made open water and opened the throttles to three-quarter speed. The boat seemed happy to be out and at cruising speed. First, he called Doug, down at the Key West VA Clinic, and explained what had happened and said that they would return to the group sessions after she was better. Doug told him he was welcome to come without her but understood if he didn't and wished Matt well. He then called the hospital and was told that Misha was asking for him constantly, that is, during the periods when the pain medications were fading off. Otherwise, she was doing as well as could be expected. Matt pushed the throttles to eighty-five percent and watched the gauges for signs of problems. Nothing abnormal occurred and he was in the Miami area in a few more hours. The challenge now was to get into a mooring area in Biscayne

Bay. Mae told him to use a certain stored position in the GPS and look for a milk jug floating just at the surface. It took half an hour, but he found the jug and tied onto the mooring chain that was attached to the small rope that held the jug in place. He also dropped the anchor and then backed up to set it and check the mooring. It was all in good order, so he pulled the dingy up and found it was swamped. He got the portable bilge pump and started the generator. It seemed to take forever to get the skiff running. He then used its bilge pump to speed up the process of getting all the seawater out of it. When the skiff was ready to go, he secured the Dreaming Moon and called Mae's cell phone. She gave him directions and said she would be at the dock waiting for him. It took ten minutes to find Mae as Matt pulled up to a restaurant's dock. Matt was concerned and Mae took him to meet the restaurant owner, Jimmy, who said, "If you eat here once in a while, you can use the dock all you want. We don't get the kind of business from it that we once did. Everybody has those huge boats that draw too much water to be up in here. Mae says you're a disabled veteran. Well sir, I thank you for your service and hope your girl is better soon." Mae said, "I will stay here and catch up with Jimmy and then go out to the boat. Just call me when you're ready and I'll pick you up. Matt handed her the skiff and boat keys and she handed him the car keys. She said, "I filled her up for you." He said, "I'll probably be there most of the day." She called back over her shoulder, "I've got time."

THE PATH TO RECOVERY

Matt arrived at the hospital as an afternoon thunderstorm hit. He waited in the car for it to abate and thought about finding a more substantial source of transportation. As he sat there, he observed that the same power pole that was hit by lightning in the last storm just got hit two more times. He made a mental note to avoid the area around that particular pole, it just seemed too coincidental that he was near, and the lightning was favoring that spot. Then he thought of an old saying and really began wondering because lightning isn't supposed to strike in the same place twice let alone this many times

When he finally made it to Misha's bedside, she was out from a recent dosing of morphine. He wandered out to the waiting area and saw a note for a free "leave and take" library and went to the designated room. He quickly spotted a *Hitchhikers Guide to the Universe* and took it back to the unit. He read quietly to Misha, and it helped to pass the time. She eventually woke up and in a feeble voice said, "You're here, I was so afraid you were gone." He said, "I had to make arrangements to get the Dreaming Moon up here and Mae is helping me." She said, "Good, I *really* need you to help me with a personal matter."

Matt was unsure of the procedures here and flagged down a nurse. He explained that he was a CNA and had done this all before and she showed him where everything necessary was in the cubicle type room. Afterward, Matt read more of the Hitchhiker's Guide to her, and she fell back asleep. Matt thought about the long road ahead. He was sure it would include physical therapy and at probably at least one round of rehab.

Shortly after nine in the evening, Matt decided to return to the boat for the night. Misha had just been given morphine and would be out for several hours, anyway. He looked at her sleeping form, quietly said, "Good night, baby," and headed for the parking lot. As he walked down the row of cubes, a man called out to him, "Hey Gabe! Come here!" Matt looked and the man repeated, "You, Gabriel, come here, I need you!" Matt stopped and quietly said, "I'm not Gabriel." The man said, "That's the only name, I could think of. Come here!" Matt walked into the cubical and asked, "What's going on?" The man said, "You have a glow about you," and reached out to touch him. Matt wanted to jerk his arm away, but something made him allow the contact to happen. The sensation was of great loss and suffering. The man's voice became weak and raspy as he said, "I was at Iwo and lost all my friends there, my dear darling wife went three years ago, son last year, and now I too must go." Matt said, "I'm sorry to hear that." The man seemed to fall asleep, and the feeling Matt was receiving morphed into canoeing down a grassy river, as if he were in the Everglades or somewhere very similar. A nurse was standing behind Matt, and he said, "That's the first time I've heard Mr. Shipman speak, he's been here two weeks." Matt turned around and met Henry Leysathe, III. Matt wanted to get out of the room as soon as possible and he and Henry went to the hallway in unison. Matt introduced himself and Henry said, "You're Misha's other half. 'Gonna be a long road with that girl. She had a lot of extensive repair and is getting heavy doses of morphine. I wish you well, my friend." Henry stuck out his hand and Matt shook it. The feeling was intense, and it seemed that only Matt knew why. They parted and Henry wondered what that was all about, as he returned to his duties. Matt called Mae on the way to the restaurant parking lot, and she said, "Good timing, I am at the restaurant getting a bite to eat and talking with Jimmy. Have you eaten yet?" Matt said, "No, I just haven't been hungry enough to find food at the hospital." She said, "We'll get something in you when you get here."

Matt arrived at the restaurant and saw it was closed. He walked up to the door and saw Mae and Jimmy at the counter, he knocked, and they waved him around to the back door. He walked around the building and was met by the kitchen crew, finishing up their duties. The apparent head cook asked, "Matt?", and when Matt nodded said, "There's a fish sandwich and fries under the heat lamp for you, it's only been there a few minutes. You want some slaw with that?" Matt said, "If it's not any trouble." She replied, "It's no trouble at all, for a friend of Mae's." Matt began wondering what was so special about Mae. Sure, she was a nice person and had been around for a long time but there was nothing in particular that he could pinpoint. He sat at the counter beside Mae, who was finishing a bottle of beer. Matt said to Jimmy, "Thanks for having the cook make me something, looks like they have closed shop back there." The woman from the kitchen came up the back of the bar and Jimmy said, "Matt, did you meet Harriet as you came through?" Matt said, "Kinda, guess I wasn't too good at introducing myself to her." Jimmy said, "Wouldn't do you any good, she's all mine. We've been married for fifty years, now, and I'm still loving every minute of it." Harriet said, "He's a liar, I gotta watch him like a hawk, else he'd take off with the first skirt that flipped his way." There was some laughter and Harriet asked, "Who needs a beer?" Everyone did. She got out four Abita Ambers and pried the tops off. Matt said, "I never heard of this beer before." Jimmy said, "Its good stuff, I think that I might be the only place in town that has it, though. I discovered it when I was working over in Pass Christian, Mississippi some years back." Matt liked the taste and said, "I may have a new favorite brand, here! Doesn't taste watered down." Mae said, "That's because you usually drink that watered down lite stuff." Matt's mind was busy calculating when Jimmy and Harriet got married and how unusual an interracial couple must have been back then. Harriet was shiny black and seemed to be the happiest person on the planet.

After food and a few beers, Mae suggested it was time to go. She handed Matt the skiff and boat keys and said, "You're driving since I filled the gas tank!" They arrived back at the Dreaming Moon, as a meteor seemed to fall from the sky in front of them. Mae said, "Who died?" Matt said, "Nobody that I know of." He immediately thought of Mr. Shipman and Mae spoke before he could, "Someone flag you down?" Matt said, "World War II vet, seemed to have lost everything." She said, "And?" He said, "The feeling changed to peacefulness before I left." She said, "And?" He reluctantly continues, "I met a man and have a feeling he has the same thing as me." She said, "Get his schedule and let's meet him." Matt said, "He looks Native American so, maybe I was just imagining it." Mae said, "From what Jim told me, you would not be able to imagine the feeling." Matt said, "Yeah, guess not. It probably would have scared me, if you hadn't clued me in."

Matt slept soundly, knowing he was in his own bed and that there was someone else on the boat. There was a chop on the water, but it provided a rocking motion that he became used to in a matter of minutes. Morning was gray and the clouds seemed to touch the water all around the boat. The chop was gone. The combination of the low clouds and reflective water surface created an eerie seascape, and it disturbed Matt in a peculiar way. It wasn't the emptiness; it was something else, which defied explanation. He decided to stand on the bow, and drink his coffee, something he had never thought to do before. The fog-like clouds seemed to thicken and envelop the boat, visibility reduced to less than fifty feet, and the boat seemed to be in a small clear, domed pocket made just for it. He stood on the rail and drank coffee, lost in thought about the challenges that surely lie ahead.

The sound of a screaming engine roared from the south and was followed by a Jet Ski heading toward the boat, at full speed. The passengers had been at an all-night sandbar party and anxious to get home before encountering a patrol boat. Matt saw the driver's facial expression suddenly change when he realized that he was about to become one with a comparatively large and stationary object. A frantic course adjustment almost worked but the laws of Newtonian mechanics held true, for yet another time, as the inertia driven vessel hit the anchor chain at speed. The acrobatics that followed rivaled the greatest of circuses and everything shifted into a surreal slow motion. The man, on the front of the machine made two full turns, the young woman on the back three and a half and the Jet Ski, skipped and rolled across the water's surface. As the slow motion reverted to live action, panic set in. Matt knew the water was over fifteen feet deep and his Navy training took over. He threw the life ring that hung nearby, ran to the life jacket locker, grabbed a handful, and jumped into the skiff. His initial thoughts of simply diving in were overridden by good sense and training. The woman was motionless in the water and the man seemed to have a broken arm and was unable to propel himself to his partner. Matt's assessment was that the woman was the higher priority, and he went full speed to her side. There was blood in the water, and he was sure that this was not going to be good.

The woman was in a bikini and the only place Matt had to grab was the chest strap of the top. He tried to lift her and get her turned over at the same time and ended up with a hand full of cloth and no success in flipping the woman. He then grabbed hair and got her face up. It looked like her nose was the source of the blood, so he grabbed under her arms and pulled with all his might. She came into the boat like a dead alligator, except that her artificial enhancements increased the resistance until they popped over the gunwale and helped hold her up while he flipped her legs in. He quickly did an airway and circulation assessment and began CPR. The man finally made it to the side of the skiff. When he saw what was actually happening, he began freaking out to the point where he was going to drown without immediate assistance. Matt stopped his compressions and breaths long enough to yell at the man in a voice that carried absolute authority to get into the life jacket he threw at the man's face. He returned to the CPR and after a minute, the woman began to breathe on her own. She coughed, gagged, and rolled into the fetal position. Matt checked her pulse and breathing and finding both present and steady, began looking for the man. A shaft of sunlight showed a body, just below the surface, and Matt went into the water. He forced the man's deadweight to the surface and toward the life ring. Mae was out of the cabin now and was about to dive in to help. Matt yelled, "Call the Coast Guard, they're both hurt bad!"

Mae went to the radio, which was always on channel 16, and made the call. A patrol boat was three miles away and was dispatched to proceed at full speed and a medevac team headed for the pad. Matt had the man secured in a life vest and was climbing back into the skiff when Mae came back into view. He grabbed the nearby life ring and used its rope to attach the man to the skiff's stern cleat. He then slowly motored over to the Dee. At the rear of the Dreaming Moon, Mae opened the swim door and secured the skiff's bow line to a cleat with a figure eight. Matt checked the woman and she had both a steady breathing pattern and pulse but was out. He then turned his attention to the man and began struggling to get him onto the deck. Mae helped by pulling on the ring's rope and the herculean task seemed to take an hour, at least in Matt's mind.

The man was blue. Once Matt got him sprawled out on the deck, seawater and stomach contents heaved onto the deck and breathing started. The man had a pulse, so Matt took this as a good sign and went to check the woman again. She was still unconscious and bleeding from her nose. Mae threw a washcloth and Matt used it to pinch the woman's nose. The fog was lifting, and the Coast Guard boat made its way alongside and the three men and two women went into motion. They were all trained in water rescue and advanced first aid. After the boat captain and Matt had a short exchange, the crewmembers took control of the situation. The helicopter appeared at the same time as Miami-Dade Sherriff and FWC patrol boats. The helicopter was determined to be the evacuation method of choice and minutes later left with both victims onboard.

Jurisdiction eventually fell to the Miami-Dade Sherriff and the other agency's boats soon departed to tend to the morning's startup of the stupid boater's parade. Matt answered questions, presented insurance documents, and gave a statement. A small barge arrived, and men loaded up the remains of the Jet Ski. The sheriff's deputies determined that since the Coast Guard patrol was not concerned with the Dreaming Moon being a hazard to navigation, they weren't either. The bell, on a pole over the top of the cabin, which Jim had installed several years earlier, was one of the major convincing factors. Two hours later, it was just him and Mae again. Matt went into the water to look for damage to the boat and Mae checked the operation of the anchoring system. There was no damage, just as expected since the anchoring point was likely the strongest place on the boat.

Matt pulled himself together, realized it was time to get ready to go see Misha and rinsed off with the freshwater hose instead of the shower, which required the generator. Mae said she would drop him off because she wanted to go into Miami for some things. Matt offered her the car, but she said that she had made arrangements to get around already. Matt didn't question her any further and she didn't volunteer anything more. As she let him off at the dock, she said, "I'll leave the skiff here, call me though because I might be nearby." With that, Matt was off to the hospital. On the way, he saw solar panels being installed at an intersection, evidently for a flashing light, and decided to see about getting some for the boat.

On the way in to the SICU, he was stopped by a black man, who was walking down the hall. He grabbed Matt's arm and asked, "Are you Azrail?" Matt felt the energy surge and said, "No, I guess I just look like him." The man looked Matt dead in the eye and said, "Have you heard the voice of the turtle?" then walked on as Matt tried not to look into Mr. Shipman's space. It didn't matter that he didn't look because a different man, in a bed, was being wheeled out as Matt passed. This told him that Mr. Shipman was gone.

Misha was asleep when Matt made it to her spot, and he touched her. There was a very faint sense of open meadows

and freedom. Matt thought, once again, that it was probably
just his imagination. She woke up and asked, "What
happened?" Matt told her about the Jet Ski accident, and she
fell back asleep. A nurse came by, said that Misha was stable
enough now to be moved to the orthopedic ward and began
making preparations. He was quietly relieved because it
meant he would not be around so many people hovering at
death's door.

There were still only a few female patients in the hospital, so
Misha was in a private room again. The orthopedic ward was
a bustling place and apparently sparsely staffed. It took two
hours for a nurse to come by, check on Misha and give Matt a
briefing on the ward procedures. In the SICU, he could visit
anytime, in this ward, there were time restrictions. Visiting
hours were two hours in the morning and two in the evening,
the rest was reserved for treatments and tests. He was also
sternly warned about intimate activity being off limits at all
times. Matt was both relieved and irritated at the new rules
and restrictions. Misha was awake and beginning to get antsy
about pain medicine time and it caused the nurse to scowl.
Matt read the nurses name tag, Bea Adams. Bea said to
Misha, "We'll be getting you off that stuff, now." Misha
weakly replied, "It hurts…" Bea cut her off, "I know, it'll be
a gradual procedure, but you'll never get better if you are
passed out in the bad all the time." With that, Bea said to
Matt, "You can stay until I get back with the injection, then
you have to comply with the visiting hours." Her tone
indicated that there would be no negotiation, or exception
granted.

Twenty minutes passed before Bea returned, Misha was
exceptionally cranky, and Matt was almost happy to be
thrown out. As he drove back to Harriet and Jimmy's
restaurant, the Alfa had a few episodes of stalling and
sputtering. It was still driving okay, so he just made a mental
note to ask Mae about it. He called Mae and she said she was
in the restaurant and was about to eat dinner and asked him

to join her. Matt suddenly felt famished and said he would be right in.

As soon as Matt sat down, a cold beer appeared in front of him, and a cute young waitress asked him if he knew what he wanted. He unconsciously eyed her up and down and said, "A rare steak and a baked potato." She asked, "Rib eye or sirloin?" He said, "Whichever is the biggest." She smiled and said, "Rib eye, it is then," as she walked away. There were probably a dozen other patrons in the dining room and there didn't seem to be a second waitress. Matt had no idea why that mattered to him. Mae asked, "How is Misha today?" He explained the room move, the visiting hour restrictions and the nurse saying that they were going to wean her off the pain meds. Mae said, "Sounds good," and showed him a newspaper article, from the thirty-third page, which seemed to indicate that the couple he rescued was going to be okay. There was no mention of Matt's heroism. Matt said that he was unable to find Henry, the nurse he got a sensation from, again and would just have to watch as he came and went to try spotting him. Mae said, "Probably scared him, maybe nobody clued him in to the gift." Matt asked Mae if the Alfa had ever acted up and described what it did and she said, "In-line fuel filter. Have to get one from an auto parts place and change it, kinda like on a boat. You only need a screwdriver." Matt thought, "Great, now I'm a mechanic too." Mae saw his look and said, "There are very few Alfa mechanics around, you might as well get the book out of the trunk and learn how to fix the little things that go wrong." He responded, "Just seems like there are a lot of challenges right now." The waitress returned with his plate and asked if he needed another beer. He looked up at her cheerful smile and said, "Sure." The waitress sauntered off and Matt followed, with his eyes. Mae said, "She's Jimmy and Harriet's youngest, and would cause you a lot of problems." Matt said, "Just shopping, not buying." She said, "Good, she's a handful and spent six months in Juvenile Hall

for assaulting a man who whistled at her while she was
wearing a bikini." Matt said, "Makes no sense." Mae asked,
"What?" He said, "Girl wearing a bikini mad at a man for
looking at her." Mae said, "I guess you're right. Those things
are designed to make men look at you. Unfortunately, it's not
just the ones you want to look."
After dinner, they headed out to the boat against the wind
and waves. The moon was just cresting the horizon out to the
east, there was a stiff east breeze, and the sky was partly
cloudy. On the boat, Matt mentioned the strange weather to
Mae, and she said, "Must be a storm out there somewhere,"
and handed him a smoking pipe. He looked inquisitively and
she said, "New special mix, you need rest." He took a hit and
tried to hand the pipe back to her. She refused and said, "You
need that more than me." He wondered what she meant but
since she always seemed to know, finished the bowl.
The moon was now all the way over the horizon and seemed
to be smaller, and further away, than normal. It was full and
Matt puzzled on its size for an hour while thinking it was
only a minute. He found his way to bed and went to sleep as
soon as his head hit the pillow. A familiar woman walked
through his dreaming mind. She had made her first
appearance when he was around eight years old and had
been in almost all his dreams until he went to sea for the first
time. She just faded away and in all the times she had visited,
he had never gotten a clear view of her. The only thing he
knew for sure was that she was the most beautiful thing he
had ever seen, and he wanted to be with her, but somehow
couldn't. She had black hair that had a shimmering blue tint
to it, like a raven. Her hair was straight and so long and thick,
that it covered her body, like a robe and its radiance
prevented him from focusing on her face. He knew that her
eyes were haunting, but he couldn't come up with a color or
description of them. She just walked into his mind and led
him to an island where he was trapped for what seemed

eternity. It wasn't exactly horrible, being stranded on an island with a beautiful woman, so his mind ran with it. Matt's body slept while his mind lived on an island with a beautiful black-haired woman. This wasn't a sexual dream, per se. It was more like living as intertwined vapors in a paradise. He woke up and found he had been asleep for fifteen hours. Mae was gone and the sun was standing at mid-day. He immediately thought that Misha was going to be pissed that he wasn't there for the first visiting hours and tried calling Mae. There was no answer, and he was torn between feelings of duty to Misha and his need to detach from the stress and strain of the situation. This was the first time that he realized how valuable of a service he provided to people with dying family members. He was lost in that thought when his phone rang.

Matt answered his phone and Mae said, "You were out, so I decided to take a turn visiting Misha." He said, "Good, I thought that she would be pissed if I didn't show up." Mae said, "You still have to take care of yourself. You can't do anybody any good if you are down, or sick." He said, "Tell her that I'll be there for the evening hours." She said, "Okay, and I'll pick up the fuel filter on the way back." He said, "Thanks." He thought, "I hope that I'm that with it when I'm her age."

Matt relaxed on the boat and eventually decided to do some fishing. His mind wandered and the black-haired woman visited his mind again. Four hours passed without him being aware of them and it was Mae, motoring up in the skiff that shook him back to reality. He was in a deck chair, fishing pole in hand and something on the line. He reeled in and found a hook full of algae. He got up, tied the skiff to the stern and helped Mae onboard. She said, "Misha is wailing about the pain medicine and driving the nurses crazy. They have her in a special bed now that's supposed to help in taking care of her, and she hates that too. You should be glad you missed this time." Matt said, "I feel like I need to be with her." Mae said, "She needs to become a little less dependent and you less co-dependent. It's just not healthy for either of you." Matt was initially taken aback by the frankness of Mae's comment but, in reality, he knew it to be the absolute truth.

Matt asked Mae "Is the new smoking mix from up here in Miami?" Mae said, "When you have been around an area for sixty years, or so, you have sources. I'll introduce you in a few days. By the way, since neither of you are working, how's the money situation?" He said, "Okay, for now but I will have to do something soon." She asked, "Wasn't Misha hurt on the job?" He replied, "Yes, but I don't know how that would work, with her having the injury from the Army and all." She threw another question out, "Maybe she could get one hundred percent disability from the VA now." He said, "I'll ask a benefits counselor that. Maybe I should get over there and find one." She said, "Let me take you to the American Legion, they have people who can handle this for you, and I don't mind visiting the older vets." Matt replied, "Okay, when?" She said, "Tomorrow afternoon before you go see Misha. I will stop by this evening and set things up. By the way, you'll eventually find out that Jimmy was in Vietnam around sixty-four and got messed up pretty bad with the Agent Orange thing." Matt replied, "Would never have figured him to be messed up, he really seems to have it together, except for having a daughter spend some *juvi time*." She said, "He has been lucky, but it's been Harriet, that's held him together."

Matt suddenly realized it was time to go. Mae dropped him off and told him to call when he got back to the restaurant, because that's where she would probably be. He spent ten minutes changing the fuel filter and was off with a smooth-running car. For some reason, Sarah, and her offers of sex, popped into his mind as he tooled along. Arriving at the hospital, he realized he was fifteen minutes early and decided to go get some flowers from a grocery store he had just passed.

Matt arrived five minutes late for visiting hours and Misha was unhappy, until she saw the daffodils. Her anxiety seemed to abate for a minute while she said how thoughtful he was. Then she turned crabby again. Matt said, "This is a pleasant start to a visit, what's wrong?" She said, "Lift the sheet and check me out." He did and found her naked, sandwiched between two mesh-like halves that held her in place. The bed was a spherical device that allowed her to be in almost all positions, except completely upside down. Matt said, "You look good in there." She said, "Evidently, every male nurse and doctor in the place seems to have been by to perform an evaluation of some kind that involved looking under the sheet." Matt said, "Everyone here is a professional, you must be imagining things." She said, "The Physical Therapist, an X-ray tech, a lab tech, a nutritionist, an Ortho Tech, a Cardio tech did an EKG, and two floor nurses. Matt said, "Doesn't seem out of line, just a lot of things going on at once." She said, "The only good thing is that my legs are strapped in individually and can be spread for taking care of business. I am just afraid a male nurse will be the one helping me." Matt said, "I have to clean women up sometimes, you know. It's just a job that needs doing. If he decides to take advantage of the situation, then that's a different story. Anyway, how are you feeling?" She said, "You should position me and take advantage of the situation, that's how." He said, "If we get caught, I won't be able to visit anymore." She said, "I have to pee, then. Stand me up a little, open my legs and hold the bedpan under me." Matt did as he was told and after she finished said, "Now, set that down and take your time cleaning me up." Matt did as she asked and ended up with an erection that ended up inside her. It was a very quick event and after he cleaned himself, and her up and she recovered, she said, "Thank you, I need all the endorphins that I can get, and sex seems to release a lot of them!" He said, "It was nice for me too, baby!" He picked up the bedpan as Bea came in and said, "I'll take that, it has to be measured to make sure her kidneys are functioning adequately." She looked him up and down and said, "Keep the hanky-panky down please." Matt looked down and realized his pants were unzipped. Visiting hours ended with Matt reading to Misha. She said, "Please put the television on," and directed him to the right channel. Matt was suddenly glad he was leaving as a pseudo-reality show about housewives came on. He kissed her and said, "Be back tomorrow, Love you, baby!" She said, "See you," and pressed the call button for pain meds.

Matt was at the American Legion the next day and the liaison officer agreed to go to the hospital to meet Misha and possibly begin working on an increase in her disability status. Two days later the claim was in the works and Matt was in a pattern that left a lot of time on his hands. Misha was cranky and always wanted sex when he visited. She worried that he would be snatched up by a healthy, young thing while she was laid up if she didn't keep him properly entertained. The only time that he had trouble with the sex was after helping her with a bowel movement, but she always convinced him to engage her.

Two weeks passed and Misha was in the middle of being weaned off pain meds and extra cranky. Matt wondered how long this was going to last and tried to keep a positive outlook. She was so upset and irritated that she stopped the sexual offers. She did try offering them to any nurse that might be able to get her pain medication, but none accepted, and the universal conversation was that she would be over the hump soon. Matt began skipping the afternoon visiting hours as often as he could come up with a good excuse.

At the one-month mark, Matt said he had to start working again and that there were some nearby nursing facilities that had promise. He found three patients in one day and two more the next. The other positive was that the rate was one-fifty up here and the payments were all in cash. A new routine of him visiting Misha in the evening, then working all night and sleeping during the day developed. It seemed normal, after a week.

One evening, Misha told Matt that she thought that she filed a Worker's Compensation claim, the day after the car wreck, while he was off doing something. He said, "I'll see what I can find out about that." The conversation changed to her getting into a regular bed soon and he better take advantage of the positional opportunities of this bed, while he could. He did, as often as she offered, and it seemed that they wouldn't be caught. A week passed and he came in to find her in a regular bed. She said, "The mesh marks will take forever to go away." Matt said, "They make you look exotic," and she laughed for the first time in recent memory. Matt said, "I had a discussion with Doug, from the group in Key West and they hope that we will come back. There are still six months of the study left." She said, "Doubtful, I was told today that I need at least three months of inpatient physical therapy and maybe six more as an outpatient. We might be up here for a while." Matt said, "Hopefully we'll finish hurricane season without a storm." As he spoke, a storm was forming off West Africa and slinking across the Atlantic toward the Caribbean.

STORM WARNING

A week passed, and since Misha was no longer in the easily accessed positions provided by the orthopedic bed, there was no sex going on. Matt missed it and after a few days, the lady with the black hair began visiting his dreams again. He was frustrated that she was always unidentifiable, and the nature of their relationship was so vague and undefined.

The building hurricane was halfway across the Atlantic and building. The forecasters had every scenario possible plotted out and named her Alison. It looked like Key West was in for a rough ride and evacuations were already happening. Rain belts were crossing Haiti and it was just over one day before landfall. Matt asked Mae if she thought it was time to move inland, or something. She said, "We can't get into Jimmy and Harriet's dock in the Dreaming Moon, the rising water would make it deep enough but would also make the bridge passage even lower. Last time Jim and I had to evacuate the Keys, we moved near here. The islands behind us reduce the storm surge and wave action but the wind will keep it stirred up. We should scout out a position of last resort." They spent several hours, in the skiff checking bottom composition and barrier island width and vegetation density. The theory was that they could tie to the leeward side and stay in the island's wake. They located a spot that also would allow them to beach the boat in sand and tie it down.

That evening, Matt was eating with Jimmy and Jimmy told him, "I got a friend, who's in the Islands for the month and his dock is open. I can call and see if you guys could tie in there for a while." Matt said, "We'd have to park the car somewhere." Jimmy said, "I'm sure his driveway has room." Matt said, "Sounds good to me then; let me know what he wants for rent." Jimmy's expression turned serious, "You were in the Navy. Don't they still say that a man in the water has no country?" Matt said, "I heard that." Jimmy said, "Real boaters always help other boaters, especially when the danger to their own vessel is minimal to none. A hurricane is a serious issue for the boating community and any boater who fails to think about the common good is a common danger. If someone doesn't secure their boat, it could take out ten others as it rolls and swings in the tide. There will be no rent for the storm period. After that, if they stay over in the islands for a while, something agreeable can probably be worked out." Matt said, "Thank you, let Mae know the details, I have to run to make the hospital." Misha was doing well, her shoulder, through intensive and painful physical therapy, had regained some of its function and the improvement curve was allowing for faster gains now. Matt was happy that she was able to get up, walk around and independently takes care of most of her personal needs. He was also happy that her case for full VA disability had been granted, on a temporary basis and there was a month of catch-up money deposited into the bank account. This, along with his retirement and cash income, meant that they were in okay shape financially, for a while. The hurricane was the biggest worry now. The Dreaming Moon was well insured but probably not easily replaced. Misha expressed worries that children on a boat might not be ideal but prices to live on land meant that they would have to move up to Homestead or something equally disagreeable to a keys resident. They both wanted to preserve the boat, if at all possible. Matt and Misha's visit was tense because she was getting tired of the hospital, and he wanted to make sure the boat was safe. On top of that, he had a patient that he was sure would die on him tonight. All this, plus a faint feeling from Misha that worried him, but he decided to keep that a secret.

The morning broke in a weird yellow hue, and everything seemed to have an odd aura about it. Matt got to Jimmy's and Mae was there having breakfast. He decided he would join her and suddenly noticed how frail she appeared. He ordered a hearty breakfast and asked Mae what was going on. She said, "Just having a down day, happens to all of us you know." Matt went to touch her arm and she moved it away while softly saying, "Not now." He retracted his hand and thought the worst. The television was saying that Key Largo was now the likely landfall of the hurricane, and it would occur at high tide that night, about ten thirty. Matt asked Mae, "Did Jimmy talk to you about the dock space?" Mae said, "We can move their today, but it's probably no better than the island spot we picked out. I believe we should move there though, since we will be closer to land." Matt said, "I'll take care of the boat and you can stay here, a hotel, or the shelter." She looked at him, with a determination he had not seen previously, and said, "I want to be on that boat! Don't ask me to be ashore, now. I belong to the sea and sometimes she is a harsh mistress." Matt said, "No problem. I'm going to be there anyway."

They left the restaurant and Matt asked where Jimmy was. Mae said, "This place floods in these storms, he is off to get the truck he uses to move out most of the equipment. If it's really bad, he'll set up a kitchen somewhere inland and feed people. That's just the way he is. Don't you worry, that daughter of his keeps plenty of strong young boys around to help." They took off into an obscured sunrise, increasing wind and a heavy chop. Matt worried about Mae's new fragility as he piloted them out to the Dreaming Moon. Once they were on the Dreaming Moon and the skiff secured, Matt got the engines going and untied from the mooring chain. The chain dropped heavy under the surface and the milk jug line followed. The boat was drifting, in the wind, faster than Matt liked. He practically ran to the controls and found Mae plotting the course to the dock. The chop was three to five feet now and rocked the boat quite noticeably. She said, "Here take the controls and get up to these coordinates. The chop evened out into rolling waves and Matt had to learn how to maneuver the boat to follow the waves and not cross the crests and fall into the troughs. It was a rough ten minutes before he managed to get the speed and rhythm. They arrived at the dock and found another boat had tied there. Matt immediately turned and headed for the GPS coordinates of the island that they had scouted before. The first rain band hit as he secured the boat with three lines to trees on the island and dropped the main anchor and then the auxiliary anchor. All the portholes were secured with the storm covers, and he checked all the hatches. Too frantic to be nervous, he closed the main hatch and dogged it. Whatever the storm brought would now have to be dealt with. He called Misha's room, feeling that the signal would soon be gone. She answered and he said, "Somebody beat us to the dock, we are going to ride it out behind an island. I'll find my way to the hospital soon as possible afterward. I love you baby!" She said, "Love you too," and just like in a movie, the signal failed. Matt tried to redial, but the signal was gone, Misha tried and instantly got voice mail. She left a message that she hoped everything went well and she would see him soon. She then begged her nurse for pain medication. She got pills that she had decided were no better than aspirin.

The rain turned to hail, and Matt paced the salon. Mae had retreated into the smaller stateroom and said she would be out soon. The hailstones seemed like coconuts, from the sound and Matt began to worry about the upper fiberglass. It seemed to go on forever and then the wind began to howl, and the boat began to rise and fall in an off rhythm that caused him to have to take shelter in the captain's chair. It had a seatbelt, for when things got really rough and he decided that it was not needed, for now. Mae yelled she was okay and would be out soon. The wind slacked slightly, and the rain sounded like running water for the next five minutes. The storm was now at Category 3, and they were sitting on the south edge of where the eye would eventually make contact and would not get the break usually provided when the eye passes over. The wind increased and the boat seemed to be rising and falling like a roller coaster. Matt was sure that waves were now coming over the bow. This went on for a good fifteen minutes and he was beginning to get seriously worried about the trees and anchors holding and wanted to open the cover over the captain's window to see what was happening. There was a slight break and he decided to look out a porthole. He undid the inner cover and saw darkness and foam. He closed the cover and worried even more. The next wind band hit, and it happened that it was the one close to the eye, and possibly the strongest. Mae took this as her cue and ran naked from the stateroom to the main hatch. He was so surprised by the absurdity of what he was witnessing that he was unable to react until it was too late. She had undogged the door and as she opened it and shouted, "Good luck to you!", as she turned the latch and was dragged into the great vacuum created by the angry gray hurricane. Matt saw her go over the stern with a wave and instinctively didn't follow. He quickly re-dogged the hatch and held on as the boat dropped into a wave. He was sure that he was drifting now and thought about what he could do about it. Matt was unable to comprehend Mae's apparent suicide and could only think to start the engines in hopes an opportunity to maneuver came his way. It didn't because the boat was still tied fast to the island. The wind screamed for a good five minutes, and the boat began heaving in a new direction, side to side with the listing approaching the limit of recovery. This was one of the best designed motor yachts on the water and was solid as the day she left the factory, so he had some confidence in her but was wondering how long this bravado could last. Then the boat seemed to turn and then list to starboard. It kept leaning over until it was at maximum angle. He was certain she was going to flip and braced himself for the inevitable result of an upside down world and all of its tumbling objects. He even worried about rolling several times and anxiously evaluated the items nearby for potential danger in the mélange. It was a brief terror and, much to his relief, the See settled on her side and seemed to stabilize there. It seemed like an eternity of wave sounds, water rushing and warning buzzers. He realized that the engine automatic low oil shutdowns had engaged when the oil inside the engines all went to one side. Then the wind seemed to be slacking and the water and wave sounds changed. The boat suddenly began moving and soon flipped back upright with a violent rocking motion. Matt was thrown across the salon and into the opposite wall. When he recovered and assessed himself, there seemed to be minimal damage, nothing more than scraped knees from the carpet and a jammed left middle finger. The storm began to lessen and soon he felt it was over and thought about looking outside. He decided he better wait a few minutes to be sure and checked the interior for damage. He worried about the engines now but couldn't do anything to check them, at the moment.

He found no internal damage to the boat and prayed the exterior had fared equally as well. Eventually, the boat stopped rocking, and he opened the main hatch.

The sun seemed to have returned and the water seemed to have reduced to a light chop that was basically nothing to a boat this size. He went out on deck to find seaweed coated every surface and he was still attached to the island. He then wondered where Mae had gone and if it was possible that she survived. He couldn't conceive her to still be alive as he went inside to go below and check the engines. All was well in the engine room, oil and coolant levels were fine and he went back up to begin cleaning off the seaweed. He soon spotted several boats that had not fared as well. The most serious situation appeared to be the people clinging to a sailboat a few hundred feet away. He yelled and told them he would come get them as soon as he got untied. He radioed the Coast Guard and reported Mae missing, the radio operator said that he would add her to the list and took the coordinates and relative time.

HERO

Matt checked the Dreaming Moon over, as he untied her, and within thirty minutes had a dozen boaters on board. He radioed the Coast Guard and got assistance to three injured people on a boat that was still seaworthy but had no working radio or cell phones. He had to find a place to drop everyone and the only place he could think of was the dock where he was supposed to tie up.

Arriving at the spot that was reserved for the Dreaming Moon before the storm, he saw the sailboat that had taken the spot did not fare well. She was on her side with the mast broken on the house that the dock belonged to. The boat owner was standing on the seawall with a blank expression. Matt called out and asked if the man was alright. The man said, "Wife's trapped below, get help!" Matt called the Coast Guard again and was told that it would be at least half an hour before anyone would be available in the area it was a real mess. Matt pulled as close as he could to the foundered boat and recruited three able bodied men from his rescues. A woman among the survivors offered to man the Dreaming Moon's helm and the men went into the water to see if they could get the woman out of the capsized sailboat. It was soon apparent that the sailboat was damaged beyond immediate repair and Matt asked the woman manning the Dreaming Moon to throw him the waterproof flashlight attached nearby.

With light in hand, Matt slid into one of the sailboat's forward hatches. Everything inside the boat seemed to have been scrambled and then blended. A mishmash of unidentifiable pieces of things floated in the dimly lit cabin, which was now just over half-full of water and almost shoulder deep on Matt. He searched in the debris, hoping for a miracle and heard a potential one. The head was on the current upper and thus dry side of the interior and the door had been jammed by a large piece of debris. He tugged at the item and found it moved slightly. He found a better perch and place for a foot to add leverage and managed to pull the salon's island bar top from the door, which remained closed. He inched up and cautiously tried to turn the latch to open the door and it was stuck hard.

Matt decided to look in the forward berth before dealing with this problem. A few minutes later, he had searched everywhere else, and decided to try the head door again. After lifting with his shoulder, he managed to get the latch to turn. Stepping away to let the door swing, the woman he was looking for, and much of the contents of the holding tank, dropped into his arms. She was limp and the smell was foul, so he immediately began working his way, carrying the one-hundred-twenty pound woman, to the hatch he had come in. It took an agonizing five minutes, but he had detected breathing and a pulse, so he was okay with taking careful time to get out. Two men assisted in getting the woman out of the hatch and up on the seawall. Matt got himself out and ran up to check.

The man from the sailboat was using his left arm to shake the woman and yelling for her to please wake up. Matt noted that the man's right arm seemed to just be hanging limply and thought, "Broken clavicle." He had seen it before while in the Navy. People were gathering around the woman and Matt took charge. He got everyone to move back and the man to stop shaking and shouting at the woman. He checked for a pulse and breathing, again and found both. He then looked her over, head to toe and rolled her up to check sides and back. The only thing he could find was an indentation in her skull. Her eyes were closed and when he opened them, they were dilated and unresponsive. He said to everyone, "She's alive, but needs medical help now." He yelled over to the woman manning the Dreaming Moon and told her to call the Coast Guard again and tell them we have an unconscious woman with a head injury.

The response was that the access street to the place where they were located was blocked and crews were working to cut downed trees and move cars out of the way. Matt asked her to try to find out if there was vessel nearby with a doctor onboard. There were no boats within five miles. He made a decision and picked up the woman to carry her to the Dreaming Moon. Two other men noticed he was faltering and took over. They all were back on the boat in a matter of seconds and Matt took back over the helm. He called the Coast Guard dispatcher, gave him the dock's coordinates, and asked where the nearest dock, or anything else, was where and ambulance could meet them. The overloaded dispatcher said, "Can you just work your way up to the

causeway and call me just before you get there?" Matt's
voice cracked a little as he said, "Roger, will do."
The causeway was not even in sight and there were several
vessels in various states of floatation in the immediate path.
Matt cautiously went as far out into the bay as far as he felt
necessary before turning north and going to full speed. When
the causeway finally came into clear view, Matt made the
radio call. Fifteen minutes later, he was alongside a public
dock and an ambulance could be heard. The woman was still
unresponsive, but still alive. The people who had been pulled
from the damaged boats began going ashore to figure out
their own lives and by the time the ambulance arrived, only
Matt, the woman, and her fast-fading husband remained.
Matt had used a piece of roped to secure the man's arm and
told him to just sit still, which he didn't seem to be able to do.
He was constantly nudging his wife to try to get her to wake
up. The ambulance finally came and then Matt was alone. He
tried to call Misha, but the system was too busy.
As Matt pulled away from the dock, he realized that the skiff
was missing. He made his way back to the island and found
it was on the sand with the rope still firmly attached to a
palm. He wondered how that had happened and hoped it
meant Mae was alive. As he unwound the rope, he could tell
that a person had not tied it and it must have been the
swirling waters that wrapped the rope around the tree. He
checked the skiff over and found it was in good condition
and the gas did not seem contaminated by seawater. The life
jackets and other required safety items were all gone. He got
a new rope from the Dreaming Moon and set up to pull the
skiff back into the water and towed it back to the mooring
point.
Except for the seaweed and scattered debris, everything
appeared normal as he retied the boat to the mooring chain.
He pulled and checked, and all seemed to be secure. He then
secured the boat and headed for Jimmy and Harriet's in the
skiff, taking a life jacket and a spare oar with him. He made it

to the restaurant and saw that it had taken about a foot of
water but was otherwise intact. The block structure was in
fine shape and the tape crosses on the windows signaled that
they were all intact. The front and kitchen doors seemed to be
damaged and open. He walked into the back door and called
out, no one answered, so he continued into the dining area
and saw that the chairs and tables were jumbled but nothing
seemed beyond repair. He neither saw nor heard anyone and
continued to where he parked the Alfa. It was still here
because there was no time to move it to the house with the
dock he was supposed to tie to. He had managed to park
uphill from the restaurant and didn't look like the car had
been underwater, but the top was damaged, and the interior
was soaked.

He lowered the top, opened the doors to let the water flow
out and then checked the oil to see it there was any sign of
water contamination. Everything seemed okay, and he tried
the ignition. The engine ran fine, and everything seemed
normal until the radio began to smoke. He shut down the car,
pulled the radio fuse and restarted it. A few minutes later he
was meandering down the street in hopes of making it to the
hospital to see Misha. Surely there would be exceptions to
visiting hours today. It took three hours to get to the hospital
and then he realized he would have to find gasoline before
trying to get back.

When Matt got in to see Misha, she announced that since
there had been a huge influx of new patients, she was
granted a three-day pass to leave. She was ready to go
immediately. Matt told her about Mae, and she said, "Maybe
we can cruise around looking for her." He said, "Good idea,
let's see if we can get back to the boat before dark first,
though." They left the hospital and stopped at the first open
gas station, the price was six dollars a gallon and as they left,
after paying twice the price as normal, Matt tried to get a cell
signal to call the gouging hotline. He was unsuccessful.

The trip to the restaurant parking lot took just over an hour and the place was still abandoned. Matt remembered that Mae said that Jimmy would likely just set up a mobile kitchen and feed people, somewhere inland. He got Misha, and her bag, into the skiff and they headed out to the boat. They had no issues on the way out and Misha asked if there was any special smoke around. Matt got it and they sat on deck for half an hour passing the pipe. He had only gotten out enough for their immediate use from custom installed secret storage space. He was worried that someone official would be checking on them sometime during the night. Sunset proved God is an artist and as it faded to black, they went inside. Matt started the generator, and they had microwave sandwiches for dinner. The dope hit them and as soon as they snuggled up it seemed to be morning. They spend a little extra time together before getting out of bed and as they went topside to have coffee, a Coast Guard patrol boat came alongside. There were some questions about Mae followed by whether he was the one who had gotten a large group of people up to the causeway just after the storm. After that, the boat captain said that the commander of the Miami station would like to give Matt a public award for his efforts. Matt said that he hadn't done anything that anyone else wouldn't have done. The officer said, "Even so, can you be at the station tomorrow at eleven hundred hours?" Matt said, "Aye, I'll be there. Can I get there in this boat?" The officer replied, "We'll set up a berth for your overnight use, at that time. I'll also make arrangements for shore power, water and a pump out. You actually helped us out tremendously because we would have had to commit resources to rescuing all those people if you hadn't done it." Matt said, "Just a boater helping out other boaters." The officer saluted and said, "Until tomorrow." Matt returned the salute and the patrol boat pulled away as the officer said, "We're still looking for your missing woman."

Matt checked the boat over and swam around it to look at the exterior. Other than a few scratches in the clearcoat, all was okay. He then checked the fresh water to see it if had any signs of saltwater by drinking a glass, it was fine. They then prepared to begin searching for Mae. He took them to the small island that had served as surf break and anchor and was amazed at how small it actually was. He asked Misha if she wanted to come with him in the skiff and she said, "No, I'm going to sit here, drink beer, smoke dope and zone out. It's been a long time in that friggin' hospital room. My skin needs to breath." He said he would be back in an hour or two and motored off toward the shoreline. Misha stripped and sprawled out on a towel on the bow.

The water was full of debris now, the tide had washed everything that made its way into the canals, storm drains out into the bay, and navigation was more difficult the closer to the shore he went. After two hours of circling and carefully checking every potential sighting, he gave up and returned to the Dreaming Moon to spend time with Misha. She was now in half a bikini, in a deck lounger, glistening with the copious amount of lotion she had applied to her pale skin in an attempt to ward off sunburn. No one came by the rest of the day. By evening, they were baked and ready for air conditioning.

Early the next morning, they had coffee and watched the sun extinguish the stars as it slowly inched its brightness into the clear azure sky. A flock of pelicans landed on the island and began squawking for handouts. It all seemed too ideal and, for once, nothing spoiled it. Eventually, they had to make way for the Coast Guard Station and Matt prepared for departure. He decided that they should go outside into the ocean to head north, so as to avoid the storm debris.

When they arrived, the station guards directed him to a slip that had power, water and even cable TV. As soon as they were secured, a barge pulled alongside and pumped the tanks. Next, they were offered a courtesy inspection of the hull and engines. Matt took them up on the offer and everything checked out. The award ceremony was attended by two television stations, the Miami Herald and the Key's Journal. The Station Commander gave a short speech, then called Matt up and read the citation that accompanied the Coast Guard Gold Lifesaving Medal. Mat had no idea he had just been handed the highest honor available but knew it had to be special based on the media coverage. He said thank you and the ceremony continued with two silver medal presentations followed for others who had also made rescues after the storm. That was the end of the official ceremony and the media quickly departed for other stories. Post-storm reporting was the hottest thing in the area.

Matt had received the Gold instead of the silver award because he had entered a capsized vehicle and rescued a woman he did not know, risking his own life without hesitation. The man who owned the boat was a member of the Coast Guard Auxiliary and had reported the action to the Station Commander. That man, Greg, approached Matt to tell him his wife was going to fully recover and thanked Matt for rescuing his wife. Matt remarked that arrangements had been made for him to be tied in that particular spot but when he got there, just before the storm hit, he had beat him to it. Greg said, "Sorry about that, I am friends with the next-door neighbor, and he told me that the owners were in the islands and no one was using the dock and he was sure that the owner would not care. That is with the storm coming in and all." Matt said, "No problem, I got through." Greg asked, "Have they found the missing woman?" Matt said, "No, she washed over as the wind and tide were reversing, so there's not much hope. Too bad, she was a real interesting character." Misha came up, was introduced, and promptly said she was tired and wanted to go to the boat. Matt agreed and they spent the rest of the day relaxing while securely tied to a protected dock. A maintenance barge came by, and the crew said that they were there to do an oil change. Matt was surprised and saw one of the men who had performed the engine check earlier. The man said, "We saw on your boat's log that you were due, got permission to service and fuel your vessel since it was used in a rescue operation. You seriously did a good thing, and these are services that we would have had to do to our boats, if you hadn't taken care of things for us." Matt agreed to let them proceed and five technicians went to work with practiced precision. An hour later, the engines and coolant were good for another thousand hours and five hundred gallons of diesel had been added to the tank. Matt asked about the cost of the services. He was told that the Dreaming Moon was now listed as an auxiliary vessel, commissioned for post-hurricane operations, and this was all free to him and perfectly legitimate. Matt thanked the men as they all left. Matt liked the way this all worked and thought he should seriously check into becoming a member of the Auxiliary. Later, a runner came by with an invitation for dinner with the station commander. Matt sent word back that they would be happy to attend.

It was a good night and dinner was great. Matt did find out that his medical discharge from the Navy would prevent him from being a functional member of the Auxiliary. That ended the thoughts of organized service, and they enjoyed the alcohol-free dinner. Back on the Dreaming Moon, the drinking did happen and so did a lot of physical exertion before sleeping.

RETURN TO MARATHON

Matt got Misha back to the VA Medical Center and stayed until visiting hours were over. She was unhappy being back in the hospital but looked healthier from the fresh air and sunshine. He tried to re-establish working arrangements but there were still issues with the phones in the area. He also needed to do something about the top on the Alfa and get new safety equipment for the skiff.

He ended up in Homestead before finding the needed items and then the car stalled out and he couldn't figure out what was wrong. A towing service, provided by his insurance company, came, and took both Matt and the car to a shop. Most of the shop employees were still involved with post-storm cleanup and only Matt and the owner, who was also the tow driver that day, were there. The owner, Tom, said, "Let's see if I can get you going here, I used to have one of these things in the seventies." It took Tom five minutes to find the problem. Water had shorted out a relay in the electrical box in the middle of what served as a cargo area behind the seats. Fortunately, it was a common relay and an easily fixed issue. Matt had a discussion with Tom about how to keep the car running and got an Internet site that sold Alfa specific parts and accessories. Matt was paying in cash, so he got some bonus advice and services. The engine and transmission were in great shape but the electrical system, and interior had a lot of suspect items. The fuel pressure also indicated a new pump was in the near future. Matt paid, went back to the store, and bought a tarp, and six bricks to hold it in place, to protect the interior until he could afford a new top.

Back on the Dreaming Moon, he tried to use the Internet from the cellular provider, but the system was still having capacity problems and wasn't able to connect. It was a lonely night on the Dreaming Moon and Matt got a visit from the woman with black hair. He woke to find he was alone. The bed sheets were balled up and he was drenched in sweat. He pulled on a pair of shorts and went topside to check the weather. The stars hung like they were painted in place by Van Gogh, and he checked his pulse to see if it was all still a dream. He couldn't decide if it was real or a dream and just sat in a deck chair and gazed heavenward. For some reason, as clear as the night sky was down here, he could never see the Milky Way like he did as a kid in the remote mountains of West Virginia. He wondered about that until a searchlight crossed the deck.

It turned out to be a Coast Guard patrol boat. The crew saw he was out on deck and pulled alongside. Matt recognized one of them and she said that several bodies and some body parts had been found and suggested he go to the county morgue, to see if the woman he reported missing was among them. Matt said he would do that tomorrow and she seemed to want to talk more but the four other members didn't. She asked, "You got what you need out here?" and Matt thought it sounded a little like she was looking for an invitation to return in a non-duty status, and said, "Doing fine, for now, that is. I'll give you a call if I need anything at all." She smiled, handed him a card, and then took the rigid hulled inflatable away from the Dreaming Moon at an idle and then the searchlight began swinging back and forth again, looking for troubles before they happened.

The next day, in the morning, he went to the morgue and after identifying himself and answering a string of official type questions, he was allowed to look at the bodies and parts. Actually, there was only one woman and she seemed to be Mae. Matt was extremely sad but managed to give the coroner's office enough additional information to begin a more thorough investigation. After completing the paperwork, he was told that he would be contacted within the week.

Misha was unhappy enough at the hospital to get a referral to an outside physical therapy outfit in Marathon. Jimmy and Harriet were back at the restaurant now and Matt asked if anybody could drive the Alfa down to Marathon for him and a busboy said that he would do it for a hundred dollars plus bus fare back to Miami. It was agreed and as soon as Misha was discharged, they all headed south. The busboy drove the Alfa, Matt and Misha were in the Dreaming Moon. During the trip, Matt got a call. He was told that the female body, at the morgue, was so highly likely to be Mae, that she was being officially declared dead. He then was asked if he knew what to do with the remains. He said she wanted to be cremated and was told that he was responsible for the arrangements and asked if he needed a referral. He called the first number that they gave him and made the arrangements. He then went out to sea a little further to lose the cell signal. The trip to Marathon took six hours and since Matt had given up the slip at the marina, they were assigned an outside mooring ball. The busboy beat them there by three hours and was working hard at getting on as a second mate for a fishing boat that used an adjacent dock when Matt finally found him. The funeral home called and asked when Matt was going to pick up Mae's ashes. He consulted the calendar and found that the next super moon occurred at a suitable time of the day, and tide, and was three months away. He asked about storage and made a deal.

LIFE ALMOST RESUMES

Matt was Misha's chauffeur now and was back sitting with Clive and Desi. Clive was still not quite dying from his prostate cancer and Desi was, from his throat cancer. Misha was getting total disability and when they arrived, they found three months' worth of Worker's Compensation checks waiting at the marina office. This, along with Matt's retirement and cash income meant that they were surviving and might be able to save a little money toward boat and car maintenance.

Matt had now replaced almost every electrical relay and most of the switches in the Alfa. It just kept developing new problems and he felt like it took all his time just to keep it running. He had started using marine switches where he could because the regular ones kept shorting out and he still hadn't replaced the top. The relays, on the other hand, were expensive and often backordered. The fuel pump was the worst. He had it in the trunk and planned to get it changed on a Saturday, but it left him on the side of the road on a blazing hot Wednesday afternoon and he spent most of the afternoon changing it out.

Misha was doing well in physical therapy and had not relapsed into addiction. They were still smoking dope and drinking beer, but it was not out of hand. She was unable to drive because of her shoulder and they were afraid to buy another car because of the payments.

The super moon came, and they drove up to Miami to put Mae out to sea. It was a strange trip. The following day, Misha decided to clean the smaller stateroom. They hadn't been in it since the storm up in Miami. Things were a mess. She picked up Mae's clothes and made the bed. There seemed to be a note sticking out of a drawer and she pulled it out to read it.

As she read what was on the paper, Misha's world spun out of control went dark and she hit the floor, hard. Matt was at the marina office at that time. He came back and had to search the boat to find Misha. When he touched her, the sensation that he received made him sit on the bed, involuntarily. He was unable to move for two hours, or, it was longer, while contemplating Misha's sudden death. Then he saw the paper and picked it up, all the while thinking it might be a suicide note. Then he read the note and almost passed out.

Mae had written the name of a Marathon lawyer on the note and that she had left her half-million life insurance and a few million in stocks and bonds to Matt. He was unable to process this information as he again looked at Misha on the floor and made the call to EMS. Two days later, the coroner reported Misha's death was the result of an aneurism of her subclavicular artery and that there was nothing that anyone could have been done to save her. It was also determined it was likely the result of stretching and strain during her surgeries. This was of little consolation to Matt, and it took him the next three months to be able to contact the lawyer about Mae and get the claim for Misha's life insurance filed.

The lawyer wanted to sue the VA for botching her surgery, but Matt said no. He had decided that he had enough money to live forever on and that the lawsuit would just force him to relive her death over and over.

SONG OF THE SIREN

Matt had dropped everything. Clive was doing exactly the same as he was before, his cancer had not progressed and his daughter, Sarah, had gone to Greece for an extended visit. Desi's cancer had taken his ability to speak, and he was probably going to die within a month. It was all just too much for now and Matt smoked dope and drank beer on the boat. He was now getting nightly visits from the mysterious black-haired lady and felt the need to take a trip. He serviced and fueled the boat and headed out to sea without a destination or a plan. A pod of dolphins kept pace off the bow and seemed to provide guidance. He saw that they were leading him southeast and as the sun set in the west, the moon came up in the southeast and its glowing reflection across the water continued to provide a pathway for him to ply. Matt was now unsure of anything, he had been finishing up the special mixes of smoking weed left on the boat and was drinking vodka straight from the bottle. His only thought was to find where the path he was being lead on took him.

The sun found Matt on a beach the next morning. The Dreaming Moon was anchored in a cove and the skiff beached nearby where he lay. A black-haired woman was approaching from over his shoulder. Frigate birds circled overhead, and he was mesmerized by their spiraling acrobatics. It all seemed like a dream and the woman came ever closer, unnoticed, and as quiet as the breeze.

A feeling of another presence brought Matt out of the trance that the birds had drawn him into, and she was there beside him with extended hand. He took the hand as if it were the most normal thing and followed her to a hut in the small dense jungle that defined the island. She was beautiful and holding her hand caused showers of color and light to dance in his brain. He purposefully let go once and found darkness overtaking him. Grabbing her hand again brought back the fireworks.

In the hut, she sat him at a table and let go of his hand. He was not being overtaken by darkness and desperately wanted to touch her again but found he couldn't move from the chair. Fruits and drink arrived in front of him, and she began feeding him. He ate and drank like he had just been rescued from the desert or the open sea after days of drifting. He was sure that this was heaven and that he had died after finding Misha, but why was he here with a different woman? Soon after he found that he could no longer even conceive Misha as he was filled with fruits and drink. The mysterious black hair seemed to engulf him, and he found she was so beautiful that he could not look away from her. She gently grasped his arm and he followed her to her bed.

Nothing else existed but the beauty and the feeling of this particular moment. The bonds of time and space were broken, and life was a collection of colors and light floating freeform in a black expanse. Matt was again sure he was in heaven until there was only blackness. Just as the cloud of color had appeared, it disappeared and there was the black vastness of space without time. He tried to look for the woman again, but she was gone, without any trace of her existence. Time was not registering and then he was awake on a beach at night.

The moon was full and so close he felt that he could touch it without even sitting up. He raised his hand and then was asleep again. The next awakening was to a moonless night and the Milky Way was plainly visible threading its way among the twinkling bodies. He thought about the dreams of youth, how many had come true and so many more had fizzled without ever being given a chance to flourish. He

thought that if he ever made it back to Marathon, he would
revisit some of those dreams and see if they were still viable.
The trouble was he suddenly forgot all of them and could not
bring any of them back to mind because she was back for
him. Her hair engulfed him, and they spiraled together out
into the stars and exploded into a million colors of light, each
going its own direction. Then, just as suddenly as they had
exploded, they came back together as one embodiment of life.
Then she was gone again, and so was everything she had
brought with her. The island was empty and the only thing
he remembered was that she said something about a son
coming. It made no sense to him, at the time.

ISLAND OF DREAMS

The sun had already crossed the sky's apex when Matt woke
on the beach again. Matt felt the sun's fiery fury on every
inch of his bare skin and wondered where his shorts and tee
shirt were. The skiff was beached thirty feet away and the
Dreaming Moon lie at anchor a hundred feet further in a
lagoon. He stood and looked at the island, all two hundred
by four hundred feet of it. There were some Mangroves
around the lagoon and three palm trees. Otherwise, it was
just a sandbar in the middle of the blue waters of the
Caribbean. He took the skiff back to the boat to get water and
found everything in perfect order. He drank water until he
was sloshing full and then sat on the deck and wondered
how he had arrived here and exactly where here *was*. He
turned on the GPS and found the battery was dead. He tried
the main engines and found their batteries were also dead.
The generator starting battery was also dead when he finally
thought about starting it.
He thought that he might be stranded here and then
remembered the small solar battery charging panel that he
had used to get the Alfa going the first time. Fortunately, it
was on board, and he decided that the generator was the first

thing to get going. He checked its oil and the diesel level in the main tanks. Everything seemed fine except all the batteries on the boat were dead. He hooked up the charger panel and began checking switches and connections. Evidently, he had left a light lit on the boat when he left for the beach in the skiff. The refrigerator and freezer contents said that might have been as long as a week ago.

The rotting chicken and fish from the freezer made good bait, so dinner was not an issue. The freshwater tank had over two hundred gallons in it, there was plenty of propane for the stove and maybe thirty pounds of rice along with canned goods that were all within date. He decided he had been hallucinating and just happened to find this island by accident. By evening, the battery for the generator was about one-quarter charged and he decided to get it well over fifty percent before attempting to start it. The sky fell dark without much of a sunset, there was not a cloud to refract the light and add colors today. He ate and then decided that he would be too hot in the stateroom, without a fan or air conditioning.

The stars were bright, and he couldn't tell if there was a new moon or if it was just late rising tonight. It didn't really matter he thought because he needed sunlight to charge the generator battery. He lay there, on the deck looking up and began thinking about Misha. This prompted him to find the last of the special dope and smoke it in the large bowl. He added warm, straight vodka to the smoke and thought he felt better.

Back lying on the deck, he looked up at the sky and as he lay there, the black spaces between the stars began swirling and formed the black-haired woman of his dreams. She descended from the heavens and made him feel so completely fulfilled that he fell into a deep and restful sleep. All fears, memories, pain, and the future ceased to exist he was just at rest. Nothing else existed in the world and he slept until late morning when a raven lit on the stern and began talking to him. Matt rose up and had to stretch before he could even think about how crazy he must be to hear a bird that shouldn't even be out here talking to him. He had slept on the deck and was thinking that pirates had grabbed him, and the boat, overnight and decided to flog him before waking him up.

The raven spoke of the one that Matt had seen and not considered. She knew the sea, and would soon make herself available to him, and then he would be happy again. He asked the bird to tell him who she was and was only told to get the boat ready to follow. Matt checked the generator battery, and it was now seventy-five percent charged so he hesitantly hit the start switch. The motor started immediately, and Matt got the battery charger hooked up and started the main engines. Returning to deck, he found the raven was waiting for him.

Matt hoisted the anchor, checked that the skiff was attached securely and manned the helm. The bird said, "West! Follow me," and Matt did. Seven hours later as the sun was turning orange in the west, he arrived back in Marathon. The bird continued to lead him until he was alongside Desi's boat. Matt asked quizzically, "Why here?" The bird simply squawked, and it almost sounded like, "She's here! She's here!" Then the raven took off and Matt watched until it was so high that it was no longer visible.

There was open dock space at the bow of Desi's boat, Matt tied in there and went in to ask Desi who owned the spot. Desi was alone, on his once luxurious yacht, and suffering from severe depression so Matt's arrival was an immense joy to him. Matt asked, "I am tied up at your bow, who do I need to see about rent?" Desi said, "I own the entire dock and the parking area, feel free to use it. You have come to sit with me, right?" Matt said, "Sure, I can do that. What happened to Vickie?" Desi said, "She's out at the grocery store. She has been gone for three days and when she came in today, announced we would have a dinner guest this evening.

Looks like it must be you." Matt wanted to tell Desi that a bird had led him here after three days on an island, which he forgot to mark on the GPS and had no idea where it was. He decided the story would likely get him fired and decided to check Desi's arm. When Matt took Desi's arm, under the guise of taking his pulse, he immediately knew that the end was very close. He maintained a straight face and asked Desi if he had been eating well and the answer was, "No," and went on to say, "I am almost ready to check out of this world, no need to eat a lot." Matt's reply was cut off by Vickie's entering the main hatch.

Vickie confidently strutted into the salon with a plastic grocery bag in each hand. She went into the galley and then disappeared into the interior of the boat. A few minutes passed and Matt looked up and the sight of her, with her long black hair, sent a shudder up his spine. He had never really paid any attention to her. She hadn't announced she was available like Sarah and now he couldn't remember if she had long black hair the last time, he saw her. She saw that he was watching and smiled a sultry smile. Desi said, "All these years and now she lets her hair down for the evening." She came to the bed, kissed his forehead, and said, "You liar!" Matt suddenly felt uncomfortable, but Vickie was not going to let him escape, she told Desi, "See, I told you we were having a dinner guest." Matt went to speak but she cut him off and asked if he was in the mood for red meat.

Matt had a dichotomy of reactions. One was to run and never look back and one to stay and see if he had gone completely insane. He chose the latter and followed Vickie to the galley when she asked him to. He was reduced to stares and grunts by her charm and that gave her the lead. She said, "I am so sorry about your friend Mae and especially about Misha. How are you holding up?" Matt was disarmed and answered, "Sometimes, I think that I am going insane." She said, "You're not, there are just new islands to visit now." Matt was unsure how it happened, but he found himself cutting the salad ingredients while she put two steaks into an electric tabletop grill. She then took out a jar of toddler level baby food, got a spoon and took it to Desi. She gave him the first few bites and then he took over and asked her to bring him brandy and a cigar.

When Vickie returned to the galley, Matt was done with the salad and wondering about the wine bottle sitting on the counter. It seemed *special* for some reason. Vickie checked the steaks, turned the appliance off, got a glass brandy, asked him to open the bottle of wine and was gone again. When she returned, she checked the steaks again and asked him to please take the salad and wine to the table. He did as instructed and then watched her get the steaks onto plates and bring them to the table. The table was already set for two and Matt wanted to ask a thousand questions but couldn't find the words. She began the conversation with, "I hope you like your steak medium rare, it's the only way I cook them." He said "That's great and…" She cut him off by answering his question before it was asked with, "Because you seem nice and take care of Desi when you don't have to." She then poured them wine, guided the conversation to everything about him and left out almost everything about her until dinner was over. Matt said he should go check on Desi and she said that she would join him as soon as she loaded the dishwasher. Matt said, "Let me help you." She said, "Absolutely not, *this time*." He looked at her and she said, "You do plan to come back, right?" He said, "Yes, I guess I do."

Desi was asleep and Matt began reading the book that he had left the last time that he was there. Vickie came in and said, "Good night." Matt waved and smiled back at her smile. He felt like he should follow her but since there was no overt invitation.

In the morning, Matt returned to the Dreaming Moon and went to bed. Vickie had told him that he was again welcome to dinner and to be tied their dock as long as he wanted.

There was something that made it seem unreasonable to think about leaving here or doing anything different. He did ask if she would drive him over to the previous marina to get the Alfa. She said for him to come see her at five in the afternoon and she would take him.

A week later, Desi died peacefully in his sleep. The coroner came and since it was a known case of terminal cancer, no investigation was deemed necessary. Vickie now owned everything, except the spot where Matt's boat was tied, which was set in perpetuity to Matt. He had no right of sale, just the right of use and access, without restriction or fee. Matt wondered what Desi and his lawyer had discussed five days before he died. Matt had also known that Desi was fading fast and tried to keep it from Vickie. She had stopped going out and made dinner for Matt almost every night, without any advances or overt intentions. On the day after Desi's memorial ceremony, Vickie insisted that Matt to come over for dinner. After dinner, she convinced him to stay and watch a movie. This became a pattern and after a week, he finally reached to touch her. As his hand made contact with her arm, an explosion of light filled his head. That's when he realized that when she initiated contact, there were normal touch sensations but when he initiated the touch, the fireworks went off. He asked if she wanted to take a boat journey out to open sea to watch the moon and stars. She said she just needed to finish the dishes and secure the boat and that he should go ahead and get his boat ready for the trip. Matt left Vickie's boat and finally decided to see if it had a name. On the stern, in small gold letters was *Raveness*, Elbow Caye, West Indies. It wasn't like the stern stencil of most boats, just small, unassuming and carrying a message more powerful than all the large and fancy scripts on all other boats. Matt felt electricity in his step as he boarded the Dreaming Moon and began readying her for a sea voyage. Vickie arrived with two small bags and asked if he wanted her to help untie. He directed her to the bow, and he unhooked the shore power and water that Desi had a contractor install for him and then started the engines. All systems were normal. Next thing was to untie the stern rope and return to the helm to turn them around. He headed out the channel to open sea at idle. As they inched along, he asked Vickie if she had a favorite destination. She said, "You mentioned a place south of Miami once. How about we go there?" He said, "Perfect," and noticed that a full moon was just turning the eastern sky light and sending a reflective trail straight to them. He suddenly said, "I think there might be a better spot for us," and steered for the moon. Vickie let her long black hair fall free and smiled a smile at him that caused more than a tingle in his spine.

NO MAN LEFT BEHIND

It was if a dream ended, Matt realized that he was not who or what he thought he was. Vickie filtered into focus in the light of a new day. He asked her, "What are you doing here?" She said, "Taking care of you. Things have been a little crazy for a while, but I think you might be coming back." He asked, "From where?" She picked up a prescription bottle from the floor in one hand and an empty vodka bottle in the other. He looked at them and then her and after a pause, asked, "How long?" She smiled and said, "Almost six months. It hasn't been all bad though!" and rubbed the small bulge in her lower belly.

Later in the afternoon, Vickie drove him to the VA clinic. It was a much shorter drive than he remembered. She saw his confusion and asked, "You don't remember bringing the Raveness down here, do you?" He looked out the passenger window and asked, "Where is the Dreaming Moon?" She said, "You ran her aground in Key Biscayne and a salvage company bought her for scrap. You seriously don't remember?" He looked at her and, as a tear rolled down his cheek, asked, "Was Misha real?" Vickie said, "Sometimes, a little too real. She did love you and it was a terrible tragedy for her to go so suddenly. But I can tell you that watching Desi go slowly was also horrible."

Matt suddenly felt like he was trapped and rolled the window down. He asked again, "Why are you with me?" Vickie said, "I knew you were the man who had haunted my dreams since I was a kid, as soon as I saw you arrive to take care of Desi, that first day. It scared me so badly that I had to leave for the night." Matt said that he remembered that she would leave almost as soon as he got there. She let him talk for a while as she circled old town in unnecessary loops. The clinic was not going to be the right place to go today.

Matt finally remembered Mae. He perked up and asked Vickie, "Did you know Mae?" She answered, in a practiced tone, "No, she died in the hurricane up in Miami and I guess we never crossed paths in Marathon. It was great that she left you enough money to live on, though." Matt suddenly realized the Misha had life insurance too and asked about it. Vickie explained that he had given half to Doug, to help fund his PTSD research and the other half went into an annuity for the son that was going to come along soon.

Vickie looked at Matt and she softly said, "I love you Matt. I loved you long before I even met you and we have a long time to be together, if you can just pull yourself together a little more." He looked at the roundness of her belly and said, "I might need help, but I will try my best to be the love of your life. You haunted me for many years before now and, now that you are real, I know that I love you more than anything else in the world. It's just been a long, strange trip to get here." She smiled and flipped her long black hair over her shoulder and said, "I'm thinking that the best part of the trip is just ahead of us." He looked back out the open window and smiled.

The End

www.ingramcontent.com/pod-product-compliance
Lightning Source LLC
Chambersburg PA
CBHW061421160726
47995CB00003B/701